REUNION IN CARMEL

Tim Comstock

authorHOUSE®

AuthorHouse™
1663 Liberty Drive
Bloomington, IN 47403
www.authorhouse.com
Phone: 1-800-839-8640

First published by AuthorHouse 6/9/2010

ISBN: 978-1-4520-1409-8 (e)
ISBN: 978-1-4520-1410-4 (sc)
ISBN: 978-1-4520-1411-1 (hc)

Library of Congress Control Number: 2010907749

Printed in the United States of America
Bloomington, Indiana

This book is printed on acid-free paper.

ACKNOWLEDGMENTS

This book was a long time aborning. The delay was mostly my own fault. Parts of my daily career interfered with the time required for a venture such as this. In addition, my normally strong sense of self-confidence was buffeted by thoughts that no one would really care about what I would write or about my characters and their trials along the Monterey coastline.

That doubt, I believe, is fairly common among authors who are less than established. Family and friends encouraged me to press on, so I picked it up again after several years. My friend Jan Haag, an English professor at Sacramento City College, a very talented author in her own right, provided much help and pushed me to make the manuscript better.

Her assistance and the marvelous typing and editing skills of Becky Goad raised the story to a level of professionalism I could not have accomplished on my own. Early drafts were typed by Janice Hayden. Her work truly kept my dream alive. The frustration of several rejections by literary agents was countered by the positive comments of friends who took the time to read the story and provide their commentary. Dick

Sanderson, Barbara Thomas, Greg Thatch, Trish and Gary Kerns, my brother Bill and many others—all inveterate readers—kept pushing me forward. My wife Nancy and sons Tim and Will did the same.

Also, great thanks to Miles Hermann for his wonderful cover. He truly caught the spirit of my story with his great talent.

Because of them, and others, the book was completed. I can't thank them enough, and I hope it proves enjoyable to all who read it.

This book is dedicated to my wife Nancy, my family—Tim, Will, Courtney and Josie—and to my late, beloved brother Bill.

INTRODUCTION

The events in the following volume occurred nearly fifteen years ago. Thus there are no references to cell phones and the like. Computers, though in use then, were not the automatic source of information and communication that they have become.

The size, scope and complexity of the police department depicted are from another era. Times, indeed, have changed, and the Carmel Police Department has become larger and more technologically savvy than in the simpler era described herein.

Some say those changes came to pass because of the havoc wreaked by Louis Peel back in the 1990s. Others say it was simply the natural progression of things—that it would have happened anyway. I will leave that to the reader to decide.

No matter what, the visit of Louis Peel to the Monterey Peninsula left a mark that will never be forgotten.

PROLOGUE

The flash of lightning was razor-true, sending the top quarter of the huge cypress crashing to the beach below. A cannonade of sparks was quickly extinguished by the driving rain. Seventy feet of the tree remained standing, its humbled form a sad monument to this savage spring storm. However, nature's reminder would not be needed, because other events of the night would engrave the storm permanently in everyone's memory.

Another maimed form lay on the wet sand, its topmost part shorn away by the flawless blade of a machete. Its wielder dropped the weapon to the ground, grabbed the ankles of the headless body, and dragged the dead weight to the edge of the swamp.

It took all of his considerable strength to lift, then heave the body a few feet out into the reed-choked fen. Even in the darkness, he could see that it wasn't fully concealed. Cursing his victim and the uncooperative elements, he stepped into the cold, thick water and moved toward his kill. Foot by foot, he forced the carcass three yards farther until it became entangled in the overgrown rushes and could be moved no more.

Back on the beach, he aimed the flashlight into the bog. Not a sign of the body. Perfect. He cleaned the machete blade with a towel, then blotted the blood from the lower part of the head. This last chore he performed with a certain delicacy, as though the severed head could still feel, and he was averse to inflicting gratuitous pain. The longish hair was darkened and matted by the rain—nothing he could do about that.

The night's work nearly completed, he pocketed the flashlight and folded the towel four ways over the head, encasing it. He picked up the machete in one hand and the towel in the other—checking to be certain that its cargo was secure—and trudged across the heavy wet sand toward the ocean. Two miles to go. Twenty minutes, twenty-five at most.

A tremendous crash of thunder startled him into a momentary stop, then he continued on. Carefully, he transferred the machete into the hand carrying the head and shone his flashlight briefly behind him on the sand. The faint pinkish trail from the towel was absorbed immediately in the soaking sand. He smiled and put away the flashlight. He needed that hand to maintain his balance, since increasing winds and rain buffeted each step. He noted the tide encroaching on the beach, and he quickened his pace. Another foot or two of high tide and his journey would be far more difficult and dangerous than his plans allowed for.

But if prudence impelled him to move more quickly now, so be it. He knew he would finish his night's work safely. No eyes would have observed his actions, not tonight. Chances were no one had even looked out of any of the hundreds of windows in the beautiful houses bordering this piece of the Pacific. Why should they? There was nothing to see on this dark vista except the rain.

Only a crazy person would venture outside on a night like this.

Saturday Morning
Chapter One

The rain finally stopped early Saturday morning. Though storm-snobbish natives who met up with each other that morning would refer to it as merely a heavy mist, the fact was it had been a cold bitch of a storm. Since late Thursday morning, when all the electrical power had gone out, Carmel had been a virtual ghost town. Heavy winds had littered the village and the beach with tree limbs, pine cones, and blankets of cypress and pine needles. Carmel's aging drainage system was choked, and the sidewalks were treacherous, especially for senior citizens. But by sun-up Saturday, the storm's leftovers did not impinge on the promise of a perfect day. The pale blue sky extended to the horizon, replacing a three-day stretch of solid black clouds. By 8:00 a.m., every block in town seemed to boast at least three little old ladies sweeping up debris from the storm. Soon all but the largest tree limbs would be out of view, consigning the storm to memory. The first sign of sun called other older citizens to advance on the beach with their dogs for an outing equally necessary to the well-being of human and pet. At that same early hour, dozens of homes disgorged children who had been housebound far too long. As parents watched with relief, the kids headed for the beach.

Sari Kempton and her brother David, who had three years on her eight, headed straight down Eleventh to a piece of the beach they had come to regard as their own. Normally energetic, after three days of progressive cabin fever, both Kempton children were frenzied in their rush to the shore. They knew that storms left many items worthy of inspection. They also realized that today the three-mile strand would truly be theirs, no tourists to clutter it up. David held Sari's hand, but she was in the lead.

"Slow down and hang on, Sari, this is really slippery," David shouted to the back of her head.

David's hair was as dark as Sari's was blonde and as straight as hers was curly. Their features, too, gave no clue that they were related, but they were closer than most brothers and sisters their age. Their father understood. Three years ago, during the family's first summer in Carmel, the kids had only each other to play with, a circumstance that had shaped each to the other's best friend. The beach was their playground and favorite place.

Will Kempton watched his children's spirited trek until they passed from view. His hair was blacker than David's and his eyes a paler blue than Sari's. Though still in decent shape, he'd never again be the 170 pounder he'd been on his college boxing team. He was still smiling at their exuberance as he climbed into his Jeep and drove up the hill to the police station. After fourteen years in the Jersey City PD, the last six years as a narc, Will found himself on a three-quarter disability leave. Though his usefulness in New Jersey had run out, there was still a big chunk of cop left in him. Unattracted by most of the stale opportunities for a used-up city cop, Will took his time looking around.

Locating the chief's job in Carmel three years ago had been an incredible stroke of luck. The position in Carmel had two benefits: It let him ply the trade for which he had been trained, and it was low stress. The three-thousand mile distance from Jersey was also a godsend; he was able to leave behind the rawest reminders of Debbie's death. Right off, Will had been smitten with Carmel's magnificent scenery. Nothing in New Jersey had even hinted that life could be this easygoing and pleasant. Most importantly, Carmel offered a peaceful home to raise

Sari and David. His only regret was that Debbie had not lived to share the pleasures of this rare place.

As Will opened the door to the tiny station house, he smiled at the aroma of fresh coffee brewing on the antique Mr. Coffee.

"Morning, Peach," Will said as he leafed throughout the stack of pink phone messages looking for anything important.

"Good morning, dear. Coffee needs a couple more minutes. You go on in. I'll bring it in when it's ready."

Peach, who came with the job, was among its blessings. As Will sat behind his battered, heavy oak desk, he wondered for the hundredth time who in central casting had managed to find Peach to play the role of secretary to the police chief.

She was a close copy of everyone's ideal maiden aunt. Mid-fifties, gray hair done up in a bun except on the rare morning she was running late—when her shoulder-length hair gave her the appearance of an over-aged hippie. Peach typed at race car speed, was good on the phone, knew all the mysteries of the recently installed computer systems and processed the flow of parking tickets, the department's dominant staple, faster than the eye could see. Hell, she even volunteered to babysit the kids on the rare occasions Will had to go out of town or the even rarer times he had a date.

Yep, life was definitely good, Will thought, as he tipped back in the old swivel chair and surveyed his empire. The building was all brick except for the handsome mahogany wainscoting, vestige of a bygone era of artisanship. The heavy ceiling beams and the rust-colored carpet made the place look more like a lodge than a police station.

Will's reverie snapped as he tipped too far back and the rear wheel on his chair gave way. As he crashed to the floor, he berated himself aloud: "Either fix it or quit leaning back, dummy."

"William, this is at least the tenth time you've done that," said Peach as she came into his office with a steaming mug.

"Hell, Peach, it's the fiftieth time," he said, picking himself and the chair up. "I gotta fix this thing. Three years here and my only injuries are from falling outta my chair—it's embarrassing."

"It's a scandal, dear, is what it is. Here, drink this. I'm going down to the post office to pick up the mail."

"You walking or driving?"

"I thought I'd walk, it's such a lovely morning. Why? Do you need me to pick something up?"

"Never mind."

Peach insisted. Finally he confessed that sitting in the back of his Jeep was a mountain of laundry that had accumulated during the storm-caused power failure. If he could get it to the laundromat this morning, he could pick it up after work.

"No problem," Peach said. "Then I can swing by the bakery for a doughnut. Want one?"

"Oh, I don't know, Peach," Will said as he eased gingerly back into his chair.

"Promise I won't watch you eat it." Her comment was a playful jab at Will's theory that whatever one ate out of public view didn't cause weight gain.

"I'll be back in about one hour. If you're not too busy, try to fix that chair before you really hurt yourself." As she closed the office door, a sturdily framed picture fell from its spot on the wall above and to the left of Will's desk.

"Jeez! Those goddamned mortar nails don't work worth a shit. Fix the chair, hang the picture—what am I around here, a handyman?"

Will pounded the nail into the brick wall with the Scotch tape holder and reached a tentative accommodation with his chair. As he savored the coffee, he decided that if a temperamental chair and the need for a better mortar nail were his major career problems, then he really did have things going his way. About time.

Compared to this, life in Jersey was an exercise in survival. His mother hadn't made it beyond her fortieth year. Will knew that it was life with Officer Bo Kempton, not the trials of life in her native Jersey City, that had steadily drained the spirit from his mother, but it was easier to blame geography for at least some of her decline. She would have had a chance if she'd lived here, he felt.

Thoughts of his parents elbowed Will's good mood aside. He had adored his mother. Everything he knew about love and warmth and what a family ought to feel like was because of her and despite his father. The old man had been a good cop, no doubt about that. He had spent twenty-five years on the streets, assigned to a precinct where petty—and not so petty—graft were commonplace, but Bo Kempton had remained an honest cop. Maybe being set apart by that was some of what had made him such a humorless man, whose companion of choice was Dewar's, leaving precious few moments for his wife and son, to whom he gave his medals, but not much else.

The sharp ringing of the phone brought Will back from Jersey City. "Police."

"It's me," the sleepy voice announced.

Jim Sequeira was deputy chief in all but title. He was also Will's best friend in Carmel. At forty-four, Jim was a few years older than Will. A fifth generation Californian, he was the first member of his family to make a living away from the Sequeiras' huge artichoke farm out near Salinas.

"Hi, Jimmy. Did you think you might come into work sometime today?" Will asked.

"Well, it's so nice out, I hate to fuck up the day with work."

Will laughed. "Maybe ya better check out that attitude with the taxpayers. Peach's out getting doughnuts, big guy."

"Oh, then I'll come in."

"Don't burn your tires. Except for furniture repair and some paperwork, there's not a helluva lot to do."

"And don't we love that, boss?" Jimmy said before he hung up.

Will took a gulp of coffee and stared at the pile of paperwork he was avoiding. It wasn't that he was tired; unlike Jim, he was a morning person. One more way in which the two men complimented each other. Will liked putting in the early hours of the day, which allowed him to get home by mid-afternoon to David and Sari. No matter when Jim showed up, he never really began to function well until late afternoon. Their agreement was that if anything big happened after dark, Jim could probably handle it, and, if not, Will was just a phone call away.

In Will's view, the fact that nothing big ever happened did not devalue the theory.

The ringing of the phone interrupted his reverie once again. The caller's shout jarred him.

"Police? Get Kempton down to the beach, now! Something's wrong with his daughter!"

***

It had started with screams. At first the screaming was indistinguishable from the normal kid noise along the length of the white beach. But soon enough the difference in the sound, muting even the rolling waves, became alarmingly clear to all within earshot.

When the shouting started, Jack Ames had been jogging. Stopped in his tracks, he tried to locate precisely the source of the sound, and honed in on a small, curly-haired blonde girl struggling frantically in the soft sand to propel herself backward—and failing.

Jack sprinted the fifty or so yards to the little girl. As he neared her, he saw it was Will Kempton's daughter making the racket. There was a pile of sand in front of her. Jack's first thought was that some other kids had probably destroyed her sand castle. But, Jesus, what a noise.

"Whoa, Sari. Come on, sweetheart, we'll build another castle," Jack said, as he dropped to his knees and reached for his friend's daughter.

Sari spun around. Her face was slick with tears and her eyes were wild. She pulled back, staring at him in stark terror until recognition penetrated the barrier of her fear. She collapsed against him.

"Mr. Ames. Get it outta here! Get it outta here!" she screamed.

Through her tangled mop of curls he looked at what had indeed been her sand castle. Resting atop the pile of sand was a human head.

"What the hell!" Jack said, then quickly realized that getting Sari away from the hideously grinning face was the first order of business. He picked her up, keeping her back to the nightmarish scene, and hustled up the beach. Only then did he yell for help. "Call the cops! Get Will Kempton down here quick!"

It seemed like an hour before Will and Jim came screeching up to the edge of the sand. But, in fact, they were there four minutes after Will hung up the phone.

Instinct dictated their actions. As Will gathered Sari into his arms, Jim ran down the hill to the spot Jack had pointed out. It was not hard to find. In response to Jack Ames' repeated shouts to call the station, nearly everyone on the three-mile stretch of Carmel's white sand had congregated at the site of Sari's defiled sand castle.

As Jim reached the onlookers, he heard the mechanisms of a high-speed camera, which may have accounted for the harshness in his voice as he bellowed, "Everybody back!" As Jim bobbed and weaved and gestured them away, he knew he was only delaying the moment he would have to look again into the face of death.

The last—and only—time Jim had seen a dead man had been when, as a teenager, he'd had to help his father carry the body of a worker, who'd had a heart attack, from the artichoke field to the row of huts occupied by the migrants. As Jim turned and knelt to confront this new meeting with death, he wished his father was there with him.

"Oh, holy shit. Jesus, where's the…" Jim's next words were choked off by a sourness in his throat. When he had the urge to retch under control, Jim glanced again at the head. With one eye closed and one open, it seemed to cast a wink from another world.

Jim stood up quickly— too quickly—and staggered backward a step or two. Dexter White stepped forward and asked Jim if he needed help.

"No. Yes. Get up the hill, and tell Will to call the coroner. Then get me something so I can cordon off the area."

"I'm on my way."

"Also, tell him to get Jeff and Jennie down here."

"You're sure you're okay? You look pretty pale."

"I'm still breathing. All right, everybody, show's over! This is police business—please clear the hell outta here!"

Saturday Night
Chapter Two

They spent most of Saturday night at Will's house reviewing the day's events. It was nearly Sunday when Jim opened the quart of Famous Grouse he'd brought to assist them in their deliberations. It's not really a quart, Jim thought, as he sauntered back into the living room carrying two full tumblers of Scotch and ice.

"It should be a quart, goddamnit! Quarts, pints and gallons—and piss on liters and milliliters!"

Will looked up from his chair as he accepted the glass and asked, "What the hell are you talkin' about?"

"I'm sick of all this foreign shit! All these liters and stuff and the Japs and ragheads buyin' up all our land. It's like a fucking invasion, 'cept we can't fight back."

"My, we sure are a little puckered up."

"Listen, Johnny-come-lately, my people've been on this land forever. It's ours. Who the hell are they to come in here and buy whatever they want and force their chicken-shit liters and meters down our throats?"

"Why you Portagee bigot, you." Will used a soft needle. The truth was, he was grateful for the small talk and suspected Jim needed it nearly as much. Anything to get their minds off the wretched day.

For Will, the day had been a swarm of competing, often confusing, emotions. The shuddering fear that had overtaken him the instant the call had come into the station almost as quickly gave way to relief when he saw Sari with Jack Ames at the top of the beach. But that relief was immediately consumed by the realization that his little girl was genuinely terrified. His first instinctive move was, of course, to soothe her. But as soon as she began to quiet down in his arms, the cop in him surfaced, and from that moment he split his focus between continuing to comfort her and finding out what the hell had happened. Thank God, Jim was there to get the scene under some semblance of control.

As for Jim's day, it hadn't been his kid disabled by fear on the beach. But children were what mattered most, always, and this child belonged to someone he really cared about. Feelings aside, Jim had packed more real police work into the day's long afternoon than he had experienced in any month since he'd joined the Carmel force.

The brutal shock that some bastard had inflicted on Sari left both men, all these hours later, still furious—determined, as Jim put it, "to catch that motherfucker and make him pay." Sari's involvement made it personal, but both lawmen were also sufficiently motivated by what had been done to the poor son of a bitch whose body had yet to be found. Who was he? Where was the rest of him?

Both men knew they were on their last drink of the night. They savored the smooth Scotch as they reflected, for what seemed the hundredth time, on what had happened.

Jim had just pulled up to the front of the station when Will bolted out the front door, yelling that Sari was in trouble. Jim swung the powerful 1992 brand new Chevy cruiser into a hard U-turn before Will had closed the passenger door. Will flipped the toggle to activate the siren and they headed noisily down Ocean Avenue. It was only hours later that both realized they'd left the station unattended.

Eventually, between Jim and Sari a fairly clear picture of the scene had been painted for Will. Sari said that David and his friends had moved down the beach, leaving her to work alone on her sand castle. She had turned to get a bucket of wet sand to fortify its walls. She dumped out the bucket and arranged the pile of wet sand, then turned back to her castle. The head was there.

That was when she started screaming.

Sari told Will twenty times that no one had spoken to her.

"It was just there, Daddy…it was awful…I yelled hard."

She hadn't noticed anyone watching her while she was playing. She didn't see anyone around her, she said.

"Nobody was there 'cept kids," she added.

Then how in the hell did that poor bastard's head end up on the sand castle? And what kind of ghoul would do such a thing to a little kid? In twelve hours, they hadn't come up with a single clue. Not a single person had seen anything suspicious—let alone someone transporting another person's head, for God's sake!

Toward the end of their rehash of the day's events, the two tired men tried to come up with the easiest way to get around—totally unnoticed—carrying a human head. Jim suggested a Dobbs hatbox as a good mode of moving such cargo. Will countered with a bowling ball bag. Their foray into black humor offered some respite from the knowledge that something evil had contaminated the beach. The suggestions piled up: a coat bag from Patrick James; a coal scuttle from Great Things Antiques; a sweater bag from The Scottish Shop; a styrofoam Igloo ice chest—ideal for both transport and preservation.

"Hey," Will said. "You know that just might be pretty close to accurate."

"What do you mean?"

"Think about it. There were, what, fifty people within a hundred yards of Sari?"

"At least—more by the time I got down there."

"Fifty people, and none of 'em saw anything unusual."

"So?"

"So," Will said. "It's a good bet this asshole wasn't walking on the beach in an overcoat wearing wingtips carrying the head out in the open."

"Where you goin' with this?"

"I don't know, but think about it for a second."

The two men walked their drinks over to the bar for a refill—having decided without discussion that their last drink would be next-to-last.

"Look," Will said. "The only thing ever on the beach besides kids is old people walking their dogs, tourists and yuppie joggers, right?"

Jim nodded and sipped his Scotch, letting Will wander.

"For this guy to get by with nobody seeing him, he's gotta look pretty much like everyone else."

"Gotcha."

"Now. For the sake of discussion, let's assume that this prick isn't gonna fit in with the oldsters walkin' their dogs."

"And why do we assume that, Kemosabe?" Jim asked.

"Because, smart ass, old people seldom have the muscle strength to cut off somebody's head. And if they do, they don't walk it to the beach and dump it on a little kid's sand castle. They're too tidy for that."

"True," Jim said. "Plus they've got trash compactors and curbside pickup for stuff like that."

"There you go. I think you've finally stumbled onto the path of my reasoning."

Jim rubbed the residue of a smile from his eyes. "So what you're saying is that our guy is twenty to forty or so and in decent enough shape to jog at least a little ways."

"Enough to get down to where Sari was and then away pretty quick."

That was their single conclusion when Jim got up to leave twenty minutes after the grandfather clock announced Sunday's arrival. Will walked Jim to the door. As they said their goodbyes, both knew that the next day would be grim, only partly because sleep wasn't likely to come easy.

"Sari all right?"

"Good as we can expect, poor kid. Jesus! What a helluva deal."

"I know. Look, you stick close to home tomorrow. I can cover the office."

"I gotta be there. Coroner's gonna call in the morning, and the papers are gonna want my comments. Besides, Sari'll be in good hands. Peach said she'd spend the day with her and David."

"God bless Peach. Will, we're gonna get this fucker." Jim said it with more than a professional resolve.

Jim himself came from a large, loud, and loving family. The rule in the Sequeira family had always been one for all and all for one. Pity the poor slob who made an enemy of one Sequeira, for he soon found himself facing an army of look-alike opponents. When it came to family loyalty, the Sequeiras, Jim thought, were like the Mafia—without guns. To Jim, Will came close to being family, and that the man adored his kids was one more bond between the two.

It wasn't until Jim got to know Will pretty well that he was let in on the fact that Will was a first-generation practitioner of this kind of family. An only child, Will rarely even saw his father. Will's youthful existence was made up of school, sports, and strained meals with his silently suffering mother.

Will told Jim that, while a teenager, he'd decided that if he ever had kids, they wouldn't be relegated to minor players in the family drama. When Debbie became his wife, that resolve became reality. Though she was an only child, she'd come from a big Italian family—she couldn't remember a dinner at home with just her mother and father. Every meal saw a cousin, aunt, uncle or grandparent at the table. More often than not, her father would bring one or two buddies from his construction crew home for dinner.

Will and Debbie were in perfect agreement about parenting. They developed an extremely open and affirming relationship with their first-born. By the time Debbie died, David had known more parental affection than Will had experienced his entire life. The security of those first four years enabled David to survive the loss of his mother relatively intact.

After Debbie's death, Will gave everything he had to ensure that his baby daughter would enjoy the same strong home environment. He supposed, he'd told Jim, that he was a bit of a nut on the subject.

But it was prudence, not nuttiness, that made Will check the locks on all three doors and every window on the ground floor. That was something he'd always done in Jersey City, but hadn't felt the need for since they'd come to Carmel. As he turned each lock, the action made him angrier. It was almost as if the tides of crime and fear he'd left on the East Coast were washing up on the shores of Carmel.

As he trudged up the stairs, that thought caused a shudder to climb his back all the way to his neck. He went back downstairs and threw the deadbolts on the front door and the back door.

Was he being paranoid? The uncomfortable thought followed him back upstairs. What had happened was surely an isolated, perverted act, and it was just lousy luck that it happened here and to Sari. He checked on David. Out like a light. There were at least four complete changes of clothes on the floor along with a baseball bat and glove, two baseballs, a toy gun, dozens of comic books and countless baseball cards. He'd get after David tomorrow.

For tonight, as he bent to kiss his son, Will was thankful that David at least had not been exposed to the horrible sight on the beach. He and his gang had been a good half-mile away. David, of course, wanted to see the treasure that had been deposited on his sister's sand castle. Luckily, by the time he'd arrived on the scene, Jim had cordoned off the area and had covered the head with a beach towel.

Will walked across the hall and into Sari's room. She, too, was sound asleep. Thank God for that. He leaned over and gave her a kiss as he did every night. She slept on. Kids were resilient, he thought. She'd be all right. He'd make sure of that.

He sat on the chaise lounge in the corner of her room, displacing two bears, a doll and a monkey, amazed in retrospect at how soon after he had gotten her home Sari had calmed down. Each time she'd told him the story, she'd done so less tearfully. By her bedtime, she seemed nearly back to normal.

For one second, as his eyes closed on him, Will wondered if the murder in his own heart matched the fury that had driven a murderer to add such a grotesque coda to his crime.

Sunday Morning
Chapter Three

He awoke with a start. A noise. Outside? He swung his feet to get out of bed only to discover he was on the chaise in Sari's bedroom. Jesus, my head, he thought. He stumbled over Sari's stuffed monkey on his way to the window. The part in the curtains allowed a trace of early daybreak to edge into the room. As he looked out, he saw a figure in the driveway and—what the hell was that? A car?

Will crossed the room in three steps and took the stairs two at a time. He grabbed his gun from the top shelf of the tall bookcase, chose the back door and crept around the side of the house as quickly as prudence allowed. He couldn't make out the kind of car, but he heard something or someone at its rear. He moved rapidly toward the sound and announced, "Hold it right there! Hands up!"

"Easy, cowboy. It's me!"

"Jim! What the fuck you doin' out here at this hour?"

"Last night? This goddamned tire was flat on me, so I walked home."

"For Chrissakes..."

"Brand new. Michelins yet. Hundred and sixty bucks apiece. Bastards're gonna eat this tire."

"That's a lotta artichokes," Will agreed. "Need help?"

"No, I got it."

"Well, then, c'mon in and make some coffee while I shower and shave."

"Helluva night's sleep on your end, too, huh?"

"You and I can't ever again be left unchaperoned with a bottle of Scotch."

"It's those god-damned liters and milliliters."

"That must be it. I'll be down in fifteen minutes. Come in the back door, front's not open," Will said, disappearing around the side of the house.

Will was still on the far side of the back door when he heard it—Sari yelling for him. He hurried inside, this time taking the stairs three at a time, and was in her room in less than five seconds. "What is it, sweetheart?"

"Daddy, where were you?"

"Just down front with Uncle Jim, baby."

"Daddy, I saw a man," Sari said.

"Where?"

She pointed to the doorway of her bedroom. Will could see in her face the effort she was making not to cry.

"Sweetie, that was probably me on my way out—I slept in here last night—or else you were having a dream."

Will sat her on the bed. As he hugged her, over her shoulder his eyes swept the room. Something was not quite right. His eyes honed in on the chaise where he'd spent the night. All of the stuffed animals were placed neatly on it, including the monkey. Will rushed to the window, threw it opened and yelled, "Jim, get the hell up here quick!"

Before Jim had taken a step, Will was on his way to David's room. He burst through the door to find his son still sound asleep. Carefully, he closed David's door—no point in waking him or his curiosity. As Will started back down the hallway, Jim appeared at the top of the stairs, gun in hand. The two of them stood ten feet apart, each holding a loaded thirty-eight. "What the hell's going on?" Jim said.

"I don't know, damn it." He shook his head, which was aching. "Lock the back door and search the downstairs."

"What am I looking for?"

"Sari thinks she saw someone standing in her doorway. I'm gonna search around here. It's probably nothing 'cept her imagination, but I need to be sure."

Each man completed his task within five minutes. The house was secure. Nothing except Sari's stuffed animals seemed out of place.

Dispatching Jim to mind Sari and start breakfast, Will walked down the hall to his room, pulled off yesterday's very tired clothes, balled them up and dumped them in the hamper. He turned on the hot water, knowing it would take almost three minutes before anything close to tepid would climb the twenty-five feet from the venerable water heater in the basement. He could hear Jim and Sari chatting away, then moving down to the kitchen. As Will brushed his teeth, he tried to sharpen his focus, but the booze had apparently disconnected a few of his brain's synapses. He spat out a little blood—damn his wimpy gums!—and gulped several aspirin with some tap water. He stepped into the shower.

Fourteen minutes later Will entered the kitchen tucking in his pale beige cop shirt. The smell of bacon cooking seemed to quicken the flow of blood through his veins.

"You're looking a little better." Jim drained the grease from a huge black frying pan.

"In this case looks are definitely deceiving," Will said. "Where's the coffee?"

"Where's the pot? Couldn't find it."

"Right there by the stove where it always is." Only it wasn't. "Where the hell'd it go?" Will opened a cupboard. "This is ridiculous. That thing's been in the same place since I moved in. I gotta have coffee or I'll die."

"Got any instant?"

"Yeah, I think somewhere," Will said without enthusiasm as he rummaged through more cupboards.

"Just boil some water and sit down. Sari's requested scrambled eggs. You want some, too?"

"About six, half a pound of bacon and four pieces of toast." He was surprised at how ravenous he was.

Over their logger's breakfast, Will asked Sari—gingerly—whether she'd picked up the stuffed animals and placed them back on the chaise in her room. Sari shook her head. Even more cautiously he asked if she remembered anything about the man in the dream. She was saying that all she'd seen was a shadow in the doorway when David appeared in the kitchen, rubbing the sleep out of his eyes with one hand, scratching at his pajama top with the other.

"What's for breffus?"

"Nothing 'til you wash your face and brush your teeth," his father said. "Bacon and scrambled after that."

"Can I drink my orange juice before I brush my teeth?"

"Okay, but move it. I've got a busy day."

David shuffled toward the refrigerator to pour his juice and said, "Is Jim here because you're gonna find the rest of that guy's body today?"

Will looked quickly at Sari, then aimed a not-now glance at David. He'd told the boy last night: No mention around his sister about the events yesterday morning.

Silence hung in the room like a low fog until David asked, "Dad, how come the coffee pot's out on the woodpile?"

Will nearly overturned his chair in his haste to look into the backyard. There, on top of the stacked woodpile was the coffee pot, cord in, standing upright.

"What the hell?" Will said.

"Jeez, you were in sorry shape last night," Jim said.

"Not that goddamned sorry, I wasn't."

Will brought the pot back into the house and, after looking at it closely, washed it and started the coffee brewing.

"Now answer me, everybody, and I'm serious," Will said. "Did any of you put that pot out there on the woodpile?"

"No, sir."

"Nope."

"No."

He motioned Jimmy into the hallway. "That pot wasn't on the woodpile when you were changing the tire."

"Hell, you prob'ly just went by it without noticing."

"No." Will's tone was firm. "When I went outside, there was still some mist in the air."

"So?"

"The coffee pot was as dry as a bone just now when I went out to get it. The top layer of logs was wet, but the pot is dry."

Before Jim could sort through those strands of information, the telephone rang in the kitchen. Will caught the receiver before the first ring had ended.

With Will involved in conversation at the far end of the long kitchen, Jim asked the children if they, for sure and swear to God, had not moved the coffee pot outside. They both said they hadn't touched it, crossing their hearts dutifully. The oath-taking was barely finished when Will slammed home the receiver on the near ancient wall unit.

"Kids, upstairs. David, brush your teeth. Get dressed quickly— you're both coming to the station with Jim and me until Peach can get you."

"Where's she gonna take us, Daddy?" Sari asked.

"I wanna go to the boardwalk," David said.

"Never mind. Hustle!" Will snapped.

The kids froze at their father's tone, then moved.

Jim started to clear. "That phone call, more bad news?"

Will nodded. "Hizzoner the Crystal Gun."

The reference was to Carmel's current mayor. As with Eastwood before him, the mayor's fame transcended his political role in the little village. A trio of fast-paced adventure films beginning a dozen years earlier had made Elliot Randolph one of the world's most popular movie stars. The "Crystal Gun" movies ranked second, fourth and seventh in all-time box office gross. Randolph's vow that he would never again repeat the role did not alter the fact that he would always be known principally and forever as the Crystal Gun—Gun or Gunner to his friends.

After Eastwood's term as mayor, the politics of Carmel quickly reverted to unbridled pettiness. Randolph, a Carmel native, couldn't stand the circus. After failing to convince Eastwood to run again, he filed for candidacy himself. He won a lopsided victory and had been re-elected two years later. Randolph had proven to be an extremely effective administrator—even managed to get the environmentalists and the developers to sit at the same table. During his forty-one months as mayor, the affairs of the city had moved forward with civility.

Of course, with him as mayor, Carmel was guaranteed far more attention from the national media than a town of fewer than five thousand residents would normally enjoy. Reporters and their crews loved the assignment—receiving pay for spending a few days in this beautiful spot beat the hell out of doing a walk-through of a homeless shelter or a piece on the latest designer drug.

The surprising part was that nearly everyone was happy with Randolph's success. Probably because there was no pretense about the man. His down-to-earth manner especially appealed to Will, and the two had become occasional golf partners within weeks of Will's arrival in town. At some undetermined later date, they became friends. Randolph and Jim's older brother Manuel had been close friends since grade school.

"What's Gun doing calling at this hour?" Jim asked, well aware of Randolph's partiality to nighttime hours.

"He wanted to know if I'd read this morning's *San Francisco Chronicle*." Will eyed the still-wrapped newspaper on the drain board.

Jim turned from the sink and threw Will a quizzical expression.

"We got a big fuckin' problem, Jimbo."

"Besides the head, you mean?"

"Some asshole had a camera at the beach yesterday and managed to market a lovely photo to the *Chron*. The goddamned head's on the front page of about a million people's morning paper." Will spoke in a low monotone. The kick he used to close the dishwasher was a truer clue to his state of mind.

"That rag'll print anything," Jim offered in the hope of moving Will up out of his funk.

It didn't work. Will said, "Guy at the *Monterey Herald* called and said they're gonna print it tomorrow."

"Shit!"

"Exactly. Gunner's shittin' all over. People been calling him since six this morning saying how bad the picture is for the tourist business."

Jim nodded. "Lots of other places to go and buy a T-shirt—without losing your head."

Will looked down for two beats, then caught Jim's eye again and said, "We gotta find this asshole, Jim. Not finding him's bad for our business, too. My contract's up in three months. I've been around politics enough to know how something like this can panic people, and all of a sudden you've got no friends. Goddamnit, I love this place. I want to stay here. And I sure as hell don't want some two-bit psycho son of a bitch screwin' that up."

"We'll find him."

"It's gotta be quick—unless he's moved on. Shit, for a town that outlaws ice cream cones on the city streets, heads rolling around seems just a bit fuckin' much."

Before Jim could respond, Will yelled up the stairway for the kids to hustle.

"Why not just have 'em wait here for Peach?"

"Because the coffee pot isn't the only thing that moved by itself." He told Jim about spending the night in Sari's room, and described how the stuffed animals had somehow made it back to the chaise from the floor, including the monkey he'd tripped over on his way to the window.

"There's gotta be some reasonable explanation." Jim said.

"Right. 'Cept there's just you, me and the kids—and none of us moved the pot or the animals."

Jim shook his head and rubbed his fist over his mouth.

David and Sari thumped and rumbled down the stairs, finally ready to leave.

As they all piled out the door, Will stared back into the kitchen as if memorizing where everything was and daring any of it to move in his absence. He closed the door, and, for the second time in three years, double-locked it.

Sunday Morning, A Little Later

Chapter Four

Their two-car caravan arrived at the station a few minutes before eight. Will had driven his Jeep, while Jim drove the department's cruiser, a powerful 2001 Chevrolet that was capable of speeds up to 150—although, truth be told, during its tour of duty in Carmel the car had never been pushed beyond 70. Yet. David and Sari, preferring the more official police vehicle to the Jeep, rode with Jim. When they reached the station, the kids barreled inside and ran back to cell A, their private playroom for the last three years.

Even this early, it was safe to predict a beautiful day. Any time the fog disappeared by early morning, sun was guaranteed until at least mid-afternoon. When he first came to Carmel, Will had disliked the fog. That June, three years ago, offered up three solid weeks of it. By the time it passed, he'd almost forgotten the feel of a sunny day. Summer on the peninsula, he soon learned, was a running battle between clear skies and misty fog. Sometimes the battle was waged several times on a given day. But winter was usually mild and clear as the fog found a semi-permanent home over much of the state's central valleys, where it moved in for weeks at a time.

Except for an occasional battering storm, Will could confidently plan a game of golf any month of the year. That was such a huge contrast from the East Coast that he soon lost his distaste for Carmel's gray ceiling. Here his golf game had been fogged out only once. In Jersey his clubs stood in the basement from mid-October to early April.

Today the sky was so sharply blue that it looked fake. Nearly as fake as the tones used in many of the seascapes in the town's four dozen art galleries. A faint breeze whispered steadily through the tops of the huge pines and cypress trees. It was already a comfortable 55°, heading for a high of 68°. Today should be a great one, Will thought. At least so far as the weather went. What the rest of it would be like, he reminded himself, was iffy at best.

He was happy to see that Jeff and Jennie, his two parking officers, were already at the station. He'd hired them and took some small pride in his judgment.

Jeffrey Akins was twenty-six, tall, blond and still built like the linebacker he'd been at Monterey Peninsula College. Jennifer Coe, twenty-four, was about half Jeff's weight, but had graduated top in her class at the Highway Patrol Academy last October. She could have gone virtually anywhere in the country to work, but had chosen Carmel because, she said, it was obviously God's country and she was a loyal patriot.

She'd winced when Will had told her his only opening was for a parking cop. "Any chance for advancement?" she'd asked.

Will said there honestly was, that the mayor agreed that the town needed two additional "real cop" positions and felt he had the votes on the City Council to get them. She would, he'd told her, have a good chance at one of them if her performance up to that time was good. In fact, it had been exemplary. So far as Will was concerned, she had the job locked.

Fifteen years ago, in the grit of Jersey, Will had doubted the value of female cops. That is until Helen Rostovsky and Kinisha James had set him right. The former wiped him out consistently at arm-wrestling. The latter saved his life. Amazing the little things that can knock a prejudice right out of you, he thought.

Jeff was due to leave for the academy in a month. His days of hell-raising seemed behind him for good, and he wanted to stay on in Carmel if he could be free of the chartreuse Cushman and the chalk stick.

Will felt his troops made a good force for the city. They all worked well together. He could recall only one moment of difficulty, and that had been dispatched skillfully by Jennie. During her first two months on the job, Will, Jim and Jeff, all single, had each made an unmistakable, if genteel, hit on her. One morning when all four were finishing coffee before the day's duties were to begin, Jennie asked for the floor. "This is really just a minor housekeeping item, gentlemen. You're all wonderful guys—perhaps a trifle on the horny side—but wonderful nevertheless. At this moment in time I am not in need of a boyfriend, but I'll sure let you know if that changes. In the meantime, you should all know that there are plenty of girls out there who'd love to go out with you. I hope you each find one—or more, if that's your inclination—soon. Now, if you'll excuse me, I have to hit the streets and protect the municipality from the perils of poor parking practices."

The impact of Jen's words was instantaneous—vaporizing a silent sexual tension which, sooner or later, could have at least threatened if not destroyed the team that Will was building. From that moment, the atmosphere in his station had been ideal.

Jen's very gentle put-down caused her stock to rise with all three of her male colleagues. Thereafter, her professional opinions were sought and valued by each—especially Will. Her instincts on policy and procedural matters were unerring. She was smarter than she was pretty, and she was damned good-looking. She also quickly became the department's foremost public relations favorite with townspeople and tourists alike thanks to an easy personality that never seemed to fail her. Will saw no limits to the success she would enjoy in her chosen line of work.

Now as his group gathered to hear the orders of the day, Will poured himself a cup of coffee. "Okay, guys, it looks like we're all going to get to be real cops for a while," he said, not failing to note the beaming faces of Jen and Jeff. He recognized that eagerness—he'd felt that way himself a long time ago. He'd learned all too quickly that cops who wanted to survive were not the swashbucklers. Those either burned out fast or were killed trying to do something glamorous or heroic. The first action he always equated with stupidity and the second he usually did. Feeling a kind of world-weariness he hadn't felt since he'd left New Jersey, he decided he had to give this very green crew a crash course in the mechanics and nuances of real police work.

"I want you to pay strict attention to what I'm about to say. Follow my instructions exactly, and we might find this guy. Even if we don't, doing what I say just might save your life." Will noticed that his words had done little to remove the first-prom glow from his two parking officers.

"Cop work is a painstakingly slow, often boring, proposition," he went on, his tone uncharacteristically—and deliberately—flat. He sought eye contact with Jeff and held it. "You talk to people and try to make 'em remember tiny things that are very forgettable. Write down everything, not just what sounds important to you."

He switched his eyes to Jennie, latching onto hers and holding on. "Sometimes a crucial lead will pop out of a seemingly insignificant throwaway comment made by someone you're interviewing."

Will had a dozen examples to give for every point he made—and was tempted to throw out a few—but resisted the urge. His major goal was to inject caution and care into their every approach, not to prepare them for an exam on procedure.

"Once you think you've found a lead—any kind of lead—you get ahold of Jim or me *before* you check it out. No exceptions. We're too small to work in teams, so if you get onto something, you get one of us. Understood?"

Jeff and Jennie both nodded. The total absence of lightness in Will's tone was making them listen with matching seriousness.

Still, lest he ever have reason to regret a lack of emphasis, he decided to say it one more time. "We're dealing with one *bad* son of a bitch here, and there's safety in numbers. I can't stress enough how important this point is. No cowboy stuff."

After another ten minutes of preaching, he knew it was time to quit. Humans were not constructed to listen attentively to long sermons. If only more ministers knew that, there'd be fuller pews on Sunday,

Will thought. Besides, he could read in their faces that he'd made his point.

"Jennie, I want you to hit the beach. Interview all the regular dog-walkers and joggers you can find. See if any of 'em saw anything or anyone out of the ordinary anywhere near Sari's sand castle calamity yesterday morning. Clear?"

"Yessir," Jennie said, as she pulled a new notebook and pen from the supply cabinet.

Will thought he caught a flicker of boredom moving through her beautiful brown eyes. He locked those eyes with his own stare until Jen looked down.

"Jeff, comb the whole beach—all of it—for anything that could be remotely related to what happened yesterday. I can't tell you what to look for, but take gloves, a bunch of envelopes and a coupla Hefty plastic garbage bags so you can bring back anything that looks promising or unusual. Got it?"

"Yessir."

Jim's job was to phone every police agency in the state to determine if there had been any kind of similar homicide anywhere in recent weeks. If the bastard was a serial killer, and if they could chart some kind of migratory pattern—then maybe they could begin to narrow down the direction in which he was moving. Also, if there were similar cases elsewhere, there was a chance they could snag a clue or a description from another jurisdiction.

Will told them to return to the station at one o'clock. He would have the delicatessen at Nielsen's Market make up a pile of sandwiches. While they ate, they'd review every bit of information that their morning's labors uncovered. Then they'd figure out what to do next.

"I know this isn't a very stimulating set of duties," Will said. "Lotsa cops got fat asses because most of their work is done in a chair. I hope this psycho is in Oregon by now, but in case he's not, I want every stone turned, and *safely* turned." He hadn't meant to warn them again. But, hell, he was professionally responsible for each one of these cops, and he *liked* all of them.

"So," he plunged right on. "Call in or come in if you find yourself following a clue that even smells like it could lead to any kind of confrontation."

Will knew the worry in his voice was also written on his face. He hoped his words had cut through the veneer of bravado and excitement Jeff and Jennie had shown just twenty minutes earlier. When they left, they looked pleased to be out of their Cushmans for the day. Will nearly prayed that they understood the utter seriousness—and potential danger—of their assignment.

After the door closed behind the young parking cops, Will turned to Jim. "Christ, I feel like I just sent two kids down a big hill without training wheels."

"They'll be fine—don't worry. What's your schedule this morning?"

"I'm going over to the *Pine Cone* and see Bob. I want to try to get all the pictures taken at the beach yesterday."

"I thought you said the *Chronicle* and the *Herald* had 'em?"

"They do, but Bob oughta be able to get them more easily than I could. You know what a low opinion those pricks in the press have of us guardians of the public safety."

"Yeah, I do. Bob's closest to human of any newspaper guy I've met."

"That's prob'ly because the *Pine Cone* is only a weekly paper." It was the first time he'd smiled.

Jim was so busy figuring, he missed it. "Hell, Will, those photos were taken no more than ten minutes after the head got dropped on Sari's sand castle...."

"I know. It's a real slim shot, but it is a shot. Maybe the asshole stuck around to admire his handiwork. Gotta try everything because right now we got nothin'."

Jim nodded, moved toward his desk and announced that he was ready to start his phone calls.

"Here's fifty bucks, Jimmy. Give it to Peach and tell her to take the kids to the boardwalk, if she can stand it. And ask her if those FBI reports ever came in. I don't see them anywhere."

Will said good-by to David and Sari, told them to behave and said he would pick them up at Peach's house around six that evening.

As he walked over to the *Pine Cone*, Will could not believe how perfect, despite everything, the morning still seemed. Carmel, on this kind of day, could cheer the coldest soul. He was almost beginning to feel carefree when the sight of a kid carrying a pail and shovel reminded him of what happened yesterday. The sun didn't hide, but suddenly its brightness seemed the very opposite of cheering. It almost seemed to be ridiculing him.

Sunday Afternoon
Chapter Five

"**D**id you cover the whole beach?" Will asked Jeff, as he eyed the remainder of the huge salami and provolone sandwich sitting on his desk.

All four starving cops were devouring specialties of the deli as they shared the results of their morning's work.

"Still gotta do the part over by the river," Jeff said.

"Give the river a good look. Those rushes are a damned good place to hide something. Good job so far, Jeff."

"Thank you, sir," Jeff mumbled around a sizable chunk of meatball sandwich.

Will was referring to the morning's major find—a dark red beach towel Jeff had found at the end of the beach, below the Pebble Beach Golf Links. The towel appeared to be two shades of dark red, but a close look through a magnifying glass told Jim that one of the tones wasn't dye. Maybe, just maybe, it was blood.

Returning to the station just as Will got there, Jeff practically dragged Will inside. He smoothed his trophy out on top of the long counter that separated the three desks from the rest of the room. Jim was on the phone; as soon as he finished his call, he joined them at the counter.

Flanked by his two men, five-foot eleven Will felt small for the first time in his life. Jim had him by two inches and almost thirty pounds. But Jeff was even taller and heftier all around, his wrists as big as Will's forearms.

As they were examining the towel, Jennie came into the office through the back entrance. She'd had little luck with her interviews; no one seemed to remember anything out of the ordinary. Will told her to use the afternoon to contact again everyone she'd spoken to in the morning, asking each of them if he or she could recall seeing somebody with a dark red beach towel on the beach yesterday morning.

"You were right, Chief, cop work can be boring." Jen blotted a dollop of mustard from the corner of her mouth.

"Old cops appreciate boredom, Jen. Means they're still alive. We've got what might be a clue—let's run with it," Will said.

"Okay, I'm outta here, gentlemen…."

"Me, too," Jeff said.

"Everybody back here at 5:30. Same drill. We'll look at everything and go from there. Luck!" Will raised his Coke.

As the two young cops headed out for their second round of real police work, Will was not displeased that they walked with less bounce. Jim stretched, touched his toes three times and belched loudly.

"Enjoy lunch, did you?"

"Loved it, but this phone duty's a dry well. If the resta my calls go like my morning ones, I'll be done soon. Okay if I go down to the beach then and help Jeff?"

"Sure. But finish them all first, hear?"

"Jesus, I'm glad Bob could get those pictures."

"Remind me to tell Jeff and Jen that Bob's got special parking privileges for a year." He was only half-kidding.

"What're you doin' this afternoon?"

"Goin' to Monterey and talk to the coroner. Hoping he can give us something on the poor bastard who ended up on Sari's sand castle. Then I'm picking up the photos—Bob's blowing 'em up. After that I'll prob'ly drive out to the mayor's place and give him an update."

Jim nodded, reached for the phone. "Hey, I forgot. Asked Peach about the FBI reports. She said she picked 'em up at the post office yesterday, put 'em down at the bakery while she picked out some donuts. After she paid and was ready to leave, the FBI envelope was gone."

"I'll be damned," Will said.

"Prob'ly somebody picked it up by mistake. With any luck it'll be returned in a day or two."

Will nodded, and left. But as he walked over to the Jeep, he wished he were more sure it was a simple mistake. Something nagged at some deeply-folded wrinkle in his brain. He needed time to focus on it, straighten it out—time he didn't have. He had a killer to catch. The red beach towel sat beside him in the Jeep. Soon he'd know for sure if those were bloodstains—and connected to the murder. One thing was sure: The coroner would have those answers.

***

Seven hours on the phone had produced nothing. Jim needed fresh air—and to move around a bit. He was strapping on his gun when the phone rang. Before he could complete the formal identification of the Carmel PD, he was interrupted by Jeff's excited, breathless voice. "Jim! Get down here. I think I found the rest of our friend!"

"Where are you, kid?"

"Down at the tules on the river."

"I'll call the coroner and be right there."

Bless adrenaline! But the promise of action nearly made Jim forget to call Will. Failing to inform his boss of this latest development would get him a major ass-chewing. He finally ran him down at the mayor's house, where Will had just finished briefing Randolph on the investigation.

"It's Jim," the mayor said, handing the phone to Will.

Will's eyes widened a notch, then latched onto Randolph's gaze and held it through twenty more seconds of cop talk.

When he hung up, Will said, "I think we've found the victim's body down at the river. I gotta go."

"Not before you promise to phone me—any hour—with new information."

"You got it, Gun."

Their footsteps echoed as they walked across the flagstone floor through the huge living room leading to the front door. Will felt Randolph's hand on his shoulder—guiding him forward. He knew his boss was shocked by yesterday's event, and that he was deeply troubled that such brutality could intrude upon this idyllic spot. He felt the same way and knew a quick solution was the best hope to erase the evil.

***

Will pulled into the small parking lot near the river. At one time, he'd considered ridiculous any reference to the rush-choked swamp as a river. He'd been set right when Jim told him that the swamp had been an honest-to-God-river, the natural pool into which the Carmel River had flowed. For generations it was the chosen swimming hole for those who did not favor the treacherous tides of the ocean. In the late '50s, he learned, the waters of the Carmel River were diverted to other uses, and the pristine pond began its decline into a large stagnant puddle—a process completed by an influx of salt water when, thirty winters ago, huge storms drove the ocean across the hundred yards of sand separating the two bodies of water. Now, the solid wall of tules, eight to ten feet high, looked like something that belonged in Louisiana or Florida. Long-time Carmelites had told him they never came upon the sight without shaking their heads at this sad outcome of someone's idea of progress.

A swamp it definitely was. Jeff's left shoe had been sucked off his foot when he and Jim ventured out into the muck to pull in their catch. They'd beached it, both gasping for air, as Will ran up to them and dropped to his knees.

The men's reactions to the headless corpse were momentarily visceral, not professional. Jeff vomited. Jim's eyes filled with tears. Will's excitement at the sight of their discovery was washed away by a wave of sadness.

Will recovered his professionalism fastest, then anger replaced the sadness. Will felt his anger was beneficial—it sharpened his senses. He'd used the emotion to focus—and ultimately win—in every sport he'd ever played. He hoped this would be no different.

"Looks like a thresher made that cut in his back," Jim muttered.

"Fits what I saw at the coroner's office," Will said, his voice deliberately brusque as he started going through the pockets of the victim. He freed a soggy leather wallet from the soaked denim pants. He squinted at the driver's license. "Brady R. Carson. Nineteen. Los Angeles address."

"Just a kid, for Chrissakes!" Jeff said. The young giant blew his nose and hitched his pants, manifesting recovery.

"Too young and too well dressed to belong with those hippie groups down by Big Sur," Jim said.

"Over ninety bucks in the wallet. Kinda rules out a robbery."

"How 'bout something drug-related?"

Will shrugged, turned to Jeff and said, "Take this license back to the station and call this guy's family or whoever's at the address. First try to find out what he was doin' up here. Then tell them, gently, that he's deceased."

Jeff took the wallet, and Will could see he was happy for any task that might get him away from here and the evidence of his nausea.

As he left, the coroner's van pulled up.

Will turned to Jim. "Stay here 'til they load the body in the wagon. Tell 'em I want everything they get on Carson as soon as possible."

"They ain't gonna like workin' on a Sunday night."

"Fuck 'em! It's not like we dump a stiff on 'em every day. They give you any shit, tell 'em their boss'll be hearing from my boss."

"Yes, sir!" Jim said, tossing a mock salute at Will.

Will didn't grin. "I'm going to get that photo that's bein' blown up. See you at the station when you're done here."

"Mind if I grab a shower first?"

"Please do. You're a little ripe."

With that, Will started across the dune toward his Jeep. He stopped and spoke to the coroner's men. Will's brusqueness, he knew, was out of character. He apologized and told the techs that the case was getting to him.

***

It was almost dark when Jim finished at the river. The coroner's people had not only groused at having to work on a Sunday night, they bitched at Jim's failure to photograph the crime scene. He told them that the body had been twenty feet out in the rushes and that this wasn't the crime scene anyway. Aside from that, they were their usual dour selves.

Hell, of course they were a bit grim, Jim thought, as he trudged across the sand toward the car. Their clientele was exclusively and consistently dead. Most of their house calls were on the side of a highway to pick up what was left of car wreck victims. Where they worked always smelled bad. And the refrigerator where they kept their lunches cool usually also held three or four bodies.

Not a professional life he envied. Why would someone bust ass to get through medical school and then elect to work only with dead people, anyway? The bright side was, of course, that coroners didn't have to worry about malpractice insurance or lawsuits.

By the time he snapped on the lights of his two-story, lodgelike living room, Jim had improved his mood considerably. He knew that his sense of humor was the safety valve that saved him from succumbing to the stress. Will had told him that that safeguard would help make him a good cop in the real world.

"No thanks, buddy," Jim said aloud as he dumped his clothes into the washer. "Here's as close as I ever wanna get to bein' a real cop."

He crossed the kitchen, grabbed a Bud from the fridge and drank most of it in two swallows. He was buck naked as he called the station. The clock in the living room struck six bells. "Jimmy, our 5:30 meeting will start at 6:30. I haven't been able to reach Jennie on her beeper. Have you heard from her?"

"No, boss. But I'll try to get her right after I shower."

After signing off, Jim's recording machine told him he had missed a call from his mother, who was worried about him being in Carmel with a murderer around. His ex-wife called to say there was a leak in the basement, and his girlfriend called to see how he was doing—shorthand for "why hadn't he called?" It took three minutes to convince his mother he was safe and to check in with his girlfriend. The leak his former wife had found in his former basement could wait.

"'Til it's up to the four-foot level, baby," Jim crowed as he went upstairs. He had no vestigial fondness for his ex. He figured that she could've found a handyman in the decade since their divorce. He placed the beer can on the tile sink in his bathroom and flipped his extra-large towel over the shower's sliding doors as was his habit. It was also his habit to turn on the hot water and do thirty push-ups while waiting for the water to warm up.

"Fuck the push-ups—too tired."

He opened the sliding door of the shower tub and reached for the tap. A warm red splash hit his forearm. He looked up.

Jennie's head was swinging from the shower nozzle.

Jim's first thought when he came to was that his ass was freezing. What the hell was he doing lying naked on the bathroom floor? Seconds later, cobwebs began to clear and memory returned. He forced himself to look at what had made him faint. Revulsion quickly gave way to panic. The fucker'd killed Jen, cut off her head and brought it here! He'd been in the house—holy shit, the bastard could still be in the house. Where's my gun! On the fucking dryer downstairs on the back porch, that's where. As far away as anything could be in the house.

"Calm down, Jimmy. Think, baby!" He prayed that only he could hear his words. He looked frantically around the bathroom for any means to make himself less vulnerable. Without taking his eyes off the door, he pawed through the clothes hamper, found yesterday's boxer shorts, and put them on. He knew it was silly to feel safer with his knockers covered, but he did. He wrapped a towel around his left arm and grabbed a can of Right Guard from the sink. Now he was as prepared as he was going to be for whatever the hell might be lurking for him outside the bathroom.

He gave a second's thought to climbing out the bathroom window. Dismissing it, he squared himself in the doorway and threw the deodorant can across the bedroom. Two beats after it bounced off the far wall, Jim leapt from the bathroom and bounded to the middle of his bed where he stood with his back to the headboard. He grabbed the long flashlight from the side table. So armed, he held his breath and listened for any sound that didn't belong. Then, as quietly as possible, he disengaged the receiver to dial the station house.

The line was dead.

Sheer instinct catapulted him back to the bathroom. He slammed and locked the door. Refusing to look again into his shower, he threw open the window and climbed out onto the two-foot expanse of roof. He yelled loudly for what seemed like a month before his neighbor, Jason Overstreet, poked his head out of his back door. "Jim, what the hell's goin' on?"

"Call Will at the station! Tell him to get his ass down here quick! Hurry!"

Jason's noisy retreat and Jim's pounding heartbeat covered the single scrape of a shoe twenty yards away as a figure stood in the row of the pines fronting Jim's property.

Look at the dumb shit standing on the roof, wearing only boxer shorts. Intolerable behavior—especially in a cop! God, what a priceless scene. Pity to miss watching it play out.

The tall, lean man lit a cigarette and, enjoying a last look at the cop on the roof, moved through the pines, his curt, harsh laugh covered by the approaching siren.

Definitely time to leave. His friends will be arriving soon. Clouds are staying out over the ocean so far. Full moon coming up. Beautiful evening. Perhaps another night walk on the beach might be nice.

Sunday Night

Chapter Six

W ill and Jim were each stunned at the sudden loss of Jennie. One, two, three—out! Her professional potential would never be realized; her engaging personality had been simply expunged from the world. Will had barely made it through his conversation with her parents. They would fly out from Colorado to deal with the remains of their only child. No parent should ever have to perform that task, Will thought, as he hung up the telephone. Nothing was as precious to him as his two children.

The previous summer Will had jumped away from a potentially promising relationship with a literature professor at Monterey Peninsula College. Early on, Dr. Jane Eddowes had twice expressed her ambivalence over the amount of time Will spent with David and Sari. But his explanation of why their role in his life was so dominant seemed to mollify her, and their liaison moved to a level fairly close to serious. Then she'd importuned him to read *Sophie's Choice*, praising it as a great celebration of human strength. He read it, trembling when the novel's heroine was forced to sacrifice the life of one of her children to save herself and her other child. It was, indeed, a powerhouse piece of writing, but Jane's recommendation had appalled him. His comfort with Jane began to deteriorate. He began to think of lots of reasons why they didn't have a future together. But if subjected to a lie detector test about why his most promising West Coast romance had dried up, Will would have said only three words: David and Sari.

Though Jennie was not his child *per se*, she was almost young enough to be his. Professionally, she was his. He'd been her mentor and had encouraged her. He'd taken pride in her work and had great hopes for her future.

If Will found it hard to regard Jen's murder clinically, her death only emphasized the urgency of the task before them. That was why, right after his conversation with Jennie's parents, Will called the mayor to inform him that all hell was breaking loose and that he'd brief him after they finished at Jim's house and after he could figure out what to do with David and Sari. Whereupon the mayor not only volunteered to keep the kids, but drove into town to collect them. The offer seemed too large, but Will was too numb to think of a better alternative; so, when Randolph arrived to pick them up, Will settled for genuine gratitude.

"Hell, I'm gonna love having them," hizzoner the Gunner said. "It's lonesome out there. Only get to see mine Christmas and summers."

Will knew that the mayor's spread was the best protected piece of property on the Monterey Peninsula. It wasn't that the mayor was paranoid; rather, the man's many fans were rambunctious to a fault. The elaborate security system was the only way he could have any privacy.

It was typical of Elliot Randolph to offer his help in such a difficult time. He was as kind and unaffected as anyone Will had ever met. When considering the offer of the chief's job, Will had been leery about working for some dilettante, world-famous movie star. His worries had been eliminated the very day he had accepted the position, when he was left with a free evening in Carmel before his morning flight back to Jersey.

Will had just left City Hall for the short walk to his room at the Pine Inn, when Randolph caught up with him.

"Got dinner plans, Will?"

"Well, no, sir. I was just going to have a look around."

"You like a good steak?" the mayor had asked.

It sounded like a test. "Real good?" Will had said.

"Come on. I'll buy you the best New York you ever had."

The mayor had driven Will out to Rocky Point, a dozen miles south of Carmel. The raw splendor of the setting was, alone, worth the trip. High on the rocks overlooking a particularly wild and desolate stretch of the Pacific, the restaurant offered a supremely picturesque view. The steak came close to perfection. The place also had a well-stocked bar, and the two spent much of the evening there, during which Will ascertained that Elliot "Crystal Gun" Randolph hadn't a pretentious bone in his body.

And, Jesus, could he drink. Will judged other men partly by how well they held a substantial amount of booze. He knew it was a pretty narrow test of manliness, but with his roots in generations of police culture, competitive drinking was a major off-hours pastime. Toward the end of that first night in Carmel, Will told Randolph that he'd have made a good cop.

Three years later, after many sociable evenings, countless rounds of golf, dozens of City Council meetings and a small movie role for Will, he knew hizzoner had more to him even than what it took to make a good cop. There was a substance to the man that Will admired. And a caring that he respected.

Will got little more than air kisses from Sari and David as they leapt into the back seat of Randolph's gigantic, white vintage Jaguar. Their excitement at the prospect of an overnight at the movie star's spectacular home had nearly erased from their minds the incredible evil that had touched them and that was now threatening the balance of the entire village.

Will watched as the Jag pulled away. As he trudged to his front door, he wished the events of the last thirty hours were scrubbed from his own mind as well. No such luck, he thought, as he closed the door and moved into his living room to join his deputy for a second night of grim speculation and, he hoped, a search for any clue that might lead to unwrapping the horror before them.

He and Jim reviewed every bit of information they could think of. Jim was amazed to learn that his neighbor's call to the station had come just five minutes after his own call to Will. The phone by his bed had simply been unplugged. That realization infuriated Jim.

"That son of a bitch was playin' with me! He knew exactly what I was gonna be goin' through," Jim said as he paced the length of the living room.

"Seems like it," Will answered, seating himself on the ottoman of his favorite easy chair—the burgundy leather one—that sat nearest to the floor-to-ceiling bookcase on the northwest wall.

"Why Jennie, Will?"

"I have no idea. Maybe she was just convenient. This guy's fuckin' with all of us," Will said. "Bastard musta been near her when she was interviewing people today."

"Crazy motherfucker!"

"Not crazy, Jim—sick as hell, but he's not crazy. I think he's got a plan he's following," Will said and looked up at Jim who was now leaning against the wall nearest to the dining room.

"Plan?"

"I don't know what it is, but I don't think we're dealing with coincidence here."

"What do you mean?"

"I'm not sure. But you gotta look for a motive with murder, unless it's a serial killer—then you throw the book out the window. Jennie, your house—makes me think about revenge as a motive. Maybe this fuck is pissed at one of us."

"Jennie was just a kid, for Chrissakes, and all any of us does here is parking tickets and drunk driving."

"I did a helluva lot more in Jersey. But with a winkie like this it might not even be related to anything any of us has done as a cop."

"You're not exactly narrowing it down."

"Jimmy, we could be looking for somebody who lost an artichoke contest to your father in a Four-H Camp sixty years ago. Or somebody who hates this place—shit. I don't know…"

"Where the hell do we start?"

"The cop angle's best. Make a list of any enemies you've got who might have a genuine hard-on for you. We start with you because he left Jennie at your house."

They continued their back and forth for an hour. Will now felt the killer was here to stay until his plan was carried out or was stopped. It was clear he had trailed them—probably for a long time—because he knew their routines. He also knew their homes. He'd been in Jim's house, and they were pretty sure he'd been in Will's house that morning. The coffee pot. The stuffed animals. Sari's vision of a man in her doorway.

The thought sent a shiver through Will. Jim simply said he wasn't going home until this whole business was over. Will agreed and added that Jeff should also move into Will's house immediately. Until this thing was over, they would stick together as much as possible. The station house was the only place any of them would venture without at least one of the others.

"The guy can't be ballsy enough to come here again," Will said.

Jim nodded his approval to Will's plan. "Fact is, I've never been so goddamned afraid in my life. I mean, I'm no wimp, but this shit's just too fucking much."

"Know what you mean. It's us against him, and he's not through with us yet. He's bound to make a mistake. When he does, we'll get his ass."

While they waited for any information from the coroner, Will had Jim call all the people on Jennie's interview list. With great reluctance, but realizing he had no choice, Will placed a call for help from the county sheriff. He liked Sheriff Buck Truitt, but he hated to admit he needed Truitt's help.

Truitt's words were appropriately sympathetic and cordial, but Will detected a hint of condescension in the sheriff's tone as he agreed to assign two deputies to the case. Will made it clear that they would report to him and only him. Truitt was equally clear that his men would brief him on a regular and frequent basis. Will had no alternative but to agree.

"Who we gettin'?" Jim asked after Will put down the receiver.

"Ainsley and Forsburg."

"Coulda been worse."

"Yep. They're both good guys," Will said. He heaved himself up from the ottoman and got his gun from the top shelf in the tall bookcase.

"Call Peach and Jeff and have them meet us at the station house."

***

In thirty minutes the foursome was in place at the station. While the coffee brewed, Will spent extra time with Jeff and Peach. His dual purpose was to provide what comfort he could to ease their grief over Jennie's loss and to determine if either of them could hold up during the investigation that lay ahead. Neither had ever experienced anything like this, and Will needed to know that they could function in their jobs and that they would be safe.

Peach was shocked and her sadness was palpable, but her resolve to see this task through to a successful conclusion was Marine-like. Her toughness didn't exactly surprise Will, though he wondered at its genesis.

Jeff was obviously shaken, but his major emotion was anger. He seemed ready to do whatever was needed to avenge Jennie.

Will felt he could build this foursome, plus the two deputy sheriffs, into an effective team to catch the killer—if he could have some time before another murder occurred. He realized how very tenuous that possibility was, so after one last but very pointed lecture on safety, he gave out assignments to each.

Then he moved over to Peach's desk. As she busied herself at her computer, Will leafed through the piles on her desk. He was searching for the photo enlargements he'd picked up that afternoon. He spotted, instead, the monthly FBI reports.

"Peach, where'd this come from?"

"Forgot to tell you. Jeff found it propped up against the front door when he came back from the beach to call Carson's parents. None of us was here, so the place was locked. Like I said earlier, prob'ly somebody accidentally lifted it from me yesterday and brought it here when they found it."

"Makes sense. I'll look at 'em later." Will looked over at Jim. "You about done?"

"Three more calls."

"Finish 'em, then we'll get out to Gunner's. I still gotta give him a full briefing, and I want to see the kids before they go to bed."

Will found the photos, opened the Kodak envelope and removed the six poster-sized blow-ups of the photos taken yesterday at the beach.

They were grainy as hell, but they revealed at least the features of people, the colors of their clothing and, in one case, the color of a towel. Will grabbed Peach's magnifying glass, bent the lamp as low to the desk as possible and zeroed in on the man in the photo holding the towel.

Even in the washed-out colors of the enlargement, you could see that the towel was a dark red—and looked one helluva lot like the towel Jeff had found on the rocks below Pebble Beach. The man carrying the towel was in the background of the photo, walking in that very direction—toward the Lodge at Pebble Beach. Longish, brown hair— maybe red, hard to tell.

"Okay, I'm done. Nobody saw nothin'," Jim said, completely unaware that he'd snapped Will's concentration.

"C'mere. Look at this. Use the glass," Will said.

Jim bent over Will's shoulder and squinted through the glass.

"Oh, shit, baby! That could be the guy right there. It's got to be the same towel, doncha think?"

"Sure looks like it. Beats the hell outta anything else we got."

Jim placed the magnifying glass on the desk very gently, walked to the large window in the outer office, lifted a single blind and stared out into the darkness. His voice was hollow and a half-octave deeper than usual. "I want to catch the fucker and kill him."

Will got up, walked to the window and laid his hand on his friend's shoulder. "Me, too. Might be better police work, though, if we first make sure this is the guy who did it."

Jim turned and looked Will in the eye. Jim's skin was nearly gray, and Will thought his friend looked like a man who had never smiled. "This is the guy, Will. I can feel it. He's just what we said we were lookin' for, remember? A yuppie jogger-type. Twenty to forty. Fits right in with the beach scene—right?"

"Yep."

"Picture's fuzzy, but the dude looks closer to twenty than forty. Hair's long. Legs are pretty muscular. What now?"

"Call Gunner and tell him we'll be another hour gettin' out to his place."

"How come?"

"We're goin' over to Pebble Beach—to the Lodge."

On the ten-minute drive to the resort Will tried to calm Jim's enthusiasm by explaining that they were operating on a pure hunch. One blurred photo and one red towel added up to barely half a clue, although the coroner had reported that the towel Jeff found was stained with Brady Carson's blood. Jim asked why they were going to the Lodge.

"Well, our guy jogs down the beach toward Pebble, dumps the towel, thinking the ocean'll sink it or carry it out. He climbs up to the golf course and becomes Joe Tourist Jogger, who nobody pays attention to 'cause he looks like everybody else."

"So?"

"So why go all the way down to Pebble unless it's near where he lives?"

"You think he's maybe stayin' at the Lodge?"

"It'd sure be nice. Otherwise, our great photographic clue is a dead end."

"We can't even give a decent description of the bas—"

"We're not going there to describe anything except the long hair— red or brown—and to Xerox the Lodge's register for the last month. We call CI&I and have them run a check on every name in that register."

"You're the cop, boss. What's CI&I?"

"The state's Criminal Identity & Investigation unit."

"Like this guy's gonna use his real name signin' the Lodge's register?"

"Shit, Jimmy, I know it sounds like nothin'—prob'ly is nothin'— but with a game like this, you gotta kick over every rock 'til something moves."

Will slapped the cruiser into park directly in front of one of the world's most famous resorts. The two men clambered up the short steps and entered the Del Monte Lodge.

***

Jesus! What the fuck are they doing here? Talking to the manager. There's no way on God's earth they can know who I am, let alone where I'm living.

The lean man moved with feigned casualness to the newsstand adjacent to the front desk. He picked up a magazine and leafed through it as he strained to overhear what the two uniformed cops were discussing with the manager.

Fucking magazine's shaking. They'll notice. Got to get out of here.

He returned the magazine to its place with marked, but unobserved difficulty. After pausing for a moment to glare at the khaki-clad backs of Will Kempton and James Sequeira, the man disappeared around the corner and continued down the richly carpeted hallway.

Men's room, thank God! Hide in the stall until they're gone. Maybe I should simply go out there, shoot them both and get the fuck on with my journey. But that would spoil the symmetry of the plan and leave too many loose ends. Stay calm. This must be pure coincidence. They can't know—they don't know. Relax. Talk to the manager after they leave. Breathe deeply. Good. Hands are steady. Pulse is slowing. That's better. Jesus! Someone just came in. Using the urinal. Flush the can, get out, wash hands.

My God! It's Sequeira. Calm, stay calm.

"Evening, officer."

"How ya doin'?" Jim's response was a reflex and covered the concern that had brought him to the Lodge.

"Fine, thank you. Lovely evening, isn't it?"

"Sure is. Take it easy," Jim said as he dumped a linen towel into the wicker basket in the corner and opened the door to leave the men's room.

Yes, I'll take it easy—until we meet again, you pig.

Alone once more, the man held his hands out until they nearly touched the mirror that ran the length of the marble double sink.

Steady as a rock.

He looked into the mirror. The left edge of his mouth curled into a quarter of a mirthless smile as he rubbed his hand through his jet black crew-cut.

Monday Morning, The Wee Hours
Chapter Seven

Monday was one hour old. Will and Jim had driven directly from the Lodge to the mayor's house, arriving there at eleven o'clock. Upstairs in Randolph's electronically secure house, Sari and David slept. At the mayor's insistence, the children would be his guests for as long as it took to find a killer who, they all now knew, had been stalking the movements of Carmel's police force.

The three men sat in the mayor's huge living room. Each nursed a short drink as Will brought Randolph up to date on the information they had about the two killings, which, in the chief's opinion, didn't amount to nearly enough to feel they were getting somewhere.

"Victim one: Brady R. Carson, nineteen, resident of L.A. He hitchhiked to Carmel to visit his girlfriend, Benita Lake. Lake is a freshman at Hartnell Community College. She indicated Carson was expected at her parents' house sometime Saturday afternoon. The coroner said Carson died from a single blow of a sharp, heavy instrument. His spinal cord had been severed. Carson had no traces of alcohol or drugs in his blood or organs. Estimated time of death: midnight to six o'clock Saturday morning.

Will stood and worked a knot out of his neck, then sat back down on the leather couch facing the mayor's chair.

"It appears," Will added, "that Carson got in too late Friday night to go to the Lakes' house. Our hope is that someone saw him—maybe with the killer—that night. We'll have five hundred posters with his picture by early tomorrow. We'll get 'em around and the *Herald's* gonna print it. Maybe we'll get lucky."

Randolph seemed glued to his chair.

"The Lakes?" he asked.

"They check out. Both forty-five. She's a nurse, he's an accountant. Twelve-year-old son, dog, cat, two cars—the whole bit. No killer in that house."

"Can you trace the towel—where it was bought?" Randolph asked.

"It's a standard Cannon terrycloth towel. We'll try, but there's thousands just like it."

Will rose again, walked to the small bar where he found more ice and Scotch for his drink. He brought the bottle back and placed it on the coffee table. Jim and Randolph helped themselves as Will sat again and moved on to Jennie, working to keep his voice businesslike.

"Time of death estimated between two and four that afternoon. She'd left the station house at 1:35 p.m. to start her second round of interviews. Three of those on her list told Jim later that she'd spoken to them again in the afternoon. Short visits. No one remembered a red towel from the day before."

"Jim's touched base with everyone on Jen's list. They're all natives, except for a young couple stayin' at the Pine Inn. I doubt our killer's on that list either."

Will touched on his still-hatching theory of revenge. "Only somebody stalking both of us could've known our routines to the degree where he could invade Jim's house, tie a head to the shower and leave without fear of interruption. Hell, none of Jim's neighbors saw anything 'til Jimmy went out the window onto the roof in his shorts."

"Maybe Jim's the target—I mean, it was his shower." As Randolph said it Jim shifted uneasily in his spot on the couch. Will interjected, "What about Sari, for Chrissakes? Also, I think the bastard set Jim and me up this morning and got inside my house." He related the strange goings-on early Sunday morning, which, he thought, seemed like a week ago.

"That's why I was so quick to accept your very generous offer to keep the kids here. This son of a bitch is after somebody—maybe all of us—and he's not quitting until he's satisfied. Our job is to catch him before then."

Will told the mayor of their visit to the Lodge, the loan of two deputy sheriffs for the duration and the living arrangement at Will's house—also for the duration.

"What a fucking mess," Randolph intoned softly, as he lowered his head and rubbed his eyes with his fists.

"Could get worse, Gunner. We haven't even found the rest of Jennie, and I can guarantee the papers'll be bat-shit crazy in the morning."

"Media's got in on Jennie already?" Randolph asked.

"Hell, yes. They're all monitoring our radio frequency and generally hanging around—will be until we nail this guy."

Randolph rubbed the stubble on his chin, squinted and gazed over their heads for a moment. "I hate to be the one to say it first, but the lines between a criminal investigation and a public relations disaster for the village are rapidly blurring. The media aren't the only ones who'll go bat-shit, you know. So will the Business Association. Every day that goes by without an arrest on this deal, those guys'll get a day closer to throwing a *huge* shit fit. Especially that little slime president of theirs."

"Barth?"

"Yep. Ronald P. Barth, himself."

"Aw, fuck him, Elliot," Jim said. "I've known that puke for twenty years—he squats to piss."

The mayor stretched his legs and for one moment smiled so big that his eyes seemed to disappear. But the next moment he was dead serious again. "You're right. The problem is, while his dick is tiny, his ambition is huge—and he's got something of an organized following. It's no secret the guy wants to be mayor."

"Shit!" Jim spit. "He couldn't lead a group in silent prayer."

"You and I know that, Jim. But a lot of folks may not find it out until too late. Barth's been sniffin' around the edges of local politics for years. He has a real need to be elected something, so he can finally be somebody. You know, the kinda guy who can validate himself only by having some sort of title."

"He's too dumb to get elected," Jim protested.

"Come on, Jim, you know better'n that. Some of the dumbest people in the world get their mail addressed to 'The Honorable.'"

"Jesus! Barth." Jim again spat the name out like popcorn chaff stuck in a molar for half a day.

"Besides, he's not stupid—totally unprincipled, yes—but don't mistake him for the village idiot."

"Besides ambition, he has another incentive to run," Will said. "He hates your guts."

Gunner smiled modestly. "Has since I first ran for this job. Can't imagine why."

"Me, neither," Will said. "Just because you're successful, popular, rich and almost good-looking."

"You're giving me too much credit. Barth's jealous of almost anybody who's halfway human. He'd like nothing more than to have these murders raise a panic so he could hang it around my tough-guy image to use against me in the next election."

"Mayor Barth. The prospect is enough to make me puke," Jim declared with a sour look on his face.

"He'll put you guys right in the middle, too, Will. If this asshole keeps killing people, Barth'll paint you as my boys and crap all over you."

"He got any skeletons?"

"Sure. But none that matter. Can't nail a guy for having a girlfriend who's homelier than his wife. Look, I'm not about to get into a pissing contest with a skunk." The mayor looked directly at Will. "What we gotta do is catch this crazy bastard quick. The longer it drags out, the more publicity for Barth."

Will nodded and rose to leave. "Hold on, Will. Take a minute tomorrow to make sure you've got all the horses you need. If you need more from Sheriff Truitt, tell me—he owes me."

Will scowled. "I don't wanta be in to him more'n I already am."

Randolph unfolded himself and stood. He placed a hand on Will's arm and said, "I know, I know. But our first goal—hell, our only goal—is to end this mess quick. Nothing else matters. If I thought it'd help, I'd get the governor to call in the National Guard. There's no room in this for pride. We get another coupla heads rollin' around here, and Barth and the media will flat fucking kill us. Let me remind you also that Avery has been known to intrude his people into local situations like this."

"That's all we need—the attorney general and his group of buttoned-down clowns marching in here."

"Bear in mind he's practically already declared his candidacy for governor. Walkin' over my back, and yours, would generate some real nice publicity for him, too."

"Is he making noises, Elliot?"

"Not yet. Once he calls, though, I can only stall him a couple days. And unless we make some real progress, he'll call—count on it."

Randolph's word signaled an end to the meeting. Will went upstairs and nuzzled his two sleeping children, and he and Jim left. At the door, Randolph said, "Get this guy, Will. Quick."

The drive into Carmel was silent; both men were too exhausted and depressed to attempt even small talk. Will knew that this state of mind was a cop's worst enemy. He also knew he hadn't been a real cop for a long time, and wondered if he could still rally the inner resources to meet this challenge. He had to get some rest and get his brain working.

Jeff met them at the front door, gun in hand. "Jesus, kid, haven't you been to sleep yet?" Will asked.

"No, sir, I been too scared to drop off 'til you guys got back. Peach's asleep up in Sari's room."

Will was not certain that he could make it up the stairs to his bedroom. He turned as he mounted the first step. "Get comfy anywhere you can. I'll set the alarm for six-fifteen. See you in the morning."

He fell on his bed fully clothed and was asleep in ninety seconds. The only good thing about a case like this, he thought, was that it made you so tired your churning mind shut off once you hit the pillow.

***

Forty yards away a man, little more than a silhouette, leaned up against the tallest tree in a copse of four huge redwoods.

Well, well, everyone's staying at Kempton's place. I've gotten their attention enough to make them cautious—and afraid. Nice. Light going out. Could just wait an hour, then go in and kill them all.

Too risky. One of them might be standing guard. Stick with the plan— it's been perfect so far. Move slowly and carefully. Don't want to screw up now. Success is so close I can smell it.

The man squinted as if that action would enable a clearer focus through the wispy fog. He moved forward two steps without a sound.

Last light just went out. How neatly symbolic. All your lights are going out real soon, you bastards. You'll have to separate some time tomorrow. That will be the time to pick you off, one by one.

Well, maybe not. Let them catch up on their work a little. Haven't found the rest of the girl cop yet. She was damned fine. Shame there was no time to know her better. Probably would've been easy, the way she begged this afternoon. Perhaps I'll move into town tomorrow—closer to the action. They won't find me on that list of lodge registrations from the last month, but if they go back another month—too close. OK, I'll move. Then it will be time to meet some of the other citizens of Carmel.

Fog and the lofty cypress and pines blocked the moon. The figure glided toward the car, leaving no trace of his shadow. The car started quickly and quietly. Del Monte Lodge was just ten minutes away.

***

Emma Jacobs' home was just four blocks away, less than a mile from Ocean Avenue, Carmel's only main street. The yellow-shingled house with white trim was surrounded by a short picket fence—straight out of an illustrated fairy tale. If her house was out of a picture book and her garden pretty enough to look slightly unreal, Mrs. Emma Jacobs herself was very real indeed. The white-haired, seventy-three-year-old widow was a widely respected figure in town, known to everyone who counted, which to her mind included almost every citizen under the age of ten. She'd lived in this very house since arriving in Carmel as a twenty-year-old bride. Only the garden had changed with the years, growing ever more full of color as Mrs. Jacobs became bolder. Eight years ago she had been designated president-emeritus of the Carmel Women's Garden Club, a devoted group of green-thumbed matrons over whom she first presided in 1953. Unlike some of the houses in town owned by more casual Carmelites, Mrs. Jacobs' property showed not a single trace of last week's ferocious storm. She had spent most of Saturday raking and bagging leaves, pine needles and limbs. The house looked, as it always did, ready for the photographers to arrive.

On the outside, anyway.

Monday Morning, By Ordinary Standards
Chapter Eight

Inspecting the third beautiful day in a row, a number of Carmel's natives noted that three days was the limit. According to the gospel propagated by the town's skeptics—and most townsfolk were adherents of this Carmel-centered sect—tomorrow would be foggy all day at best.

But today was perfect. The Garden Club's luncheon meeting would be well-attended as it always was when a clear sky reminded the club's membership that, on a good day, there wasn't a place on the planet worthier of the tender, loving care that beauty, by its very existence, deserved.

Alicia (Mrs. Barrett) Noble and Sally-Ann (Mrs. Brewster) Hartshorne were having breakfast together at the Pine Inn on Ocean Avenue. A kind of pre-celebration celebration, complete with mimosas. After all, today was a big day for both of them. At the meeting, Alicia would be turning over to Sally-Ann the Garden Club's gavel—never-yet-needed by any president to keep a meeting orderly, but a cogent symbol of power nonetheless.

As soon as the waiter brought their bill, they would without discussion divide it equally, even though Sally-Ann had ordered a mushroom omelet and Alicia only cereal. If they were careful not to display any twinge of frugality toward each other, Alicia felt perfectly comfortable knowing that Sally-Ann would figure precisely fifteen percent for the tip on the pocket calculator she always carried in her Gucci handbag. Over-tipping, the ladies had agreed the very first time they had lunch together, was a working class failing.

Though others were responsible for setting the tables for the luncheon, both women had an interest in checking the results to make certain that the event would be as special as each of them earnestly believed it to be.

At precisely 10:00 a.m., Mrs. Noble caught the waiter's eye. And at ten past, they were on their way to the clubhouse.

While Alicia and Sally-Ann were sipping mimosas, Will was briefing his new recruits. The very need to expand his force made it clear as this particular morning that Will's strategy had better be good.

Both Clinton Forsburg and Tom Ainsley were around forty. Experienced. But in Will's judgment each carried something more in his kit of qualifications. Clinton Forsburg, tall and fair like his Norwegian ancestors, arrived at the Monterey Sheriff's Office after ten years with the Oakland P.D. He made no secret of the fact that he was drawn by the peaceableness of Monterey. But Clint was also, Will knew, the nearest thing he had to a real cop on his reinforced staff. Oakland did not have as many generations of crime as Jersey, but it had every bit of the desperation and viciousness that marred its Eastern counterpart. As for Tom Ainsley, another linebacker type, he'd known Jim for almost thirty years—and when Jim vouched for a man, Will knew he could count on him.

"Clint, I'm gonna partner you with Jeff. You're the pro. Jeff's a little green," Will said. "I want you two to talk with all of Jim's neighbors. See if any of 'em saw anybody near Jim's place yesterday afternoon who didn't belong there."

Will then turned to deputy Ainsley. "Tom, you and Jimmy meet with everyone on Jennie's interview list. If anyone smells—even a little—bring 'em in."

Both teams were told that they were not to move, even to the bathroom, except in two's. Will indicated that he would most often be with one team or the other; when he wasn't, more than likely it would be because Peach had summoned him back to the station. Will trusted Peach's judgment on that, and she would be at the station throughout— no brief errands today, no donut runs. He didn't need to tell her that; Peach's face said she knew today was to be all business. Will did give her one order: to keep the office locked. Each team was to contact her by radio every thirty minutes to let her know its destination.

At one o'clock, everyone was to show up at the station. Over a quick lunch, they'd share what they'd learned during the morning, and Will would make new assignments as appropriate.

Will told Tom and Jim that they were to interrupt their interviewing immediately to respond to any call from Peach. Will would be in constant radio contact with Peach and could provide back-up if needed. Will explained the sleeping arrangements at Fort Kempton and suggested the newcomers move in.

"Is that mandatory, Chief?" Ainsley asked.

"Well, let's think about it. It's obvious this son of a bitch has been shadowing us for quite some time. Once he sees you two, he might transfer his affections to you—that might not be something you want to take over to Monterey."

Ainsley and Forsburg looked at each other. Will could see that the preceding hour had eliminated any thought on their parts that this assignment was going to be akin to a vacation. Will knew the sheriff's theory that usually, Carmel was a playground so far as police work was concerned. He knew that theory had been set aside for the duration— partly because of the respect they showed him. Where he came from and what he'd been through were not secrets. Their serious demeanors about the task at hand were also clinched by what had been described to them this morning. No question, what had happened was close to the top of anyone's scale of malevolence.

As one, as though they'd talked it over, they nodded now. They'd join the troops at Fort Kempton.

"We'll go over and get our stuff tonight and bring it back to your place," Clint said.

"Be better to call a buddy over there to collect your stuff and bring it right here to the station." Ainsley didn't miss the gravity in Will's tone; he got up and walked to the telephone.

"Okay guys—back here by one o'clock. I'll hit the river—maybe he put Jennie's body there, too," Will said. "I wanna find her before some civilian does."

"Or some asshole tourist with a camera," Jim added. His comment earned a grimace from Will.

After sending his troops off, Will poured a cup of coffee and sat down to read the *Chronicle* and *Herald*. He read both papers' coverage carefully, determined not to miss any reference that might be troublesome—or titillating. He was pleased to find no photos in either paper. Aside from a characteristically garish headline in the *Chronicle*, both papers covered Jennie's death with straightforward brevity and relative dignity.

The *Herald* story was longer and mentioned the expression of "concern" by a spokesman for the Carmel Business Association. Will was relieved to find no reference to Ronald P. Barth. *Good—you little turd! Keep your soft little ass outta my way.* Will knew that any additional incidents would not only give Barth a public forum—but would bring a swarm of reporters from all parts of the country to the village. Both prospects were distinctly unappealing to Will. He knew time was running out—that he had to get this guy quick—but, goddamnit, where the hell to begin?

"Peach, you gonna be okay here all alone?"

"You just leave the coffee on, lock the door, get back here on time with lunch, and I'll be fine."

"Every one of us has a key. So don't you go opening this door to any—"

"Will! Stop worrying. I'm a big girl."

"I know that—and you know I do—but we're dealing with a certifiable cretin here."

"Will, your place is going to be pretty crowded tonight. I was wondering…"

"Peach, you're not gonna go home 'til we catch this bastard."

"Oh, I know that, dear, but if you wanted to do a charming, middle-aged lady a favor, you'd move *her* out to the mayor's house."

The twinkle in her eye made Will smile.

"Peach, you scandalous old broad…"

"Gotta grab for that brass ring whenever you get the chance, youngster."

Will smiled deeply into Peach's eyes. She was as close to being family as anyone except his kids. What the hell. "I'm gonna call and tell him that you're comin' out tonight."

"Oh, no, dear, I was just…"

"You're goin', Peach. I'm not going to have anything happen to you. The mayor's place is wired so if a skunk farts, all the lights go on."

"Will, I'll be fine…"

"Jennie wasn't, Peach—and she had a gun. No, you're goin'. I'll call, and after lunch we'll go to your place and get your stuff. You can leave for there tonight after work."

"I can tell you're not going to change your mind on this. I think it's silly, but…"

"I'd rather be silly than worry," Will said as he reached for the phone.

The mayor said he'd be looking forward to adult company.

"Says he hopes you play dominos or gin rummy," Will told Peach.

"We'll find something in common, I'm sure, dear." She winked at Will.

"What's your schedule this morning?"

"I've got to pick up Jen's parents at the airport at 11:15. I'll get them settled in town, then I'm gonna try to meet with Bob at the *Pine Cone*. He's gotta get next Wednesday's issue put to bed, and I want to give him all I can. He's already been helpful. I wish they all had his integrity. Anyway, I'll stay in touch by radio. Right now, I'm gonna scout around and try to find the rest of Jennie. See ya."

"The poor, sweet girl," Peach mumbled to herself as she double-locked the door behind Will. She filled her cup and returned to her desk. The first thing her eyes fastened onto was the large envelope from the FBI. She looked at both sides of the envelope, checked the postmark.

As she pulled the materials out to review them, she glanced at the clock on her desk. Hard to believe it was only 9:05 a.m.

***

There's the recess bell. Just made it. Jesus, look at 'em all. Like baby horses penned in for days. There's the second-graders. What a lovely day— I'm glad I decided to come out here. Where the hell are the fifth-graders? Ah, there they are. Now, move this way, children—come on.

The man knelt down with both hands grasping the chain-link fence that surrounded the entire grounds of the elementary school.

***

Will had just parked in the lot by the Carmel River when he got the call from Peach.

"Will, a teacher at the academy just called in. There's a loiterer out by the far northwest fence."

"Any description?"

"Gray windbreaker, dark shirt and pants, dark knit hat."

"On my way."

Will made a gravel-crunching U-turn and gunned the Jeep back toward the town's elementary school.

***

Where the fuck are those kids? Been here ten times in the last six weeks, and they always come right over here. Did he keep them home? No, why would he? He doesn't know, not yet. Careful, hands are shaking. If they're home, they're as good as dead. Go visit them later in the morning and ... Jesus! What's this? Two people comin' over here! Fat old bitch and a guy in a suit. Shit! There's a car comin' up the hill. Fucker's spotted me!

***

In forty seconds Will stood in the precise spot the man had occupied moments earlier. He looked through the chain-link fence and saw Miss Klast, a teacher, and Mr. Jameson, the principal, running toward him.

Miss Klast threw her bulk against the fence and wheezed, "He took off over the hill straight into the forest."

Will disappeared over the same hill, unsnapping his holster as he headed down into the forest. He ran three or four hundred yards without seeing a thing except trees or hearing anything except the rustle of branches. Out of breath, he stopped hard and hid behind a bent oak to get a second wind. No sound except his breathing. Then a blur way off to his left and below. He took off after it. *C'mon, you cocksucker, slow down.* His words were little more than a hiss. Fifty yards took him into the middle of a residential enclave. He stopped and listened again. Nothing! The utter absence of noise was eerie.

He retraced his steps. A quick session with Jameson and Klast provided a mediocre description. They agreed to report to the station house after school to meet with an artist who would try to wring a portrait from their agitated brains.

He was still huffing as he walked toward the Jeep. The son of a bitch could run. That fit their scant profile of the killer. And he had headed in the general direction of Pebble Beach. Very general—but it also fit. He wondered if it could possibly be the same guy. Logic said not—most likely just some weenie-waver looking to get it up in front of an audience of kids. Still, Will's instincts darted in and out of his reasoning. Something told him this wasn't a routine exhibitionist call—and made him damned glad he'd told Randolph to keep the kids out of school.

As he neared the door of the Jeep, which he'd left swinging in his hurry to get down to the schoolyard, the police radio crackled, and he rushed to hear its static-covered rendition of Peach's voice: "Mobile Unit One, Mobile Unit One. Come in, please! Mobile Unit—"

"Peach, for Christssakes, it's me. I'm here."

"Oh, thank God! Will, we've got gunshots at City Hall."

"Jesus! On my way."

Monday, Mid-Morning
Chapter Nine

City Hall was a hundred feet south of Ocean Avenue. When Will had made less than half that distance, a mass of people and seemingly abandoned cars barred the Jeep's progress. Will had no choice but to park where he was stuck, and proceed on foot through the milling crowd. As he passed Jim's Chevy patrol unit, the crowd burst into applause. Sounds that loud from a crowd were never good news to a cop—in this case the sound was a mix of cheering and a kind of joyous jeering. Whatever it signified, it did nothing to ease the tension that had begun in him as soon as he took out after the loiterer less than fifteen minutes earlier—and only became thicker when he came up empty-handed.

Before Will could shout at the heedless crowd to get out of harm's way, Jim and Tom appeared on the walkway of City Hall with a small wiry man. Handcuffed. The little man beamed at the assemblage. Another cheer erupted. He bowed to his audience.

When he was still twenty feet away, Will managed to catch Jim's eye. His friend just shook his head: Suddenly, a new day in the life, his bemused face said. But that didn't keep him from doing his job. He bellowed at the crowd to move along even as he wound his way through the assemblage, his hand gripping the handcuffed prisoner just above the elbow.

The surreal tableau so threw Carmel's police chief that he yelled over the heads of the crowd: "Jimmy! What the fuck is going on?" Several disapproving looks were thrown his way. They just bounced off him.

"Just meet me back at the station!" Jim yelled back. "Lemme get this dummy locked up, and I'll tell y'all about it."

Finally, stumbling past a last gaggle of onlookers, Will reached Jim. "Anybody hurt?"

"Five holes in the door of City Hall—that's it."

"What the hell?"

"Just follow us." With that, Jim pushed his way through the maze of spectators in the general direction of the Chevy. The main show obviously over, the crowd, which had disregarded all orders to do so, now dissolved to partake of other fascinating pursuits.

Will walked back to the Jeep, his feet suddenly more mobile than his head.

***

The raucous scene at City Hall a half mile away fell short of intruding on the sumptuous interior of the Carmel Garden Club.

"Oh, Sally-Ann, doesn't it look beautiful?" Alicia Noble said.

Her recent breakfast companion quickly agreed. The two had just entered the clubhouse. They saw six long, linen-covered tables. Each table was set with sixteen place settings and four artfully arranged vases of spring flowers. At the far end of the room, there was an elevated head table with a short podium. It, too, was decorated with tastefully displayed blossoms.

"It's never looked better, Alicia."

They began to walk the length of the room, stopping to smell the arrangements. "A day like today and a setting like this just makes one glad to be alive. Sally-Ann, would you start opening the drapes? I'm going to put my speech up at the rostrum, then I'll do the drapes on the other side."

***

As soon as Jim got his prisoner to the station and confined him securely, he went into Will's office. He made a mighty effort to keep a straight face, but failed. He surrendered and laughed out loud.

"And just what is so goddamned funny, for Chrissakes?" boomed an almost totally exasperated Will. "Who *is* that asshole?"

"Jerry Whiting, Will. You met him."

"Attorney?"

"Accountant. Does people's taxes. Part-time. Does mine."

"What the hell was he doin' shooting a gun at City Hall?"

"Haven't you been readin' 'bout what he's been going through lately?"

"No, I haven't. Quit asking me questions and give me some answers instead." Will's patience was gone, and his puzzlement at Jim's good humor was on a fast roll toward anger.

Jim nodded, moved quickly across the room and sat down in the old, green armchair in front of Will's desk. He looked down for a beat, then up at Will, making sure his voice was conversational, not condescending. "Eight months ago Jerry went to the Planning Commission for permission to cut down a huge Monterey pine. The tree's ten feet away from his living room wall, and its roots are threatening his house. Already's fucked up his front porch. Any of this coming back?"

Will shook his head.

"Well, I'm not surprised. Kind of thing we old-timers love to read. Anyway, the commission farted around with his request for three months and then denied it. Said the tree was too big, too healthy and too beautiful to destroy. Said it was an integral part of the natural peninsula forest, or some such shit," Jim said.

"Okay, I missed this one. But the commission comes up with mindless decisions like that all the time. Most people just appeal their stupider rulings—haven't heard of any of 'em deciding that the appropriate recourse is to unload a goddamned pistol at City Hall. This guy's in serious—"

"He did appeal, Will. Jerry's a tree-hugger, a real environmentalist. He went back to the commission. Told 'em he was going to tear down his house and rebuild it so as not to disturb the tree."

Bewilderment again took over Will's features. He bent forward across his desk, but before he could voice his mounting confusion, Jim snorted his own reaction to the goings-on.

"So," he added derisively, "the commission fiddle-fucks around for another few months and finally tells Jerry that he can't tear the house down—can't even touch it—because the house is ninety years old. According to them, it's of historical significance."

"You're shittin' me," Will said, temporarily hooked on yet another tale of the strange politics of his adopted home. It wasn't that he'd forgotten the events of the last forty-eight hours, but somehow this distraction put into perspective for Will real life in Carmel—that murder wasn't the only way to separate a citizen from his head.

"Wouldn't do that," Jim said. "Jerry's spent the last few weeks trying to show those clowns that they've dumped a perfect catch-22 on him. He's gotten no satisfaction—not one whit. This morning, he took his last shot—or least it seemed that way to him for the moment. He talked to some guy on the commission who told him that the beauty and fame of Carmel can only be maintained through constant struggles and self-sacrifice."

"But it's his house, his property...it's where he lives," Will said incredulously.

"S'right. They didn't give a shit and more or less treated Jerry like a leper 'cause he didn't agree with them. He went back there, to his house, and mulled it over, and I guess he figured out he still had another shot, so to speak. He went down to City Hall and registered an informal complaint with a .22."

"Jesus."

"Mosta that crowd out there were his friends and family. He made some calls to spread the word—kind of invited his kin and some pals— and I guess they called some more folks to come out and view his symbolic protest—that's what he's calling it."

"Symbolic? Real gun, real bullets, weren't they?"

"Yep," Jim answered. Jim stretched forward and placed both arms on Will's desk.

"You think what he did was OK—am I reading you right?" Will asked, meeting Jim's eyes directly.

"Oh, he fucked up. But nobody's hurt—he wasn't out to hurt anybody. Just shot the door. Incidentally, he looked in first to make sure no one was standing on the other side of it." Jim sat back in the chair and folded his arms across his chest.

"People move around, he couldn't be sure. It's still reckless endangerment."

"Disturbing the peace."

"Jim, the man had a gun. DP is too light…"

"Okay. How 'bout DP with destruction of city property?"

"He's gotta pay for the door…"

"Shit, he'll fix it himself. He's a carpenter."

Will shut his eyes, tried to rub a little reality back into his temples. "I thought you said he was an accountant."

"Part-time. Resta' the time he's a carpenter. Did my kitchen cabinets. Good job, too."

"Get him outta here, Jimmy. Book him on City Property and DP and just get him the fuck outta here. And tell him if he so much as spits on the sidewalk during the rest of his life or mine, I'll arrest his ass and send him someplace bad."

"Thanks, Will. Lemme go release him, and I'll come back to compare notes with you on where we are on the other stuff."

***

Sally-Ann Higgins was opening the third drape on the east side of the room when her contented musing was interrupted by a blood-curdling scream. She looked in the direction of where the terrible noise had come from, just in time to see Alicia Noble fall across the head table—as though she had been shot. Alicia's impact knocked a large vase of yellow daffodils crashing to the floor.

Sally-Ann had taken two steps toward her stricken friend before she noticed that the table-top lectern was tipping slowly toward the main part of the clubhouse.

She quickened her pace, impelled by the belief that she could minimize the damage to the lovely room if she could catch the lectern. She could see that it would be close, and hurried even more.

It fell just as she positioned herself under it. She caught its full weight—which propelled her backward two steps. As she righted herself, she glanced down at the burden cradled in her arms. Looking back at her from the lectern's opening, normally reserved for speeches and other papers, was the face of dear old Emma Jacobs.

Sally-Ann screamed, dropped the lectern, and in her haste to get away, tripped over a chair. She bounced off a table and hit the floor so hard that her chignon came undone and her glasses flew off. On hands and knees, she felt madly around for her glasses—then stopped short. Why was she doing that? She could see well enough without them to get the hell out of there, which was the only thing that made sense to her horror-benumbed mind. Just as she braced herself on all fours to get up, the head of Emma Jacobs took a last half-turn, coming to rest on the right hand of the president-elect of the Carmel Women's Garden Club.

***

Will had just finished telling Jim and Tom about chasing the loiterer away from the school and into the forest. Before they could even put their heads together to see if there was some connection to be drawn between the loiterer and the murders, an ashen-faced Peach threw open the door to Will's office. She very uncharacteristically interrupted the conversation between Will and Jim. She was nearly breathless.

"Will, I just took a call from the Garden Club. Emma Jacobs has been killed…and, and…she's…her body…her *head* is there…"

Peach ran out of words and quickly gave way to tears at this latest heinous assault. Will swung his look of disbelief from Peach to Jim, jumped up and began issuing commands.

"Jimmy, get Clint and Jeff over to the clubhouse. Tell 'em I'll be there soon's I can. You and Tom get over to Emma's house. I want both places sealed off as tight as possible. No civilians. No press! And no fucking cameras."

Jim started for the door. Will called after him, "Dust everything in both locations for prints."

"Gotcha."

"Peach, call Randolph and tell him. Tell him to stay outta town and activate every goddamned security device he's got out there. Tell him I'll be in touch as soon as I have anything. Then call the coroner. Tell him Garden Club first."

The ever-professional Peach scurried back to her desk and picked up the phone. Will quickly arranged for the *Pine Cone's* staff artist to be at the station at four to meet with Miss Klast and Mr. Jameson. He then allowed himself thirty seconds to fight off the sadness and fear that threatened his balance. No use. He spent the entire half-minute wondering what kind of monster was loose in Carmel.

***

Jeff and Clint did their best to secure the Garden Club. It had taken them just four minutes to respond to Jim's call. During that brief period of time, Mrs. Higgins and a resurrected Mrs. Noble had managed to set off a discordant—but very loud—din right in front of the clubhouse.

Fortunately, the Garden Club was on a side street, six blocks from the main drag. Nevertheless, by the time Jeff and Clint arrived, three dozen people were milling about, peering through the two-and-a-half uncurtained windows. The long tables precluded the gawkers from gaining any kind of view inside.

Jim and Tom had a much easier task—initially. There was no one in sight as they pulled the cruiser into Mrs. Jacobs' cobblestone driveway. Guns drawn, they approached the front door. Sunday's and Monday's papers were on the porch. The door was unlocked. Tom pushed it open with his boot. Before his heel hit the threshold, the stench leapt at them like an animal caged too long. Jim didn't know the smell; Tom did. It didn't make much difference. Recognition didn't make Tom gag any less.

"Got a handkerchief, Jim? Hold it tight over your nose. Help me open the windows—that'll help a little. Old people always keep their house too hot—speeds up the decomposition."

The word "decomposition" released a new wave of nausea deep in the pit of Jim's stomach. He'd intended to enter the house before Tom, but lost a step to queasiness. The handkerchief didn't help much. The smell was incredible. Jim felt that he could actually see air melting in front of him.

***

To a distant observer, the man at the window overlooking the famed 18th green of Pebble Beach looked like any other vacationer enjoying the magnificent view. A closer look, though, might have provided a different interpretation. The man was rigid except for his hands, which shook in spite of his best efforts to reclaim some semblance of serenity.

Son of a bitch! Plain stupid to go there today without a disguise. Could either of those old farts have gotten a decent look at me? Stupid, stupid, stupid! All that planning—and one fuck-up can cost you the ball game. Goddamn hands! Trembling like an old lady's! Calm down. Look at that ocean—smooth as a lake. I could leave. They'd get complacent, careless. Then, in a few months, I could sweep back in and finish the play. No. No hiatus. The show goes on. There's no way they can know me—no way. Stay put. Stay right here or move to town? Settle in. Listen to the police band—see what they know. Relax. Let them fuck up.

The Longest Monday Morning
Chapter 10

Heading down the hill to the Garden Club, Will felt skittish as hell. Damned adrenaline. He knew if his body felt hyper, his brain was exhausted. Bad blend for a chief of police. Even on the worst cases in Jersey, he and his partner, Phil Curry, always had a plan, always had one another to depend on. Besides, they were always following someone's orders—more or less.

Here, his partner was Jim. Best guy in the world, but not cut out for this kind of pressure. He hadn't even applied for the chief's position three years ago. He liked the number two job, didn't want the responsibility of running the show. Which left Will on his own so far as decision-making went. Great spot to be in when he had no time to formulate a plan—the bastard was hitting so fast, all Will could do was react.

My troops look like a Chinese goddamned fire drill, and we're up against guerrilla warfare! God, I wish Phil was here.

Just the thought of Phil eased the smallest smile onto Will's face. Curry was a cop's cop. The last of seven children of a black Baptist minister, Phil was blessed with two traits that set him apart from nearly everyone—cop or not. He had a great sense of humor and a tremendous mind.

He rolled through school, getting exceptional grades. Any local punk who ridiculed him for being a "teacher's pet" simply got the shit beat out of him. At five foot eight, weighing anywhere from one eighty-five to two-thirty, Curry was as close to a tank as a human could get. Destructive and impregnable.

Phil was the first Curry to attend an accredited, secular college. He chose a school in the deep South—he thought the experience would "toughen him up," he told Will years later. Three years later, he returned to Jersey City. Toughened up.

His parents had expected him to become an engineer or a doctor—both of which were within his reach. His decision to become a cop pleased only Phil. He had explained to Will early in their Jersey partnership the joy he felt at being a cop. "I just fucking love it. All my life I had to fight the pukes of the world to get anywhere. Now I get paid to do that. We're the good guys, Will. And we win most of the time."

It took twenty years and three bullets to put a small warp in Phil's enthusiasm and move his thoughts toward an easier career path. The partners spent the three days before Phil's retirement chopping wood, playing cards and drinking vast quantities of Old Ancestor at the lakeside cabin owned by Will's father. Over the next few days, while Will recovered, Phil signed his retirement papers, grabbed his pension, started divorce proceedings against his wife—who had a doctorate in nagging—and landed a job in California as Chief of Campus Police at Fresno State University.

He and Will never lost touch. After Debbie's death, Phil was convinced that in California Will could get a jump-start on the rest of his life. He brought Will out to the Golden State and showed him the sights and the lifestyle. One night in San Francisco, after a great meal, Phil told Will, "Shit, you can't miss out here, nice white kid like you. Look at me, livin' like a fuckin' king. You'd love it, and it'd be heaven for your kids."

Will's grief held him back. It was easier to slip back into the old routine—work hard enough to sleep at night. Then a gunshot by a fifteen-year-old drug dealer shattered that routine and Will's right kneecap.

Halfway through his two-month rehabilitation, Phil appeared in Jersey City and said what needed saying: Will's knee would never be as good as new; he'd never be the street dick he'd been; a job as a desk-jockey would make him retch. "Grab your disability and get the fuck outta this dump before it's too late," Phil ordered.

Will was convinced. And the last three years in Carmel had shown him how wonderful life could be. An artificial kneecap helped him forget on all but the coldest days that he had a disability.

***

Will pulled up at the Garden Club, having decided. He needed help, and help was spelled P-h-i-l.

How badly he needed Phil was apparent the moment he saw the crowd—now over a hundred people—hugging the front of the clubhouse. As he pushed his way toward the doorway, he heard someone demand, "Why don't you people do something about this outrage, Kempton?"

Will spun around to locate the face of Ronald P. Barth. The nasty mouth had a face to match. Tinted spectacles shielded two small eyes nearly lost in folds of fat. Will had never seen a human form that so resembled an egg. Barth was nearly shoulder-less. The pads in his cheap sport coat curled around his upper arms like two small dead animals. If Barth had ever had a muscle on his body, Will thought, its final vestige was long gone. The man's pompous style and his looks made many people dismiss him. Barth turned that to his advantage, eventually becoming a force in local politics. Barth always did his homework and was a tireless opponent. Will's awareness of these realities had failed to build any respect for the man. Even maintaining civility toward the man strained Will.

Still, he offered his hand, and feigning innocence, asked, "Why, Ron, what brings you out to a crime scene?"

Calling the little man by his first name was a barb that Will loved to shoot at Barth any time he could. Barth, who had a Ph.D., liked to be addressed as "Doctor." Will felt the title should be reserved for people who could heal. Barth couldn't.

Will glanced down at the soft, moist hand lying in his and remembered the mayor's line about shaking hands with Barth: "Shit, I've had a better grip returned from a small breast."

Will's thought was washed away by Barth's querulous question. "I asked you first, Kempton—what are you doing to stop these horrors in our fair city?"

"Everything we can, Ron. The sheriff's office is working with us, and…"

"Perhaps the sheriff should be leading the investigation. He has more resources and more familiarity with running a major investigation of this type."

"Not more than I have, he doesn't," Will said tautly, as he leaned up against the white clapboard clubhouse and shaded his eyes from the strobe effect of the sun through the tall pines that riffled in the steady breeze.

"But your rough and tumble New Jersey background doesn't seem to be proving terribly effective here in Carmel, does it?"

Will put his arm around Barth's shoulder and half-turned the man toward the building. To all close enough to see the gesture, it appeared conciliatory—even friendly. Will placed his mouth a half-inch from Barth's ear and whispered, "Listen to me. If you obstruct my investigation, in any way, you'll be in a world of shit. And guess who'll be shoveling, Ron?"

Barth's small eyes got as wide as nature would allow and he started to sputter. Before he could actually get out a word, Will was telling the crowd, "Thanks for coming by, folks. But we can handle things here now, so go on home. I'll be making a statement later today about our progress to date."

He turned to Barth and asked, loud enough for all to hear, "Ron, want to go in with me? We can always use an extra hand."

Barth was not yet sputtered out, but suddenly realizing that he was in a crowd of voters, he gained control of himself. "Uh, no, Chief. You're the experts here. Carry on, my friend."

Will allowed himself a moment of satisfaction as he entered the vestibule of the clubhouse. Usually, Barth's enmity felt like balm to his singed spirit. But right now, Will had a job to do. Politics could wait. As bad as Barth was, something a helluva a lot worse was walking the streets of Carmel-by-the-Sea.

Will spotted Forsburg at the far end of the long room. "What's the deal, Clint?" he said, covering the distance between them. He noted the tasteful décor, the perfectly set tables, and he smelled the blossoms that seemed to cover every surface in the hall.

"Pretty cut and dried, Chief. Oops. Sorry. Coroner's about finished here. Then he's on his way to the victim's home."

"Hi, Doc," Will began.

The fastidious Dr. Edwin Parker looked up at Will. Parker was diminutive, with tiny hands and feet. His small head was dominated by two large, pale blue eyes, which he focused on Will. "Chief, incidentally, I'd appreciate it if you remind your people that I am the medical examiner, not a coroner."

Will nodded. "What's the story, Doc?"

Parker sighed at Will's disregard for the proprieties. "Very preliminary....But I'd say she's been dead well over twelve hours. Decapitation—looks pretty much the same as Carson and Coe. I'm about ready to get over to the home."

"Thanks, Doc. Join you there as soon as I can."

As Parker walked toward the clubhouse door, Will turned to Clint, who began to talk as if a switch had been thrown. "Old broad, sitting over there, apparently found the victim—uh, the head—inside the lectern. Up at the head table."

"Ah, jeez." Will looked around the long room. "What're the lectern and head doin' halfway down the center aisle?"

Clint's second-hand description of Sally-Ann Higgins' juggling act would have made Will smile under other circumstances. He knelt to examine the severed head of Emma Jacobs. Poor Emma, Will thought. Everyone loved her. She was David and Sari's favorite babysitter. His mind shifted instantly—first to revulsion—then to the hatred he felt in his bones for the son of a bitch who'd done this to her.

"Any prints, Clint?"

"Dozens of 'em. Most prob'ly belong to club members, but I got a few promising ones off the sides and top of the podium."

Clint walked from the head table down the center aisle to within fifteen feet of the kneeling chief of police.

"Run 'em all through DMV and the FBI soon's you can shut this place down." Will began to turn away, then turned back to Clint, and said, "I'm damned glad you're here, Clint. This thing's just bustin' our ass. We couldn't handle it alone, though I hate to admit it."

The lanky deputy sheriff seemed pleased by Will's compliment, which he responded to with a shrug.

"The scene at Emma's must be pretty bad," Will said. "While you're running the prints, have Jeff take Peach home to pack some stuff—she's gonna be staying out at Randolph's for a while."

Will stood, felt the familiar ache in his knee and limped over to Clint and spoke again.

"And tell Jeff to use caution takin' Peach home—and lock the station door when they're gone."

"I'm a big boy, Will."

"Clint, just lock the fucking door. I don't want to lose anybody else," Will said as he idly plucked a perfect red rose from the nearest vase and smelled it.

As he walked toward the clubhouse door, Will stopped briefly, shot a glance at Clint, got an affirmative nod from him and continued out of the building.

***

The tourist pushed a ten and a box across the counter of the Pebble Beach Apothecary. "For my wife," he smiled. The tiny, tidy store reeked of the wealth of most of its customers. High-end cameras and expensive sunglasses vied for space with the world's leading newspapers. The floor was black and white marble squares—like a giant chess board.

The clerk rang up the sale on the antique cash register, and the tourist strolled out with the small bag containing a box of hair dye. On the way to his suite he mulled over his plan one more time.

New color…a mustache, glasses. It would work. They'll never know, even if those people at the school got a good look. Close call—never should've happened! But now it's almost over. Give them a day or two, then swoop down like a hawk.

***

As Will drove toward Emma's house, he found himself praying for some breathing time from the avalanche of shit. But he knew there wouldn't be any, not until they caught the son of a bitch. And then, he thought, he's doing it to me? Or Gunner, or Jim? One of them had to be the murderer's main target. He knew a cop should never take it personally when his watch was being destroyed by some crazy perpetrator. Yet, sometimes it did happen—sometimes it *was* personal. Once, way back, it had been.

He fought to shake the feeling, to bring order to his mind, but exhaustion defeated the effort. There was just too much going on, too fast. Damn, he had to get a handle on this case!

Will parked in the street in front of Emma's perfectly kept Cape Cod cottage. His department's cruiser and the medical examiner's van more than filled the driveway. Other than the extra cars, the place looked as tidy and inviting as always. No crowd here, thank God, Will thought.

He disengaged himself from the Jeep and trudged across the property toward the porch with all the eagerness of one sent to repossess a car from a gangster. The smell of something very spoiled hit him on the third step. He'd never forgotten the pungent odor of flesh too long exposed. Jesus, this was going to be bad, he thought, as he entered the arched doorway.

It was—as bad as anything he'd come across during his years on the force in Jersey. He'd been in Emma's home on a half-dozen occasions. It was typical, little-old-lady neat. Knitted shawl on the loveseat; a large, well-used family Bible resting on the baby grand; antimacassars on the arms of every chair. The last flowers Emma had cut never made it to a vase. They were strewn on the floor. Dried blood speckled the length of the mantle.

The kitchen was a scene from an unspeakable nightmare. Dried blood seemed to cover every surface. Will found it hard to believe a single human body could yield so much blood. Especially one so small as Emma's.

"Anything?" Will asked Jim.

"Yeah. There's prints all over the place, and I got three shoe prints so clear you can read the Reebok label in the blood."

Will shook himself to attention.

"How 'bout you, Doc?" Will asked, as he walked through the dining room into the kitchen where Dr. Parker knelt over Emma's headless form. Will did not kneel—he was close enough.

"She's been dead a long time. Judging from the level of decomposition, I'd say sometime Saturday afternoon or night. The house is warm—thermostat's at seventy. She's pretty far along."

"That wound in her back looks—"

"Carbon copy of the wound on young Mr. Carson," the medical examiner interrupted.

"Over there on her left shoulder it looks like…"

"Two gashes," Parker said, again finishing Will's sentence. "From the looks of things he caught her in the living room as she came in the front door. He hit her once, back there by the coffee table. She ran or staggered into the dining room. He hit her again. She kept running. He finished her off in here. Used the butcher block as a workbench to cut off her head."

"Jesus, poor Emma," Will said.

"Nice old gal," said the medical examiner. "She was our fourth for bridge whenever my sister-in-law came to town. Helluva good player, too. Told me she used to play in duplicate tournaments all over the country…."

"Doc, for Chrissakes…" Will said. He averted his eyes, then turned away. He'd seen all he needed and wanted to get the hell out of the house.

"Yes, well, as I said, the attack was at least two days ago. Cause of death, a severed spinal cord—that'll do it every time. I'll call you with any other information I turn up at the autopsy."

"You almost done here?"

"A few more photos, then we'll bag her up and take her back to Monterey."

"Call me if anything pops up that I need to know about," Will said as he drew aside a curtain on the back door and peeked out on Emma's perfect backyard—ablaze with the blooms of a dozen different flowers.

"Already said I'd call you, Will. Always do, don't I?"

It was clear that the pressure of the last two days was wearing on Dr. Parker. Will had come to think of the last forty-eight hours as his own special trial, but everyone close to the case was tired or edgy or scared. Or all of the above.

"Sorry, Doc…I'm a mess, and…"

"No apologies. Me too, Will…I'm about out on my feet," Doc answered.

After Parker and his crew departed, Will and Jim surveyed Emma's kitchen for what they hoped was the last time. Jim leaned against the counter and folded his arms across his chest. He looked completely spent.

"What now, boss?" Jim asked wearily.

"Damned if I know, Jim. Damned if I know. Gimme a couple of minutes and let me think."

Jim nodded, walked through the house and out the front door.

Will shook his head slowly several times, sat for three minutes, uttered an audible curse, got up and retraced Jim's route.

Monday Afternoon
Chapter Eleven

Will had broken all speed records in his cop-Jeep to make a tarmac pick-up of Jennie's parents. He had met the Coes—Warren and Meg—on their first visit to the peninsula to see their daughter's new home. That was just six months ago—a happy time.

This was not. The Coes seemed a decade older and their grief-ravaged faces tore at Will.

"I'm so very sorry..." Will began.

"What the hell happened, Chief?" Warren asked.

"We got a serial..." he began again.

"Did she suffer?" Meg asked in a tear-stained plea.

"She..." Will offered, but was again interrupted by Warren.

"Have you got the son of a bitch yet?"

The back and forth continued as they loaded suitcases in the back of the Jeep. His half-answers to their questions didn't satisfy them or Will. His embarrassment was made worse by the fact that, because of this morning's jarring discovery, he had a powerful desire to get away from them—quickly. Every cell in his body impelled him to get back to the hunt, yet it didn't seem rightly decent to be itching to get rid of this couple who had lost their only daughter.

Guilt tugged at Will as he sped them back to town, deposited the now-silent Coes at the Pine Inn, and arranged to see them in the evening. Fortunately, he thought, their shock seemed to make them oblivious to his state of distraction.

Will navigated the Jeep across Ocean Avenue and then up three blocks to Nielsen's Market. He parked in a red zone directly in front of the tiny, hyper-exclusive grocery. On his way to the deli counter at the back of the store, Will's olfactory senses were overloaded by a concert of smells from the incredible cheeses and cooking meats. Normally, he would pause just to enjoy this. Not today. As he strode past his favorite aisle lined with dozens of the world's greatest Scotches, he didn't glance—even once.

He grimly shook his head, frustrated at his inability to halt the craziness, and fought off the growing sense that his carefully nurtured world was spinning out of control.

Will realized he hadn't felt so lost and alone since Debbie's death. He tried to snap out of his deepening funk by thinking of David and Sari, but even that offered only an instant's respite. As he arrived at the tall deli counter, his reverie was broken by a familiar friendly voice.

"Hey! Ya can't talk to the guy who's your second major source of income?" boomed head butcher Joe Moretti—one of Will's poker game regulars. He had been in the "operating room," as he called it, cutting up sides of beef. Joe was huge—nearly filling the doorway connecting the O.R. with the shop's counter area.

"Sorry, Joe. I got a lot goin' on," Will said, moving behind the counter to shake hands with his massive friend. Joe's apron was covered with blood. The sight usually bothered Will, but not today—not after what he'd just seen. The brown mottling on Joe's apron was the product of honest work. This blood belonged where it was.

"Still haven't found the son of a bitch, huh?" Joe said as he leaned against an ancient butcher block.

"Christ, Joe, we're workin' on it. Around the fuckin' clock to nail this guy. We don't even have a decent lead yet. Plus there's a third victim—Emma Jacobs. Just got back from her place." By now Will had started pacing the length of Joe's domain.

"Aw, jeez, poor Emma…." Joe's words drifted off. Then Joe blocked Will's path and said, "Everybody's pulling for you, pal. Everybody."

"Wrong, Joe," Will said as he slapped the butcher block with his right hand. "Everybody isn't. Barth is having a good time watchin' me stumble around on this. Gunner thinks if we don't stop this bastard soon, Barth's gonna use this case to start runnin' for mayor." Will backed away from the block, rubbed his chin and tried to shake away the thought.

"Barth? C'mon—he's a joke," Joe offered. "Nobody'd vote for him. Look, standing behind this counter, I'm in a pretty damn good position to take the pulse of this town, believe you me. Folks here are not dumb. And it'd definitely require a dose of dumbness to be taken in by the likes of Barth." Joe emphasized his point by driving a large meat cleaver an inch into the well-seasoned butcher block.

Will looked at the imbedded cleaver, then at Joe and said, "Maybe that's true enough of the people who know him, Joe. But there's a helluva lot of 'em out there who don't know him personally. They may be smart—but they aren't mind readers. And the guy's a hustler—always out there makin' noises that sound good. Turns out most of the good is for him, but sometimes you gotta be looking hard to see how that shakes out."

Will walked to the block and yanked the cleaver—Excalibur-like—from its confinement and said, "Fact is, longer this shit goes on, the more Barth'll be runnin' around sayin' the cops—mainly me—are incompetent and that Gun's a shitty mayor. Hell, it's the story of his life—climbin' onto somebody's back to make himself look taller," Will walked across the sawdust-strewn floor and handed the cleaver to Joe, who waved off Will's comments and said, "Heard you got two sheriff's guys over to help."

"Yeah, Forsburg and Ainsley. Good men. But we gotta get something going to help us nail this crazy son of a bitch. If this keeps on much longer, it's gonna start hurtin' the tourist business. And once that happens, Barth'll have his issue and a whole shitload of fans."

Will added, "Hell, Joe, you know as well as I do, this town'd dry up and blow away without tourists. The townies couldn't even keep this store open, let alone thirty T-shirt shops and twenty shoe stores."

"Don't forget forty art galleries…"

Will tossed a palms-up gesture at Joe and said, "Exactly. Joe, I gotta go. Gimme a pounda ham and turkey and put it on my bill."

Will watched Joe slice the meat with skill honed over three decades. He handed Will the wrapped package of meats and said, "Take it, Will. S'on the house. Go get the bastard!"

On the elevator down to the store's underground parking garage, Will felt himself drop back into his funk. Not even big Joe Moretti, self-described happiest wop in the world, could nudge Will significantly away from the anger, frustration and fear that the last two days had brought. He could barely summon up a memory of the Monopoly game he and the kids had enjoyed in front of the fireplace three days earlier during the storm. It seemed like a month had passed since that cozy family evening.

As the elevator door opened, Will wondered if anything would ever again be as it was. Certainly the town would be tarnished for a long time to come with a lurid reputation that it really didn't deserve. Sort of a loss of innocence, he mused. If it was possible for a town to be innocent, Carmel had been that place. Innocent, fun and safe.

Until now.

Innocent, fun and safe also described Sari—at least until Saturday. He was deeply worried about how she was handling the horror of two days ago. She seemed all right on the surface, but who knew what turmoil might be brewing under her mop of curls. He desperately wanted to spend some time with her and talk her through the whole thing. He knew kids were resilient as hell. But they were also great at hiding things. He didn't want Sari to bury this somewhere only to have it come blasting out at some point in the future. He knew he would have to watch her closely and consider getting her professional help.

On his way to the station Will continued to focus on his daughter. His inability to give Sari any time now, when she most needed it, grated on him again. But now, for the first time since his arrival in calm Carmel, he realized he had a real detecting job to do. His future—the kids' future—depended on it. Maybe even the town's, at least for the foreseeable future; when a resort town went down on the destination wish list of tourists, it couldn't usually manage to move up again with alacrity. He had to catch this bastard. Then he could be "Dad" again.

He slapped the steering wheel with his right palm and said aloud, "To get there, I gotta be a better cop than I've been in a long time."

The afternoon session at the station house was electric. The two deputies fit so well into Will's force, it seemed the group had been working together for years. Will knew both Forsburg and Ainsley were good cops, and they were following his lead with total professionalism. They appeared as angry and indignant at recent events as he. Why not? This was their home, too, and some son of a bitch was doing his best to ruin it.

Will told them to keep the same two teams together. They'd handled the morning's baptism by fire just fine. During the thirty-minute lunch and strategy meeting, Will ducked phone calls from a dozen media types, but there was no way he could avoid taking the mayor's call.

After briefly noting that David, Sari and Peach were all doing fine, the mayor's tone changed.

"Media are all over me, Will. We gotta have a press conference," Randolph said.

Will paced as far around his desk as the phone's cord would allow and said, "I don't have time to fart around with those assholes. I've got a killer to catch."

"You got time to royally piss off Barth, you got time to talk to the press. We gotta convince these guys that we've got something going...."

"We do, Elliot, but it's all fingerprints and bad photos. Maybe a drawing that'll get done this afternoon if I can use the time the way I need to. If there were something sexy to give to the press, I would. But there's nothing yet for them to salivate over." Will sat on the edge of his heavy desk.

Suddenly, the mayor's voice got real quiet, a sure sign, Will knew, that Randolph had remembered who was boss. "Will," he rasped. "Let me give you a quick trip through the real world. Your job—and prob'ly mine—is hangin' by a goddamned thread. If you don't nail this bastard, we're both up the creek. You, for sure. Me, most likely. Now, I've got a little somethin' to fall back on and a shitload of money in the bank. I could survive. You'd be out on your ass and prob'ly finding it hard to get a position as a night watchman."

"Oh, now listen…," Will blurted.

"I'm makin' a point here, kid. Shut up a minute."

Will shifted the phone from his right ear to his left, kicked his desk and swallowed the impulse to tell Randolph to stuff it. "Sorry," he managed, not without considerable effort.

"If you catch him today," Randolph said without acknowledging the half-hearted apology, "you'll be a hero in and to the media. I can praise you in every newspaper and on every television in the land. But—you hear this now—if you don't catch him for three or four days, *and* he kills more people, you're gonna need some friends in the media. Real bad. An unkind word or two from one of those pecker heads—especially the TV guys—can make you look like homemade shit. Be nice to 'em now—make 'em think you're cooperating—and if worse comes to worst they'll give you a break and make you look like a man who's trying. That, at least, gives you some time. Be snotty to 'em and they'll cut your balls off. All of a sudden you're outta time, an idiot standing naked in front of the whole world, mumbling incoherent excuses."

"Yessir. But…" Will knew he was losing the argument and knew he probably should lose it, but was struggling against his temper to find any level of reasonableness.

"No buts. I'm not tellin' you how to do your cop work, but I *am* tellin' you how to deal with the press, and that's somethin' I know a helluva lot more about than you."

"What do you want me to do?" Will asked, attempting to shake the anger out of his words.

"Be down at City Hall at four-thirty. I'll see to it that the press and television guys are all there. Make a statement and take some questions. I want you to sound as optimistic and forceful as you can. I'll handle the rest."

"Anybody else gonna be there?" Will asked, again stretching the limit of the phone's cord as he walked around to the front of his desk.

"Like who?"

"Like the sheriff or Barth?" Will said, wincing at the thought.

"No chance. This'll be our shot at the story. The media very likely will seek out one or both of those guys, but we sure as hell don't hafta invite 'em to feed at our press briefing."

"I'll do my best."

"Do better'n that. We need all the friends we can get."

The mayor's statement of the obvious further antagonized Will as he placed a death grip on the phone receiver, but he was able to quietly say, "I'll be there."

But as soon as he heard the click of the mayor's phone, Will slammed the receiver back into its cradle.

The Lengthening Afternoon
Chapter 12

Will slumped into his creaking, aged chair. The thought passed briefly through his mind that he and the chair had much in common. Weariness and depression closed in on him with claustrophobic pressure. This was worse than a bad hangover. Headache, gut ache and burning eyes—all at once. He knew Elliot was absolutely right. He also knew that Randolph was just about the only important friend he had right now, and without the mayor's huge reservoir of popularity and good will, the media might already be calling into question the credibility of the Carmel Police Department and its chief.

A communal throat-clearing from his office doorway jolted his attention back to his troops. God, they weren't exactly a platoon, were they? He could use a goddamn regiment right about now.

He looked up at them and told them about the press conference wrinkle in the schedule for that afternoon. He figured they'd probably been registering every nasty thought his face expressed during his conversation with Randolph. Will ushered them all out to the station's bullpen and reviewed their assignments, reminded them again to be cautious, and dismissed them to go do their duties.

Before they left he added, "I don't want to see any of you dropping by the press briefing either. Bad enough I have to waste my time coddling the press. We meet here," he checked his watch, "6:30 p.m. Sharp."

If any of them were disappointed at Will's order, he failed to notice it.

The office was quiet after their departure. Will felt as though he were stuck in a mental tar pit. For a moment he couldn't move or think. So he gave up, sat cross-legged on the cold floor, and felt almost like a prisoner in his own jail.

Will rarely succumbed to self-pity. But when he did, he went all the way. All the way back.

***

Will knew he had inherited a good measure of his father's toughness, but it was balanced by his mother's sensitivity and intellect. He had been both an excellent student and athlete. His baseball skills earned him a scholarship to Princeton, but Will learned very quickly that those skills, while impressive, were not exceptional enough to take him further than college ball. Nor was there much major league demand for a first baseman just barely 5'11", not quite 180 pounds and with very little long ball power. He wasn't heartbroken. He'd always thought he'd end up a cop. In the innermost compartment of his heart, he got a definite kick out of the very idea: a cop with a degree from Princeton in political science. *Cum laude*, no less.

At the Police Academy, he managed to excel in practically everything in the curriculum. Most of his marks, in the classroom and in the rigorous physical training, still stood as state records.

It was at the academy that he met Debbie Gilardi. She had been one of six females who started the cadet training program. At the conclusion of the ten-week course, she'd been the only woman to graduate.

One of the things that drew Will to her, in addition to her light brown hair and dark brown eyes, was that her background was remarkably similar to his. Both were the only offspring of parents who wanted more children. Both felt compelled to compensate for the absence of siblings by being over-achievers. And, maybe even more of a bond, each had a cop for a father. Will and Debbie, both cautious by nature, fell deeply and rapidly in love, to their mutual surprise and delight. They married within a week of their academy graduation.

Debbie was, at first, impatient with the mundane assignments she was given. There was probably nowhere in New Jersey, in the 1980s, that could—or would—boast of being a bastion of liberalism regarding the equality of women. So far as police agencies went, these strongholds of macho righteousness were not even vaguely familiar with the concept of female equality. After six years of battling "Neanderthals," as she called her fellow police officers, Debbie resigned and started law school. She was in her third year, managing straight A's despite being the mother of two, when she was murdered while standing in line at a 7-Eleven.

When the call came, Will had been working undercover for a week. They had talked on the phone that morning. Mainly small talk—nothing really important. The *I love you's* that ended their conversation were perfunctory, however deeply felt. Will would be back home, through with his undercover assignment, in less than a day. They'd planned a quick trip to his father's cabin with the kids—to reacquaint him with normal humanity and themselves with each other. Then, she was gone. No warning. No reason. Just gone. The victim of a drive-by shooting in which the shooter used an automatic weapon.

To this day, Will believed that, if not for the children, he would have given in to the blackness that hovered over him since the phone call telling him Debbie was dead. Even so, it had been touch and go for a long, long time. He would keep slipping into the darkness and have to claw his way out again. For his children's sake he would not let himself become immured there.

He remembered that the spaces between the black times stretched. He knew that it was watching his children continue to live that showed him it could be done. They had given him the desire to go on, if only to be able to spend time with them. For a long while, that time spent with them was all he lived for.

Climbing to his feet, Will recalled that slowly work had taken on importance again, although never the place it had assumed in his life before Debbie died. The blast of a car horn interrupted his trip back in time and made him flinch the way a gunshot might. Memories gone, back in Carmel with the clear realization that ever since this madman had walked into town—into his life—every sound or sign of potential violence had taken on a fearsome weight.

In three steps, Will was at the window of the station house. But all it was—this time—was a Mercedes owner a half-block down from the station relieving himself of frustration at someone stealing a parking space he obviously thought was his by divine right. Let them work it out, Will thought.

As he walked across the room to the coffee pot, he was grateful there were still enough people in town to incite a typical Carmel traffic problem. But if the murderous path lengthened…. He had to get back on his pace—whatever that was. Reflections on the past and on Debbie sure as hell wouldn't help him catch a killer. Or killers?

"No more self-pity. No more ghosts. It's time to move. C'mon, Will, let's get our shit together."

He moved to his desk and sat, determined to do whatever it took to end the craziness. No headache, no gut ache, and his eyes were alive.

The first thing to contend with was the media later that afternoon. As he began to clear an open space on his desk for a place to draft his press statement, he noticed a note from Peach he'd overlooked before. The red ink was the code for "important." Holding the note at arm's length, he read:

Will,
I reviewed the latest FBI reports. I think one of the profiles
(CR 1403) is missing. Both 1402 and 1404 are in the report.
Should I check on this?
Peach

Will grabbed the small stack of FBI Criminal Records Reports and riffled through it. The reports were distributed regularly by the Bureau to all local law enforcement agencies. They listed the whereabouts of certain known and dangerous criminals and also provided information on escapees and bail-jumpers. Since his arrival in Carmel, Will had found little use for the reports. Desperate criminals didn't seem to be among those seeking a haven on the Monterey Peninsula.

One day a few months back, when he and Jim had been plowing through a similar pile of reports, Will had suggested, "Think maybe being on the lam impacts their golf game?"

"Nah," Jim said. "This place is prob'ly just too expensive for them, too."

Despite the seeming uselessness, as chief Will had gone over the data faithfully each time a new batch arrived, and he had Jim, Jeff and Jennie go over the reports as well. Never could tell when a desperado might show up at the table next to you at Fresh Cream or the Sardine Factory.

The thought of Jennie was in the present tense. Followed fast by the reality hitting him all over again: Jen was dead. And they hadn't even found the rest of her yet. Where the hell had the bastard put her?

"Jesus," he muttered. "Gotta find her...her poor parents...Jesus!"

A vision of Jennie and her ignominious, pendulous finale in Jim's shower brought Will to a new pitch of fury. He welcomed the anger like an old friend, knowing it would force him to focus and act. That's what he needed now—action! Any form of it was better than what he'd been doing. Jen was gone. Emma was gone. Despite her brave show, he damn well knew that Sari had been traumatized.

I have to lay out a battle plan. He regarded his now semi-cleared desktop as the starting point for formulating his plan. The first order of business was to compose a statement for this afternoon's press briefing. Second, get Jim moving quickly on the fingerprints found at Emma's house. Third, meet with Jennie's parents tonight at 6:00. Fourth, stop by the *Pine Cone* and try to persuade Bob to put a favorable spin on the story.

When he finished his statement for the press conference, the station house clock said 2:43. Jim hadn't phoned in yet. Will knew he wasn't in the mood to stick around the office waiting for reports from his crew. By pressing a single button on the telephone, he could make the instrument ring in his car or at his home. He didn't know how the hell it worked, but it was convenient. He wasn't about to leave anybody, let alone Peach, in the station alone.

He checked the clip in his gun, put the safety on and holstered it. He grabbed the three handwritten pages of his press statement and stuffed them into his back pocket. He was almost out the door when he remembered the FBI reports. He picked up that bundle from Peach's desk, locked the door and headed to his car.

Peach's red-ink note remained where he'd put it—in the middle of his own desk.

Monday Afternoon, Still

Chapter Thirteen

$\mathbf{A}$s he sat in the straight back, wooden chair across from Bob Abram's desk, Will knew his afternoon had been busy, if not productive, insofar as catching a murderer was concerned. Abrams, editor and publisher of the *Carmel Pine Cone*, had offered personal sympathies as well as professional assurances of fair treatment in the paper's coverage of the triple murders. He'd Xeroxed Will's script for the afternoon press briefing and told Will that he was moving the weekly paper's deadline back a few hours in order to be able to include as much information as possible. He also told Will that Barth was clamoring to get in a piece representing his personal view of the events.

"Oh, Jesus, Bob…" Will's lament was interrupted.

"Don't worry. I lied to the little turd. Told him the deadline was yesterday. Offered to print a letter in next week's issue. Hell, he huffed and puffed 'til I almost gave in. I mean, anything to get his ass outta here."

"Thanks, Bob. I don't need that little shit climbin' up my ass…" Will rose from the chair as he spoke, carefully avoiding two large stacks of back issues on the institutional brown linoleum floor.

"He is a puke. But, Will, he's got a point. This stuff is bad for everybody's business."

"I know it. Believe me, I know it. We'll get the fucker before you have to worry about Barth again."

"You don't—we're all fucked. Good luck," Abrams said as he waved to Will's back.

I need that, all right, Will thought, as he left the *Pine Cone* and walked to his Jeep. Luck to bring clues, of which he had zero useful ones. Jim's rundown of fingerprints had made that depressingly clear. He pulled the Jeep back onto Ocean Avenue. The shoe print found in Emma's kitchen was of a size ten Reebok, probably one of a thousand on the Monterey Peninsula at any given time. There was a chunk of rubber missing from the letter 'O' in Reebok, making it resemble a 'C.' That would be helpful—but only after they nabbed its owner. And they weren't any closer to that than they had been Saturday morning. He turned the car left and headed home.

He needed a shower. The rest of today ain't gonna be easy. Facing the next three or four hours relatively clean and fresh is the best I can hope for. He turned the Jeep into the half-circle driveway and pulled it around to the front of his house.

The outside looked as inviting and cozy as it always did—until he got inside where it looked like Fort Kempton. He shook his head as he walked through the downstairs. The living room was littered with blankets, pillows and full ashtrays. The dining room table, his favorite antique, was covered with bags full of clothes and suitcases. A single white sock was draped unceremoniously over the tall back of one of the dining room chairs.

He was pleased to see that Clint and Tom had dropped off their clothes and toiletries earlier in the day—one duffel bag and two large shopping bags-worth.

Will loved his home. As far back as he could recall, he'd always loved to be at home. At first, home had meant his room in his parents' house. Later, his dorm room at Princeton. Still later, his first apartment; then the house in Jersey City; finally, this house in Carmel-by-the-Sea. He'd always needed a place where he could shut out all the things he couldn't control and all the noises he didn't want to hear.

Even back in the old neighborhood, where he was a popular kid, there were times he ignored all entreaties to come out to play and simply stayed in his room to read comic books, sort through baseball cards or draw and, of course, to listen to music—usually the Stones. Those occasions were never predictable—they just happened. Friends then and throughout his life chided him for that preference for his private sanctuary. He didn't care—his home was where he was happiest.

When he joined the force in Jersey, he felt sorry for his fellow cops. Most of them spent as little time at home as possible. It didn't seem to matter whether they were married or single, young or old. In Will's mind they seemed to have descended from gypsies.

Now, though his home looked more like a fraternity house, it still kept out the stuff he didn't want in. When this was over, he thought as he walked into the kitchen, he would shovel out the mess, and it would again be home as it should be.

His biggest worry was how to squeeze five—even lukewarm—showers from his archaic water heater.

Right now, according to the clock above the back door, he had only fifteen minutes to shower before the press conference.

"Better shave, too," he said aloud, running his hand over his chin. "Might as well look as good as I can. Sure as hell don't have any great news to distract those bastards."

***

The surface trappings of the press conference looked like City Hall business-as-usual—except in size. Forty media denizens and ten television cameras crowded into the City Council chamber. This was twice as many as had shown up for Randolph's swearing-in, and that had been the largest non-golf tournament media event ever on the Monterey Peninsula.

The event was more a media gang bang than any press conference Will had ever seen. "A fucking disaster," Randolph offered as he and Will exited through the back door on their way to Randolph's car.

Randolph, used to having things go his way when cameras ran, was at first furious. But he quickly reminded himself that the session had been his idea and, burying his anger, apologized to Will for the pounding he'd taken at the hands—mouths, actually—of the media.

"I'm sorry, kid. I didn't think the vultures'd be out so quick."

As they walked around the building to Monte Verde Street where Randolph's car was parked, Will was quite aware that his own performance had been less than stellar. His anger was at the media—and himself. Still, he snapped, "Maybe now you'll let me concentrate on runnin' this investigation. I don't have time to dick around with those self-important assholes."

He knew before the words were out that it was a stupid thing to say. Dealing with the press, especially on a sensational case like this, was an integral part of his job. He started to apologize, but Randolph cut him off. "No apologies, Will. Bad as it was, I think the conference bought you a couple days. I'll talk to 'em all myself tomorrow—more'n once if need be—to keep 'em off your ass."

"Thanks."

"But you gotta keep me fully informed. I gotta know what's goin' on every minute. Anything comes up—and I mean anything at all—you've got to let me know."

Will nodded and the two men rounded the corner and headed up the street. Before they could negotiate more than a few steps, the early twilight was split apart by two dozen exploding strobes.

Three grisly murders in this improbable setting, together with Randolph's widespread fame, had brought the media to Carmel from all over the state. Both men knew that, in another day or two, the village would be crawling with news hounds from every major market in America. In three days, their brethren from all over the world would be descending upon Carmel.

They stopped abruptly as they saw the huge crowd milling about in front of City Hall.

"Jesus, look at them all!" the mayor said. Just as they saw the media horde they were spotted and the questions—this time shouted—began anew.

"Lookit the bright side, Elliot. With the tourists gone, at least the boys and girls of print, radio and TV are fillin' up all the hotels and motels."

"Yeah, but they're tight. They don't buy T-shirts, shoes and good food. Hotels and bars'll make dough. Nobody else will want that gang."

"My car's across the street and down a block, Gun. I gotta go."

As Will began to cross the street toward his house, he heard Randolph exclaim, "That little cocksucker!" Will turned. Off to the side of City Hall, Ron Barth was holding court with a gaggle of reporters. The mayor was three long steps ahead of Will.

Everything appeared to Will to be in stop-action as he reversed course through the crowd in an attempt to catch up with the mayor and stop him from voicing his reactivated fury. Barth's voice was coming through loud and clear: "Furthermore, if our own police and city officials can't do a better job than this, then I say it's time to get some professionals in here to protect the innocent citizenry of our community."

He was basking in the glare of floodlights from three different television cameras. Microphones circled his pasty face like an electronic nosegay. Will had never seen the little man look so rapturous. Clearly the thought of his own voice, Barth's favorite sound, hitting airwaves all over California, was physically exciting to the eager politico.

Barth was in the middle of telling the reporters that he would have a "major statement" tomorrow morning at nine when Will heard the mayor interrupt in his unmistakable voice of command, familiar from two dozen films when he'd been pushed an inch too far, "Barth, you self-serving, second-guessing little prick—shut up before I bust those beaver teeth down your throat."

Will cringed at the clicking and whirring sounds made by the seemingly endless number of cameras.

The threat forced Barth two paces back. Will watched as Barth stood as tall as he could, cleared his throat and spoke directly into the microphones, "Well, Mr. Mayor. Do you disagree with me? It's clear your police need help. This isn't a movie script in progress. This is real, and your little squad isn't getting the job done. We need to do whatever it takes to make our streets safe..."

Will grabbed the blur of Randolph's left arm two feet short of Barth's soft and inviting jaw. In doing so he prolonged the mayor's political career and probably saved the defenseless Barth a broken jaw—if not a full-blown concussion.

Will held onto the mayor's arm. "Let's get outta here," he hissed," before you do somethin' you'll really regret."

Randolph turned a furious set of eyes toward Will, who waited, every muscle tensed to keep holding the mayor back physically. The mayor was as strong as he. Randolph's glare went back and forth between Barth and Will. Finally, Randolph muttered, "Fuck it," turned and walked away briskly.

Will looked back. The cameras were again trained on Barth. The last sight Will could make out, as he and Randolph ducked under a low, overhanging tree, was Bertha Barth moving to her husband's side. At least he assumed it was Big Bertha in uniform. How many size eighteen, bright yellow house dresses could there be in Carmel-by-the-Sea?

An unspoken decision had been made to leave their cars parked at City Hall until the crowd disbursed. The four-block walk to Will's house was quick. "Jesus, Gunner," Will said, realizing it was risky for a protégé to lecture his mentor. "That was pretty close to a bad scene."

Their pace was a clear indicator that their adrenal glands were functioning on high. Will nearly had to trot to keep up with his boss.

"Goddamn, I do dislike that ugly little man. I just flat lost it, Will. Thank you for stopping me."

"Like you said, sir, we're in this together."

"Yeah. We sure are. Woulda looked a bit bad, having my own, hand-picked Chief of Police arresting me over the prostrate lump of that little shit."

"That's not why I stopped you, Gun," Will said, placing a hand on Randolph's back to guide him into a right turn on Ninth.

"Oh?"

"Hell, no. I was afraid if you'da planted Barth, then Big Bertha woulda decked you, causing major harm to your macho image, and possible maiming your movie career."

"Good point," Randolph smiled and slowed a bit.

"Just saving myself, sir. If I can't find a job as a night watchman in the near future, I sure as hell want to have your movies to fall back on as a means of gainful employment."

As they turned into Will's driveway, the mayor's brushed leather boot snapped a small branch. The dirt and gravel crunched underfoot. The sun was nearly gone and the moon was climbing into place. The huge cypress trees billowed slightly in the whispered breeze from the ocean. The smell, the trees, the sea, the air—all were simply perfect. Will felt momentarily contented—despite three days of horror and tension and one miserable press conference. Carmel could do that to you, Will thought. That was why he loved it so much and why he had to free it from the shattering nightmare that threatened its very existence.

"C'mon in for ten minutes, then we'll go back for your car," Will said.

"I'll go, Will. You keep workin' on this thing. I can take care o' myself. Gotta shot o' Scotch somewhere in.... Jesus! What the hell's goin' on in here?" Randolph asked as he stepped over a pile of clothes.

"I got my whole force stayin' here. Safety in numbers..."

"Christ, you're gonna need to sandblast this place when this's over," Randolph said on his way to the kitchen where he knew he could find a drink.

Will joined him at the sink, grabbed a bottle of Famous Grouse and filled a large glass half full.

"Ice?" he asked as he handed it to Randolph.

"Nope," Randolph said, as he made a small turn and leaned against the counter.

The ten minutes were consumed by Will's promise to inform his boss of any new development.

"I gotta see Jennie's parents in a few minutes, and I want to try to get out to your place later to see the kids. C'mon, let's go get your car," Will said.

Randolph opened his sport coat just enough so Will could see the butt of a large hand gun.

"I'll be fine, kid."

"Gotta license for that thing?"

"Yep. And I know how to use it, too."

As Randolph walked through the disarray that Will's house had become, his final comment was, "Y'know if this was a goddamned movie, I'd yell 'Cut!' right now."

Will started to answer, but stopped as his front door snicked shut behind Carmel's most famous resident.

Evening into Night, The Long Long Monday
Chapter Fourteen

Who is that pathetic little shit on TV? There it is—Barth, Business Association. Jesus, what a hideous little fuck he is. Oh, God, look at that beast next to him! His wife—how perfect.

The man edged forward on the overstuffed loveseat in his luxurious room. The ocean's rolling waves were easy to hear with the Pacific less than 50 yards away.

He's right, though. This is most assuredly not a movie, Mr. Mayor. This is very real, and before I'm through here, you and your silly force of cops will be nothing more than bad memories.

The badly scraped thumb increased the volume on the TV's remote control.

What a priceless press conference. Obviously, that dumb shit Kempton doesn't have a clue about me. And the good citizens, aided and abetted by the media's taste for sensationalism, seem to be losing their patience with Kempton's fumbling. They want action—and if their own cops aren't up to it, they'll get it somewhere else. Fuckin' movie star isn't giving 'em anything. Another murder or two and this whole place'll blow up. Anarchy on Ocean Avenue—that'd be fun.

Oughta go after that toad from the Business Association. He's sure got a hard-on for Kempton and the movie star. No, no—let him alone—let him do his damage for another day or two. He's a mean little shit. Maybe get his wife—Mrs. Business Association. Fuck her up real good—put parts of her all over town. People'll go nuts!

Feels good. Feels right.

Tomorrow. Final phase. It's all going so well. Move into town tomorrow. Closer to the action. And there will be plenty of action.

He snapped off the television and settled back into the comfort of the loveseat and the warm darkness of the room. He enjoyed the darkness.

***

Will arrived twenty minutes late for the 6:30 p.m. meeting at the station house. The time spent with Jennie's parents had been enervating. Her death was a staggering blow, but, because he had a job to do, he had postponed his own mourning. But her parents' devastation was overwhelming and seemed to choke off the air in the small room he'd reserved for them at the Pine Inn. Despite a strong urge to run from the room and their pain, Will had waited until their tears and questions were exhausted. He owed them, and Jennie, that much at least. He owed them a helluva lot more, but he didn't know how to make good on the rest of the debt.

Those poor goddamned people, he thought. They can't even leave here until the rest of her is found—if it's ever found. Three people dead. Beheaded, for Chrissakes....

His black reverie was broken up by greetings from his squad as he walked into the station house. "Thought I told you guys to lock this door!" was his curt response.

"Shit, Will, there's four of us in here. Nobody's gonna get the drop on all of us," Jim said. He had given Clint his desk; Tom sat at Jen's desk, and Jeff was at his own work station. Jim had apparently been pacing throughout the bullpen area.

Will grunted and asked a one-word question: "Anything?"

He knew that they would have contacted him if they'd come up with a single clue of even dubious value. Their bleak expressions confirmed what he already knew.

"Not one fucking thing, Will," Jim said. "It's like the son of a bitch is able to disappear into thin air."

"Bullshit! Don't go getting weird on me. There's nothing supernatural with this fuck…." Will slapped the raised countertop that separated the public area from the bullpen as he joined his troops.

"Chief, we know that," Tom said. "But we've run through everything we got ten times and we keep turnin' into the same dead-end alley."

"Christ, Will," Jim said dourly. "We don't know whether to shit or go blind. Where the hell *do* we go from here?"

Will leaned against the tall counter. "I wish I had something brilliant to offer, guys. This chief's badge doesn't mean shit as far as brains are concerned. I'm as punched-out as you, so if you think I know where we go from here…" He shrugged helplessly.

"How'd the press conference go?" Jim asked.

"Disaster—and after it was over, the Gun damn near put Barth to sleep with the TV cameras rolling."

At that point, everyone chimed in, not precisely taking turns. Ten different topics, most of them related to the three murders, were covered. Will let them vent for nearly twenty minutes. He knew, first-hand, that the exercise of generalized bullshitting was one of nature's best ways to calm the troops before a battle. This may not be war, he thought, but it's pretty damned close. After the small talk played out, he moved through the waist-high gate to join them in the bullpen and instructed them to switch partners and to go over everything, interview every person they'd already seen.

"We need a clue—anything—to help us find this guy. So we're gonna plow the same ground, and we're gonna listen with new ears. Take the best notes you ever took. Get started tonight and go 'til about ten. I'll be home by then to let you in—if I'm not back in time, Jim's got a key. Tomorrow morning, pick up interviewing again. You two hit the beach at 7:00 and try to find somebody else who mighta seen our guy on Saturday. Sorry, guys, that's all I can think of. My house tonight by ten and back here tomorrow morning at eleven."

As his uninspired soldiers grabbed notebooks and pens and swapped lists of interview subjects, Jim sidled up to Will and asked, "What're you gonna do tonight, boss?"

"First, I'm gonna get something to eat. Then, I guess I'll try to stay awake long enough to drive out to the Gun's to see the kids."

Jim looked beat himself. It was obvious to Will that he'd been mightily shaken by his discovery of Jen. But it was obvious Will was in worse shape. Nevertheless, Jim tried to give him a shot of optimism, "We're gonna get him, Will," he said as he kneaded his left shoulder with his right hand.

Will slumped and looked at Jim with eyes that could see through the faked confidence. "Maybe, buddy. But it better be awful fucking soon, 'cause we're running out of time."

"Why don't we patrol the city tonight?" Jim asked. "In split shifts."

"The guy's too smart. He'd see us and go hide someplace. It's obvious he's got us and our routines down pretty good. Besides, I want all of us to be fresh tomorrow—fresh as we can manage."

"You're the boss."

"Kinda wish I wasn't, but I am," Will said. "For now, anyway."

Jim clapped him on the shoulder, told him to keep the faith and started to leave the office to conduct another series of interviews.

"Thanks, Jim," Will said as his deputy walked by the tall counter against which Will continued to lean.

"For what?" Jim stopped walking, turned and faced his boss.

"Just thanks, that's all," Will said as he made full eye contact with Jim.

Jim paused, nodded, walked the few steps to the doorway and left.

Will walked into his office, re-hung the picture that had again fallen off the untrustworthy mortar nail, sat and started to neaten the mess on his desk. He'd made little progress when the phone rang. He grabbed the receiver and had it to his ear in one quick move.

"Police."

"Chief Kempton, please," came the voice on the line.

"Speaking," Will said, propping himself on his left elbow, while holding the phone with his left hand.

"Ah, but not half so eloquently as you sounded on television before."

"Pardon?" *Great, now I've got a critic.* He continued to sort the day's accumulation of paper with his right hand.

"A nice little press conference, wasn't it?" the voice teased.

Will was in no mood. "Look, buddy," he said, preparing to slam the phone back onto its cradle.

"Check out the Dumpster at Carmelo and Eighth."

"What...?" Suddenly, Will swung his full attention toward the caller. He couldn't swear to it, but he thought he heard a soft chuckle just before the line went dead. Two more seconds elapsed before the dial tone confirmed that his caller had hung up.

The entire conversation occupied roughly twenty seconds of the event-filled day. He felt the adrenaline scour the rough spots from all his senses. He knew there wasn't a prayer of tracing a call of such short duration, so he quickly wrote down every word that had been uttered. He knew he'd just talked with a triple-murderer.

Unless the Dumpster housed number four.

Oh, Jesus, he thought, don't let this be another one. He locked the station house door, ran to his Jeep, started it and the siren, radioed Jim to meet him at Carmelo and Eighth and took off down Ocean Avenue.

***

It was after eleven when Will finally got out to the mayor's house. The kids had gone to bed at nine. His call to the mayor regarding the find at the Dumpster made it clear that he wouldn't be there in time to tuck them in; so, around nine, Randolph had gotten them to bed.

Now, after looking in on them, he came downstairs to brief his boss. Peach had prepared two tuna sandwiches for her boss. He was in mid-thanks to her when he noticed that her hair was fixed differently and she was wearing, perhaps, a bit of extra eye shadow. The old girl is looking positively pretty, he thought. His inward grin didn't reach his eyes but, for a brief moment, it eased his burden.

He had explained to the mayor, on the phone, that the Dumpster contained Jennie's body. He didn't relate the dread he had felt when he approached the Dumpster or the soul-crushing discovery inside it. Nor did he reveal to Randolph or Peach that his sadness was nearly matched by relief at being able to close that small part of the case. Presumably by morning the medical examiner would be finished with the body; that way Will could talk to her parents and help them schedule a return trip home—for three.

Now, seated in Randolph's huge living room, he felt strangely excited. The last four hours of activity had given him a jolt of energy. Even though the progress made had a bleak cast to it, at least something in this case had moved. Waiting, without clue or control, had damn near driven him into the ground. Finally, he could face a new day with a trace of confidence. Too, he was more certain than ever that his earlier phone conversation had been with the killer.

"How can you be so sure it was him?" Randolph asked.

"Can't. Couldn't prove it, but I just feel like it was our guy. Instinct, cop intuition—hell, I don't know, but I really think it was him."

"Is that good….I mean, is it good if it was him?" asked the mayor, as he leaned forward on the large ottoman on which he was perched.

"Maybe—might mean the son of a bitch is getting a little cocky. Up to now he's stayed in the shadows, quiet as hell. Did I tell you he mentioned the press conference?"

"Yeah, you did. So what?"

"Well, he gave me a little jab on it. On my performance. Implied what a shitty job I'd done and how lame we were…" Will said. He, too, sat on the edge of his seat, which was directly across and three feet away from Randolph.

"Will," Randolph interrupted. "Those opinions are probably shared by most everybody who watched tonight's news."

"Yeah, I know. But only one guy knew where the rest of Jennie was…" Will idly picked up one of the mayor's People's Choice awards.

"Coulda been someone just strolling along who stumbled onto the body, kid."

"Not likely. Nope. Strollers don't look into Dumpsters, and, besides, the caller asked for me, by name, like he wanted to stick it in and twist it a little. Kinda like it was personal."

"Personal?" Randolph repeated.

"Yeah. I've had this theory that this whole thing's personal, probably at you or Jim or me. Anyway, that thought has been with me on and off since the killing started..."

"I don't see it...," the mayor said.

"Well, I can't explain it any better'n I can explain why I think I was talkin' to the killer on the phone tonight," Will said, as he replaced the award on the glass-topped coffee table.

The mayor got up, walked to the bar and dropped three ice cubes into a heavy, short glass. He splashed a few large fingers of amber liquid over the ice and took a healthy swallow before he turned to Will, who was still seated on the oxblood cordovan couch. "If all that you say is dead-bang true, I still don't see how it helps."

"If I'm right, it means the son of a bitch is beginnin' to relax, and he enjoys watching me flounder around on the tube. Maybe we can use that to our advantage."

"You're losin' me again, kid." Randolph poured a second drink, walked it over to Will and sat down after noting that Peach's gin and tonic had barely been touched.

"Let me work on it a little. I've read a lot of stuff on these crazy bastards. I gotta figure out what buttons to push on him...maybe smoke him out that way. They all got buttons..."

"Christ, Will, while you're trying to find buttons on a phantom, we got a town about to go total batshit here. One more murder and we're outta control."

"We been outta control since Saturday."

"No, I mean you and me. One more death and we're through. The Attorney General called an hour and a half ago to volunteer his assistance."

"Fucking politicians. Is he comin' in? Sorry, Peach."

Peach waved him off from her seat at the far end of the massive couch.

"Like I said, he will if there's any more killing. Otherwise, I got him to give us 'til the weekend."

"I'll get the bastard before then. I feel closer now than I have all week…"

"But not close enough to stop him from executing another poor son of a bitch if he feels like it," Randolph said, rising to stalk the length of the room and back.

Will couldn't dispute the mayor's statement. Instead, he took a deep sip of his drink, stood up, stretched and reached for his coat. "Tomorrow's a new day, Elliot, and it's gonna be *my* day. Now I'm goin' home to get a few hours' sleep."

"Stay in touch, Will," Randolph said as the police chief bounded up the three stairs into the entry hall.

Will turned, focused his stone cold eyes on Randolph, nodded and said his goodbyes.

Tuesday Morning

Chapter Fifteen

It was just past midnight when Will let himself in the front door. The sound of multiple men snoring beat a strange rhythm in the darkened living room. He snapped on a small table lamp so he could negotiate a path through the body-strewn room. As he turned to survey the layout, his first sight was a wide-awake Jim, wearing only boxer shorts, sitting in Will's easy chair. He was cradling a twelve-gauge shotgun.

"Jesus Christ, Jim!" Will's comment was more hiss than whisper.

"Just standin' guard, pal."

Reverting to a normal whisper, Will invited Jim to join him in the kitchen. His deputy explained that they'd all agreed to take a two-hour shift with the shotgun in order to "ward off any untoward evil."

"What, like the milkman?"

"He'd a been okay long as he didn't try to come in."

"Jesus, we're all goin' nuts." Will shook his head as he filled a small glass with water and walked toward the back staircase. He stopped and turned toward Jim.

"Why the hell's everybody in the living room? There's beds upstairs."

"The kids' beds are too small for me, Clint and Jeff. And Tom didn't want to sleep up there alone," Jim answered with what he obviously considered impeccable logic.

Will failed to stifle a huge yawn, pointed to the breakfast table, and both men sat. They quickly reviewed all of the evening's activities—a final run-through before bed just to make sure that not even the smallest detail had slipped by either of them. Then Will told Jim of his inclination to use the media to smoke the killer out into the open. "I'll work on it more in the morning. Meantime, I'm goin' up to get some sleep. I'll set the alarm for six."

"Who's manning the station tomorrow?" Jim asked.

"Nobody 'til we all get in at eleven. We'll figure it from there. Night, James," Will said as he shoved the chair back into its normal position at the table.

Jim started to move back to his sentry post, then stopped. "Will, how come you brought the FBI reports home? You never do that."

On automatic, Will moved back to the kitchen table and hefted the package from the FBI. Then his frozen expression cracked into a frown. He stared straight at the material as if the act could force his memory into clear focus. It finally worked. "Peach left me a note today or yesterday sayin' there was a missing profile, or something…"

"Where's her note?"

Will thumbed through the FBI report and came up empty-handed. "Guess I left it in the office." He shrugged sheepishly as he looked at Jim.

"Want me to check it out in the morning?" the deputy offered.

"One of us'll do it, Jim. I'll probably get back to the station house before you, so I'll do it early."

***

By the time his alarm sounded, a restless Will had showered and shaved. The five hours he had allotted himself to sleep had turned out to be fewer than that and less than restful. His mind hadn't seemed to stop moving even during the short time he'd actually dozed. Visions of Emma, Jennie and Brady Carson floated in and out of his brain. They were replaced by a duel between the Crystal Gun and Ron Barth. A rawhide-clad Randolph had been disarmed by thousands of direct hits from Barth's pea-shooter. Then the three victims returned, walking toward him, each one cradling his or her head in their right arm and carrying a copy of the FBI reports in their left hands.

On the short drive to the station Will thought about his dreams. Generally, he gave little if any credence to dreams, and definitely none to modern breakthroughs in dream interpretation. Hell, it had been years since he'd even remembered a dream. He'd always felt that people who routinely discussed such things were a little addled. Harmless, but addled.

But today was different. He knew this goddamned case had planted those dreams squarely in the forefront of his consciousness. He felt silly—such thoughts were reserved for shrinks and psychics. Still, as he entered the station, he was surprised to find himself trying to remember the articles he'd read about how psychics had helped police on crazy cases—cases like this. He paused only to pour water through Mr. Coffee. The machine was gurgling and chugging before he sat in his chair.

The desk was awash with papers, but Peach's note was right on top. Only Peach would catch the broken numerical sequence, he thought. "Probably a simple clerical error or editing mistake," he said aloud.

He would check it out. It had been a minor nag through most of yesterday, vying for the back of his mind with Miss Klast's description of the school loiterer. Now, he looked again at his notes on her comments: "Six feet, maybe six-one; one-seventy; medium complexion; sharp nose; high cheekbones—almost Slavic-looking and a big cleft in his chin."

When he'd taken down her words yesterday, an alarm had sounded faintly in a distant part of his brain. Competing events had cut short his trying to locate the source of the alarm. But now it began to bleat in his mind again. He hoped the *Pine Cone* artist would keep his promise to deliver his final rendering of the loiterer early this morning. That might help. Something that would definitely help was the phone call he'd been wanting to make since this madness started. He grabbed the telephone and punched up a number he'd long ago memorized.

After a ring and a half came the familiar husky, Jersey-stained voice. "What!" The word was a challenge, not a question.

"Nice telephone etiquette. Don't you academic types have any class at all?" Will asked.

"Willie-boy!" The voice was a half-tone brighter. "Do you know what time it is?"

"Same time zone, Phil—it's almost six. Now wake up and talk to me."

After a moment of muffled sounds, Phil Curry returned to the line. "Thanks for the wake-up call. Makes home seem like a hotel. How you doin', boy?"

"Shitty. You been readin' the papers?" Will put the phone on speaker as he walked over to the coffee pot and filled his oversized mug.

"Enough to change my vacation plans. That's a scary place you're livin' in. Caught you on the tube last night. Helluva job, kid. You were the shits."

"Thanks, partner. Apparently, there's a whole bunch of people who agree with you." Will left the phone on speaker as he returned to his chair.

"And your contract's up pretty soon."

"That, too. Got any room in Fresno for a beat-up old cop?"

"'S'all we got now—includin' me. Besides, I really need a woman or a minority. No offense, but...."

"Goddamned affirmative action. How's a WASP s'posed to get a job these days?"

"Not my problem, whitey. My duty's to help society right the terrible wrongs perpetrated on the various proud tribal leaders of Africa and generations of their descendants."

"I thought that's what the postal service was for," Will said as his chair creaked under his weight.

The back and forth with Phil was a welcome relief to Will. He truly missed his buddy and loved their semi-annual get-togethers. They spoke by phone at least twice a month or whenever either had a particularly tasteless joke to tell. Their days together in Jersey had forged a friendship well beyond being good buddies.

Will hated to end the repartee, but he had to get back to the real world. "Phil, you gotten your FBI reports yet?"

"I think so. They're either at the office or the lieutenant's got 'em. I make him read 'em. It's a waste of my time."

"Do me a favor. Soon as you get to your office, get hold of the reports and see who number 1403 is."

"I'm playin' golf today—takin' sick leave and everything. Not goin' in at all. Can't you get this stuff from somebody else?"

Will allowed that he could, but something in his voice must have changed Curry's mind and tone. "Wait a minute, wait a minute. I'll get the information. Gimme the number again."

"1403."

"Okay, listen, lieutenant's doin' his turn on graveyard, so it's gonna take me a little time to get back to you if he's out in a car somewhere."

"Thanks, Phil." Will sipped his coffee. It was too strong—just how he liked it.

"No sweat. Is this part of all that shit goin' on over there?"

"Right now, it's just a loose end. I got about a thousand of 'em, and I'd like to tie just one of 'em off."

Phil asked about the case, and Will told him there were no decent clues yet. He described the phone tip about the Dumpster and his feeling that the caller and the killer could be one in the same. Curry said it might be a stretch. "But sometimes you gotta go with your instincts, kid, 'specially when it's all you got."

"Another instinct I got, Phil, is that this nut is doin' all this to get at somebody in particular—like me, or Jim, or Elliot."

"But you got not a single live clue to back that up, right?"

"Right."

"That pony won't run too far, child. Listen, lemme partake of my morning ritual, and I'll run down that report for you."

Before letting Curry go, Will laid out his idea to smoke the killer out into the open. Phil agreed that it was a dangerous approach, but allowed that things could hardly get worse.

Will refilled his cup from Mr. Coffee's offering and returned to his overloaded desk. The first order of business, he decided, was to move all the papers and files to the top of the sturdy oak file cabinet. Then he plopped a single pad and one pen down on the desk and sat himself down to outline a plan to bring the killer forward.

Writing things out was Will's way of corralling details. His memory was decent, but writing reassured him that he wasn't missing anything. He'd been a list-maker as long as he could remember. Though he could laugh when others made sport of this particular proclivity, he always felt a bit unprepared when he wasn't carrying some sort of list.

The early morning sun streamed through the large window behind Will's desk. It warmed him as he struggled to bring focus to a world that had moved too fast in the last few days.

That was one of the problems with this case, he decided. Things had happened too fast for him to have time to make his trustworthy lists. A small problem in the middle of lots of big problems, but a problem nevertheless. He glanced at his watch. Almost six-thirty. His troops would be hitting the streets soon. Nobody would be in the office for over four hours. As he jotted his first note on the fresh white pad, he reminded himself that his final written product would be barely more than a gamble—not to mention dangerous as hell. He would run it by everyone, including a shrink or two, before he let it fly. Hell yes, it *was* a gamble. But it might work—especially if the perpetrator cooperated by failing to leave any additional bodies or heads in public places. But it *could* cause the bastard to explode and do God knows what.

"Got no other cards to play. Might have to try it," he said aloud, as he hunched over the pad and began to think through which verbal chips he'd use to bet with.

***

The lean man pushed away from the table that held the scant remains of his room-service breakfast. He moved into the large bathroom, washed his hands and stared at his reflection in the wall-length mirror. He smiled.

Going to be a busy day. Hate to leave this place, but if I'm going to do Mrs. Business Association, I need to be in Carmel. Could just shoot her. But that's so impersonal. Much nicer to feel her squirm under the knife. Need to feel that. Then I can get those kids. Can't go back to the school, though. They'll be watching. No unnecessary risks. No more heads. Takes too long. Can't very well hide the machete while I'm trying to blend in with the tourists—if there are any left. Timing's got to be perfect. Relax tonight.

Move tomorrow. Find the fat bitch, trail her, kill her. When, though? Need to be patient. Couple days go by, they might forget about me. Not fucking likely. Still, they might think their killer is gone. Might loosen them up a bit. Let them get complacent—comfy. Then, maybe we can have a nice little get-together. A private reunion. It's been a long time comin'. We're almost there.

He snapped off the light in the bathroom, returned to the table and popped a perfect strawberry into his mouth. The slightly bittersweet taste matched his mood. He sat again at the table and began to plot out his agenda for the day.

Tuesday Morning, Fresno
Chapter Sixteen

"The fuck do you mean you don't know where they are?" Phil Curry bellowed at his lieutenant.

"I mean they're either back at the office, or I took 'em home night before last. What's the big fucking deal with FBI reports, Phil? Shit, we got six feet of 'em at the office, and I'm the only one ever looks at 'em," Alan Kelso shouted defensively into the radio mike in his patrol unit.

Phil had gone through his department's dispatcher to locate Kelso, who had just finished breakfast at Coco's on Blackstone, three miles west of the Fresno State campus.

"Just flag your ass back to campus and see if they're there," Phil said. He was angry that it had taken the student dispatch kid almost an hour to locate Kelso. Another delay could threaten his tee time. He'd been looking forward to today's golf match for two foggy, damp weeks. Of course, he thought, today is sunny and perfect. He didn't want the game to slip away from him, but he wanted to keep his promise to Will.

"Okay, okay—but what if I left 'em at home?" Kelso asked as he picked at a small circle of half-crystallized syrup that decorated his navy blue uniform necktie.

"Al, I don't give a fuck if the reports are on Mars. Just get me the fucking name of the guy. Shit, call the real cops downtown."

"Gotcha, Chief. What's the number again?"

"One-four-oh-three. Write it fucking down."

"Ten-Four, Chief," Kelso said, racking the receiver back into the radio unit before Curry could respond.

Phil looked in disbelief at the dead phone in his hand. He walked over to the mirror to see if his suspicion was accurate. There it was, sure as hell—that big vein had popped up right in the middle of his forehead. Years ago it appeared only after particularly nasty disputes with his ex-wife. Recently it had been showing up with increasing frequency—most often when Phil was trying to rub away some of the green from his young staff.

Christ, he thought, I gotta drive twenty minutes for a tee-off in fifty minutes. Won't get any warm-up in, gonna feel rushed. *Son of a bitch!*

His golf clubs stood by the front door. He walked over and fondled the six iron. It was the latest in an ever-changing list of Phil's favorite golf clubs. A couple of bad shots with a favorite club would relegate it to Curry's long list of untrustworthy clubs. Half a dozen consecutive bad shots could qualify a club for Phil's list of truly evil instruments—a status his three-iron had earned in perpetuity. His two-iron had been in the basement for eighteen months.

"Ring, you son of a bitch!" he yelled at the phone. Its silence infuriated him. He did not want to miss this game. He felt ready to win—it was his turn to win, and he relished the thought of beating his favorite opponent, Eddie Markarian, field rep for Fresno's congressman. As he nestled the six-iron back into its resting place, the phone rang. A quick look at his watch told him he could get the name from Kelso, call Will, drive to the golf course and still take a few practice putts. He smiled, crossed the room, grabbed the phone and said, "Curry."

"Got it, Chief." Kelso sounded as proud as if he'd collared a major Colombian cocaine lord.

"Name, Alan—gimme a name."

"Louis Baker Peel."

"Mother of God." Phil's voice was barely a whisper. He hung up without another word, walked into the family room and picked up both of his guns. He grabbed a box of bullets for each and placed those at the bottom of a large Macy's shopping bag. After loading the bag to the top with underwear, socks, extra Levis, a toothbrush, and his razor, he walked out the front door. He walked by his golf clubs without so much as an acknowledgment. He'd call Markarian from his car phone and cancel.

Phil hoped there was still time. The huge Cadillac burned rubber in Curry's driveway. Two miles to Interstate Five.

The call from Curry came in just as Will was finishing the draft of his plan of action. Their conversation took fewer than thirty seconds. It was only when Phil disconnected that the wave of fear hit Will. His stomach knotted and a tremor ran through his hand as he cradled the receiver. He pulled his wastebasket close as bile foamed into the back of his throat. He managed to swallow the need to vomit, but the fear continued to roil.

Staggering up to a standing position and lurching into the department's common area, Will entertained an opaque hope that distancing himself from the telephone would somehow give the lie to Phil's information. It didn't work. As he shuffled back toward the station's tiny bathroom, he picked his shirt away from the sweat spots on his torso. He washed his hands and splashed water on his face. He knew he would soon have to focus on Louis Peel, but first he had to make sure his kids were safe. And his men. Christ! None of them would have a chance against Peel.

Back at his desk Will looked at his watch. Phil would be in Carmel within three hours. The fewer your blessings, boy, the more important to count them. His grandmother's creed. On this blessings-short day, that Phil was on his way was definitely worth counting.

Will reached his men and told them to be at his house by 12:30. He described Peel to them, as close as memory allowed, and told them to use extreme caution if they spotted him. He was certain they wouldn't get near him—Peel was too cunning for a confrontation unless it was strictly on his terms. He alerted the sheriff, then dialed Randolph and told him there would be four sheriff's deputies on round-the-clock duty at the mayor's home.

He said just enough about Peel to silence Randolph's protests. Elliot put the kids on the line, and Sari told Will that Peach was reading to her about a place called Oz where wondrous animals could talk and couches could fly. David reported that "Gunner" was teaching him to play snooker. Randolph came back on the line and asked Will what his plans were.

"Be at my house by 12:30."

"That doesn't answer my question—I need to know what you're gonna…"

"Elliot, you'll know more'n you ever wanted this afternoon. Right now I got some calls to…"

"Now look, Will…"

Ignoring the impatience in his boss's voice, Will cut in sharply. "Elliot, get off the fucking phone. I got work to do. I'll see you at 12:30." Will hung up and watched as the green light on his phone disappeared in two slow beats.

The brief contact with Sari and David triggered an ache Will knew he'd carry until he caught or killed Louis Peel—or until Peel got him. His theory had been right, by God. This case was personal. Louis Peel was in Carmel to exact revenge. He'd already turned the town upside down in his sick quest for retribution. This idyllic spot where Will had built a new life for his family had been traumatized to its core. The city couldn't begin to recover until Peel was driven out. The price for doing that, especially to Will, might be unthinkable. But finding—and stopping—Peel was his job. His only job now.

A short, hard storm of emotions swept over Will, leaving a feeling of pure energy in its wake. All his senses felt razor sharp. He'd been a great finisher on the streets. He could do that this time—he was sure of it. Now that he knew what he was pursuing. He'd caught the son of a bitch once—he'd do it again. He only prayed he could do it quickly enough. His fear a few moments earlier gave way to a contained fury he'd not known for years. He knew his life hung on his ability to control his rage and use it wisely.

His plan needed revision now that he knew who he was after. He placed a call to Directory Assistance for a Jersey listing. His next call would—he hoped—give him what he needed to round that plan into final shape. Before dialing the number, he got up, walked to the bathroom, took a leak and washed his hands again. Back in the front part of the station, he brewed a fresh pot of coffee. He knew he was finding things to do in order to postpone, even for minutes, the tide of memories that would carry him a decade back and a continent away.

Over time Will had succeeded in banishing Louis Peel and that one terrible night from his thoughts. Keeping the devil at bay was what every human did to maintain mental balance. Dwell on the crazy, sick things and they'll consume you. And Peel was the worst—the most evil—person he had ever run up against. No choice now—time was up. Will had to roll the rock away and release the foul odor of the long-buried past. With the countervailing aroma of Mr. Coffee wafting around the room, he returned to his desk to deal with what he knew would be the end of Louis Peel—or Will Kempton.

As he sat unmoving at his desk, Will had no doubt now that Peel was Carmel's triple killer. Everything fit together too perfectly to allow for coincidence—or for him to continue looking for other possible suspects. Such thinking wasn't very cop-like, he knew. Will had been taught, along with countless generations of cops, to explore every option and clue, to eliminate everything until only a single probability remained. That approach worked—it made Sherlock Holmes a legend and Will's favorite reading material—and it is practiced by every cop and detective with an IQ above his belt size.

But this time he was going to skip over days of gathering and sifting through clues. It was cut-to-the-chase time: How could Will bring Peel to ground without further carnage?

Will pondered that question for a full ten minutes. A revelation eluded him, so he put pen to paper and wrote a three-page scenario, complete with actors, cues and stage directions. His plan, which he would share with his comrades, was to trick Peel—lure him out into the open and nab him. Every move was designed to prompt a counter-move by Peel. *Killer chess*, Will thought.

He shifted slightly in his chair and stared hard into middle space. Caution, patience and finesse were required—qualities Will knew did not abound in his make-up. If the information from Jersey matched his suspicions, he'd have to make another appearance on television—

today. His performance probably wouldn't enhance his or Randolph's popularity, but that wasn't his aim. He wouldn't go public with Peel's name because he believed that would cause one of two reactions, both bad. Once named, Peel would either disappear completely or would launch a murderous rampage far worse than the one already underway. Will couldn't risk the latter. And though Peel's departure would bring quiet to the village, Will knew the reprieve would be only temporary. He would see Peel's shadow everywhere. He couldn't live like that—waiting for Peel to return. And, allowed to get away now, he would return. To hurt Will. To finish him off.

There was a time, Will thought as he focused on the papers covering his desk, when he wouldn't have been so cautious. Years ago, his sense of immortality and boundless fatalism would have propelled him into a figurative, perhaps literal, shoot-out with Peel. Circumstances—working where most of the realities were pleasant—had changed him. Life here was too good. He hadn't been a real cop for years. He'd grown soft. He'd felt it happening. It hadn't bothered him in the least—he'd actually celebrated it as his well-earned reward for the brutal lessons and bitter losses he'd had in Jersey. Life now was centered on David and Sari. He was all they had, and they needed him just as he was now—not the way he'd been. They had no memory of his life on the streets of Jersey. He wasn't sure how well he could remember that person either. Or even that he wanted to make himself do it.

Will dropped his pen, got up and walked to the coffee pot. As he filled his cup, he thanked God the kids were safe. The realization that Peel had been within a foot of Sari on Saturday launched a shudder so strong that coffee slopped out of his cup onto the table and floor. Peel could have destroyed him right then. Ten years ago Peel would have killed her there, on the beach. Why hadn't he? Something had changed in the man. *Find that. Find it and use it against him.*

Peel had been the well-dressed dandy. As for his killing style, he had given no warning and taken no risks. He worked in the dark, preying only on the relatively weak and defenseless. Now he had showed up in daylight. Now he also killed men. Now he sent warnings—so it seemed—to his ultimate intended victim. *He's hardened, while I've*

softened. Surviving at Rahway—and escaping from it—shows the change.
He hates and is driven by vengeance. I am his target.

Back in his chair a film of sweat formed on Will's face as he struggled
to find the edge he needed to bring Peel down. As he placed the call to
Rahway, he knew he was beginning the last relatively peaceful minutes
of what would be one goddamn lousy day.

Tuesday, Forenoon

Chapter Seventeen

The lean man stood again before the mirror in the large bathroom. He was pleased at his reflection. He removed his shirt.

Hair looks very natural. I'm getting so good at this, I could get a job as a colorist. A little Revlon pencil to darken the brows and that fake tan shit, and I'll look like a full-blooded Eye-talian. Ah, the glasses—perfect! Could walk right into that asshole's office and he wouldn't recognize me. The weights have added thirty pounds of muscle.

He backed up a step, flexed his biceps and smiled.

Hungry. Not even noon yet. Early dinner tonight—room service— right here. Celebrate my last evening at Pebble Beach with a perfect meal. Caesar salad, extra rare filet, fresh asparagus with hollandaise, Chateau Margaux...oh, say, 1979. Lovely. Back from Carmel by three. Dinner at five-thirty. Pack, shower, dinner, early to bed. First thing tomorrow, move into town. Kill the ugly broad. Barth. Let Kempton twist on that for a while. A little more work here—one, two, three, nice and neat—then get away without a trace. After that, there'll be only one more big fish to fry. I'll hit the road, find her and kill her, too. When? Who knows? Somewhere, I'll find the right spot to settle.

Have to remember to pick up some of those great cigars at that little pipe shop in Carmel. Life definitely is good and getting better. Pretty fuckin' fine shape for forty-one. Body's near-perfect. Not a blemish except for these scars. That whore! She paid. He'll pay, too. In full, Mr. Kempton, in full. Not quick either. That's too kind for you. Your career's already hanging by a thread. We'll finish that off tomorrow. Then your kids. Then you.

He turned and examined his profile in the mirror. Another smile. He walked out of the bathroom and drew back the curtain that covered the sliding door overlooking the eighteenth hole at Pebble Beach.

Where are your kids, Will? You were lucky yesterday, but I'll find them. Time's on my side. Nobody knows me—can't see me coming. Kill the ugly broad tomorrow, and while you're caught in the vortex of yet another murder, I'll track down your kids. If I can't have my kids, you can't have yours. Fair is fair, William.

Gray out there. Fog or rain coming? Better run now—don't want to get stale. Can't run in the rain. Might slip and get hurt. Can't have that. Rain's good killing weather, though—let it come.

***

Rahway Penitentiary put Will on hold. His zeal to get started and the flavorless Muzak on the line made the delay nearly unbearable. Still, he held the receiver to his ear. As minutes passed, the delay allowed Louis Peel to force his way into the front line of Will's consciousness.

Peel had been a highly successful stockbroker who'd made a pretty pile of money by the age of twenty-eight. Estimates of his fortune exceeded fifteen million dollars. No one could pin down the exact amount because, by the time he'd struck it rich, Peel was living a double life, rat-holing money all over the country under false names.

When the final bell would ring out at the New York Stock Exchange, signaling the end of the day's labor, Peel moved out into the darkness and his second career.

Over the bitter winter of 1988, New York and Jersey City were hit by a series of seventeen brutal slayings, which bore sufficient common elements so that police on both sides of the Hudson River concluded all the killings were the work of a single mind.

Will had stumbled onto the case quite by accident. In his eyes, a terrible accident. Usually prompt, he'd been held up by a dumb debate at the station house over who was responsible for misplacing some paperwork, and arrived late for an appointment with one of his informants, a nineteen-year-old hooker.

As Bebe Jones had learned to trust Will, he had learned that she had no intention of staying in the life permanently. That was just one reason that, as they grew close, he continually urged her to hasten her departure. Two months earlier, she had actually begun crossing off the days on a pocket calendar. Less than four weeks remained to cross off when Will found what was left of her, twenty feet from the door of her apartment. From all evidence Will had missed the killer by only minutes.

Tears of fury blurred his first survey of the scene. Bebe had obviously put up a tremendous fight—no surprise to Will, who knew what a hunger for life she had. He found her long gold nail file across the hall from her torn body. It was covered with blood. Will's intuition told him the blood wasn't hers.

He called Homicide, as dictated by department policy. He managed to be matter of-fact in outlining the crime scene. That done, he slipped the bonds of all the police procedures he'd ever learned.

In a frenzy that careened from pure melancholy to blind rage, Will pounded on the doors of the three other apartments located on the ground floor of the building. His reckless agitation probably scared any potential witnesses into silence. Finally, he gave up and resigned himself to protecting the crime scene until Homicide arrived. He was alone on the steps of Bebe's building for ten seconds when a young boy approached him.

Before Will could shoo him away, the kid said, "You looking for a guy hurt?"

"Yeah. Know where he is?"

"For ten bucks."

Will took out a five and held it firmly in his hand.

"That ain't ten."

"It's what I got."

The boy shrugged, held out his hand. Will shook his head. "First tell me."

The kid stared.

Will didn't glance away. "Two more seconds, I'm going to put this money away," he said.

"I was playin' ball in the alley out back," the boy said, speaking quickly now. "Dude come out doubled up, gruntin' and stuff. Looked fucked up bad."

After wrenching a workable description from the kid, Will gave him the five and told him to get straight home. Not a minute later, the first of what would be a small parade of police cars pulled up noisily. The Homicide cops parked as though the street was their private driveway. In a way it was, he thought, and would remain so for most of that night.

Will led the detectives inside and told them—almost—everything he knew. He pointed out the bloody nail file and his belief that the victim had stuck it so deeply into her attacker that he'd had to pull it out—possibly leaving traceable fingerprints on it. He identified Bebe and outlined their working relationship.

He didn't tell them—it was none of their business—that Bebe Jones had been in the life since she'd fled an abusive father in Ohio three years earlier. Or that, after a brief fling with heroin, she'd kicked completely and developed a fierce hatred for the producers and pushers of the junk that poisoned the streets of her adopted home. He did report that it was a desire to damage the drug network that made her seek a police connection and begin her partnership with Will. (They no doubt understood without his spelling it out that his *quid pro* to her *quo* was immediate freedom without any hassling whenever she was busted for hooking. Her part of the bargain was to provide him with information useful to his work in the Narcotics Division.)

In moments the lobby was crowded with cops, and the Homicide boys were asserting their authority with their typical priest-like condescension. Will slipped, unnoticed, out the front door.

As he stopped to lift a large flashlight from one of the patrol cars parked in the street, he couldn't help but flinch, recalling how well the arrangement had worked for him—Bebe's tips initiating a series of busts that had made Will a superstar in the department. For eighteen months, he reminded himself, the arrangement had worked for her, too. The absence of legal entanglements enabled Bebe to make, and keep, a sizable cache—enough for her to go to college and become a teacher.

How she wanted to be a teacher—believing that her own experiences on a thousand streets qualified her to relate well to kids, especially kids in trouble. To Will's mind, Bebe had indeed acquired a wisdom that surpassed her bitterness. Heading quickly toward the alley, he dismissed a twinge of guilt over keeping the kid's information from the Homicide dicks. But, he rationalized, they were busy securing a crime scene—plastic envelopes, yellow police tape, interviews of residents of the building and an inch-by-inch, hands-and-knees search of the vestibule. There was no way their actual hunt for the killer would start before hours had been lost.

His hunt could begin immediately.

Only a few people ever heard the full story of Will's odyssey that night. These didn't number among them Will's superiors on the force, and none was a member of any branch of the media. Public knowledge of his actions that night would have ended his ties to law enforcement forever.

Prowling the alley, Will silently reviewed the kid's description of the stricken man: tall, thin, short blonde hair, three-piece gray suit, yellow shirt, red tie. Good-looking, clean-cut guy, the kid had said. Shit, yeah, helluva nice guy. The small pools of blood he found in the alley almost persuaded Will to go back for a Homicide cop. His chances of catching the killer were remote—a well-organized search, with many participants, was far more likely to succeed. But he did not go back. Something drove him forward—alone.

The Muzak ended abruptly, the phone's receiver emitted two clicks, and a voice spoke on the other end.

"Dr. Washburn here."

Will was grateful to have his painful reminiscence interrupted by a businesslike voice on the Rahway end of the telephone.

Will sat up as straight as he would if Washburn were in the office with him.

"Dr. Washburn, my name is Will Kempton. Chief Kempton. I'm Chief of Police in Carmel, California, and I need your help."

Tuesday Afternoon

Chapter Eighteen

The first thing Will saw as he turned into his driveway was Phil Curry's long, tan 1978 Coupe de Ville. Then he saw Phil, a small chocolate mountain, leaning against the far left pillar of the front porch. He parked the Jeep and quickly closed the distance between Phil and himself.

"Goddamn! It's good to see you, man." Will gave Curry a bear hug, not failing to notice that his arms couldn't quite complete the circle around the massive back of his old friend.

Releasing him, Will said, "Sorry about the circumstances."

"Hey, no sweat, kid. Been gettin' bored on campus. Department's already set a new record for parking tickets, and our baddest criminals are the ones with tenure. Plus, I gotta bunch of vacation time that I'll lose if I don't take it soon. Camera's in the trunk. Got some Bermudas and all my really ugly shirts…"

"Some vacation, pal…"

"Ah, fuck it. We'll pick this guy up quick, then get in a little golf."

Both men knew that "vacation" talk was wishful thinking, but there'd be enough time to be realistic after Phil unpacked. After they'd pulled two bags and a large cardboard box from the Jeep, Will led his guest into the house. Before Curry could ridicule the appearance of the living room, Will explained the sleeping arrangements he'd forced on his troops.

"Looks like a stakeout in the old days back in Jersey," Phil said, stepping over a pile of dirty underwear and socks. "Where's the kids?"

"Stayin' at Elliot's 'til this is over. C'mon and help me set up the dining room. You hungry?"

"Does the Pope shit in the woods?" Phil answered, grinning with self-satisfaction as he simultaneously destroyed two metaphors.

"I gotta bunch of sandwiches. All my guys and Randolph will be here in a few minutes. We'll eat and then we'll figure out what we're gonna do about this crazy fuck."

"You gonna tell 'em the whole thing, kid?"

Will stopped laying out the food and looked directly at his former partner. "Don't see that I have any choice, do you?"

"Not my call—just wanted to make sure you'd thought it out, that's all."

"Oh, I've thought it out, believe me. And much as I won't enjoy talking about it, there's really no reason to hold back the truth from them at this point. Wouldn't be fair, anyway. My guys have a right to know what we're up against—and if that means telling them everything, then that's…." Will shrugged just as a slamming car door announced the mayor's arrival.

By the time Elliot and Phil finished trading insults over one another's golfing skills, Will's rag-tag force had shown up and was circling the food. After making introductions all around, Will told them to help themselves to lunch and take a seat at the kitchen table.

Ten minutes of small talk had created a semblance of calm in the room—and inside himself—that Will felt was necessary before he filled everyone in on Louis Peel and his plan to nail him. Now he unloaded seven manila folders from a shopping bag and distributed them to the men at the table. Two out-of-practice cops, two nervous deputies, two completely inexperienced men and a movie star. The odds weren't terrific.

"Everybody got a pen or pencil?" Will asked. The murmur of assent from his troops sent him forward. "Okay, gentlemen, let's do it. Page one is the most recent photo of the son of a bitch we're after. Sorry about the quality, but it's the best I could get on FAX from the FBI."

"Who is he?" Randolph asked.

"Pages two and three'll give you that. Take a couple minutes to read them."

Will waved off a question from Ainsley. Silence filled the room—punctuated only by exhalations and curses from all but Curry and Kempton. One by one, the men closed their folders and looked expectantly at Will. Jim was the last to finish. "Bad motherfucker, Will," Jim offered as he shifted uneasily in his chair.

"The worst I ever met or even read about, Jim. This place's never seen anything close—and if we don't catch him damned quick, he'll tear the town apart."

"Could be the guy in the picture at the beach with the red towel," Jeff offered.

"It is," Will answered. "Okay, boys, smoke 'em if you have 'em. I'm gonna tell you the full story about this fucker and yours truly."

The smoke that soon filled the room seemed appropriate as Will transported his companions back in time to a cold and windy night in Jersey City. He quickly covered Bebe, her death and the scene in the vestibule of her building. The quiet in the room was a perfect counterpoint to the agitation Will felt as he began to narrate the second act of the play he had directed on that night so long ago.

"I caught the bastard that night—followed a trail of blood for blocks. Just as it started to rain, I found blood on the steps of a deserted brownstone. It was rainin' pretty good—if he hadn't gone into that building when he did, I'd'a never found him."

Will made eye contact with each man at the table. He gave Randolph an extra second. No one moved.

"I went in with my gun drawn and cocked. Stood there for half a minute to let my eyes adjust to the dark—there was no electricity in the place. My heart sounded like a goddamn bass drum. The other noise came to me *under* that one somehow. All the hair on the back of my neck stood on end. I thought maybe it wasn't him but an animal in there with me.

"Then that fuckin' noise started up again. Awful sound. There was nowhere to hide—it was a tiny hallway, with a staircase along the far left wall. I was halfway up the stairs before I knew I'd even moved. Then, nothing—not even a fuckin' roach movin' around. Seemed like an hour. Was crouched on the stairs—didn't know whether to shit or go blind. I figured I couldn't stay there, so I started goin' up. Tryin' to be quiet, but every step creaked like a fuckin' banjo. My eyes were focused on the landing, 'cause that was where I was heading.

"Just as I lit up the landing with the flashlight, I heard this scuffling sound below me. I slammed down my body as fast and flat as I could. Stopped breathing so I could hear—again, *nothing*."

Will cleared his throat and continued his narrative.

"Then there was a whimper and a cough. Without movin', I fired off three shots and started yellin' like a banshee for the motherfucker not to move another inch. Shined the light between the struts of the banister. Still couldn't see shit. Couple more minutes went by—I'd almost grown onto that stairway. Then I heard a voice cryin'. 'Don't shoot,' it said. 'I'm bleeding, can't move, help me.'"

Will's voice was hushed.

"Inchin' down the stairs, I finally spotted the fuck. Flat on his stomach. Gray suit, blonde hair. I went fuckin' nuts. I *knew* it was the guy who did Bebe, see...

"Anyway, I was over the banister and on toppa him so fast he didn't know what the hell was happening. Cuffed him hard. He was makin' so much noise I whomped him with the flashlight, and he went out. When I rolled him over, I could see what a fucking mess he was. Bebe had really fought him good. There was blood everywhere—floor, walls—everywhere.

"He started moanin' and shit. I put the light so he could see me, and I told him one more sound and I'd kill him. I musta looked pretty bad 'cause he nodded and shut up."

Will paused to collect his thoughts. "So that was Louis Peel?" Jim put in. "And you were the one caught him and took him in?"

Looking at his friend, Will sighed deeply before he picked up the story. "That was Peel all right, Jimmy. But the other part didn't happen quite so neatly. First, I took him on a short trip."

A puzzled look came over Jim's face. His palms-up motion with both hands urged Will to continue.

"First, I gagged him. Then cuffed him to the banister. Then I left to go get some supplies."

"What kinda supplies, Will?" the mayor asked.

"Let him talk, Elliot." Phil's ominous tone was devoid of the warmth and respect he normally showed Randolph. The mayor's protest was cut off by Will's continued recitation. His audience noted the changed inflection, the cadence more like someone's at the confessional than a storyteller's. Will sat back and tried to ease the tension in his neck with a repeated twisting motion.

"I wrapped him, head to toe, in big plastic garbage bags. Tore a hole just big enough for him to breathe through. Then I scrubbed every inch of the floor. There wasn't a trace that he—that anybody—had been there.

"When I was finished there, I carried Peel out to my car, shoved him into the trunk, and headed for the South City Dump. Drove way back in there so nobody'd see me. Then I got him out of the trunk and propped him up on a wall of garbage and slapped him awake. I worked out on the son of a bitch, threatened to cut his balls off. He was scared, but not enough. Then he smelled the can of gas I was holding. I showed him my trusty Bic lighter—flicked it for him a couple times so he'd know it worked. Gave the fuck ten seconds to start talkin'. He was so fuckin' afraid he'd'a confessed to being Lee Harvey Oswald.

"Next day's papers made me out a hero—fulla stuff about my single-handed capture of the 'Slasher.' He signed a full confession to all eighteen murders, including Bebe's. Hospital people at Jersey General reported how I'd gently carried the guy into the ER, demanding quick attention for him. Said I was a pain in the ass 'til they started fixin' his wounds. One orderly was even quoted sayin' they'd have let him bleed to death if they'd known who he was, 'cept the cop kept gettin' in their face.

"My story was that I'd stumbled onto Peel a few hours after Bebe's murder. Said I'd been checking every doorway and alley in the vicinity when I found him unconscious in an alley a mile south of Bebe's place.

"I reported that the suspect regained consciousness just as I approached him. Said I told him I was a cop. Suspect's story of being a mugging victim did not sound right—his wallet was full of cash, and he was wearing a Rolex and two nice rings. Advised suspect of his Miranda rights and told him I'd been at a crime scene where I'd observed a rat-tailed nail file with blood on it. Told suspect if the blood on the file matched his, he was in trouble.

"Then I assisted the suspect to the hospital. On the way there, he thought he was dying. Confessed to killing Bebe and all the others. Gave me details about the 'Slasher' killings that only the perp could know. I listed those details in the appendix section of my formal report. Peel signed a statement on hospital stationery—owned up to all eighteen murders."

Will looked up briefly from his folded hands. His eyes darted to each man in the room. He blinked a few times, shook his head, then went on, his voice husky with emotion too vividly remembered. "That statement was identical to the one I forced the fucker to sign out at the dump after I'd scared the shit outta him. The only thing true in my formal report was that he really did cop to all the other killings—not that I cared. Hell, I only cared about Bebe. But Peel was so scared he spilled it all."

Each man at the kitchen table gave Will his full attention. Their continued lack of movement was unnatural.

"So I took it and ran with it. That's the basic story, gentlemen. Peel was tried, convicted and sentenced to life without possibility of parole. I was the star witness and the most celebrated cop in Jersey. A very small amount of rationalizing got me through the doubts I felt about my own behavior. Bottom line was we got the right guy, and he was off the streets—so procedures be damned. Right?"

Jeff's mouth hung open and his eyes were wide.

"I thought once he was sent up, Peel'd only be a bad memory. And that's what he has been—until now."

"He must really hate you," Jim said hoarsely.

Will shoved his chair back a foot or so and said, "Hate's a two-way street, Jimbo."

Tuesday Afternoon Moves On
Chapter Nineteen

Nothing in the room, not even air, seemed to move. Will looked around at the men trying to take in all he'd told them, then stood up. "So now you know. I nailed Peel by violating most of the Bill of Rights and several of the commandments."

He swallowed, looked grimly at his hands, then placed them on the back of the chair he'd just vacated. "I'd'a killed him if he hadn't owned to killing Bebe. I've regretted my actions that night a thousand times. Not any more. I'm sorry I didn't kill him. If I had, three good people'd still be alive. Peel is just solid, fuckin' scum—the world'd be a helluva lot better off without him."

He saw five of the six men look at him as if for the first time. Jeff's jock-macho coolness had melted. Will could see he was almost in a state of disbelief that his smallish boss had brought down one of the country's most notorious killers in a single night of calculated viciousness. Forsburg and Ainsley seemed less taken aback than Jeff. They were cops, and any cop with time on the streets could probably understand what had happened to Will that night. Both shook their heads and Clint said, "Helluva catch, Chief."

Will's wry smile belied his worry over what they—especially his boss—thought of his story. He sensed Randolph's discomfort. So did Curry, who punched the mayor lightly on the shoulder. "Sounds kinda like a movie, doesn't it, Gunner?"

The mayor shook his head slowly, looked up at Will and said, "Jesus, Will—I never knew…"

"Well, Gun, I did leave it off of my job application." Will's even wryer smile fell short of Randolph's side of the table.

Curry leaned toward Randolph and rasped, "It gets real out there, Gunner. Runnin' with dogs turns you into one sometimes. The trick is to find your way back to the human side. Lotsa guys don't make it back. Will and I both did, but we hadda get outta Jersey to do it."

Randolph nodded, though it was clear he couldn't fully comprehend the merciless brutality described moments earlier. Clint's cigarette lighter was the only sound in the house as the mayor struggled for words.

Finally, straightening his always good posture, Randolph said, "Guys, you all know I'm no member of the ACLU, but Christ, Will, if Peel had all that money, why didn't he get a big-time lawyer and just rip your ass off? All that shit you did to him—they'd'a taken your badge and thrown out the whole case against Peel."

"Don't think that didn't worry me," Will said. "But he never said a word. The whole thing, from arraignment to sentencing, was the weirdest thing I've ever been through. Peel never talked—not once. Whenever we were in the same room, he just stared at me."

"Jesus," Randolph said. "I just don't understand…." The mayor splayed his hands in the palms-up international signal of puzzlement.

"It was like a game, Elliot," Will interrupted, as he moved to the sink for more water.

"A game?" Randolph asked, as his eyes followed Will on his journey across the room.

Holding the now full glass, Will turned back to face his boss and said, "I think he was lettin' me know, 'Okay, asshole, you won the first round, but I'll be comin' after you.' His fuckin' eyes, man, I've never seen anything like 'em."

Aside from Curry, who knew all about Will and Louis Peel, Jim seemed the least surprised member of the audience. He looked up at

Will, who still stood near the sink and said, "Always knew there was a part of you that you hid. You're a lot tougher than you look, boss. I'm glad you got the bastard, and I don't give a shit how you did it. You're my friend, and that's all that matters."

Will was moved, inclined his head in Jim's direction and said, "Thanks, Jimmy." His voice was husky with emotion.

"How the fuck did he get outta Rahway?" Ainsley asked.

"Didn't get all the particulars," Will said. "But it was almost two months ago. Busted up one guard pretty bad and somehow just slipped by the others...."

"How the fuck can a mass murderer psycho like this guy just slip quietly outta a hole like Rahway?" Clint asked.

"According to the guy I talked to at Rahway," Will said as he circled back to his chair, "Peel's escape made the papers and stuff back there, but wasn't picked up by the national wires. He thinks it's possible the Feds hushed it up."

"What in the fuck for?" Clint asked. He slapped the tabletop to emphasize his anger.

"They're hidin' Peel's wife and kids in some witness relocation program. Apparently she wasn't as supportive of Peel during the trial as he thought she should be. Also, he'd been scaring the shit outta her just before I caught him. She wanted out, big time."

"Why put her in a relocation program once he was sent up for life?" Jim asked.

"She told the Feds that he had money all over the place and that she was afraid he'd pay to have her hit."

"Jesus!" Randolph shook his head. He was still a half-step behind most of his tablemates.

Will focused on the mayor.

"Lucky the Feds believed her. Peel's type is usually damn low in any prison's pecking order. Feds figured he'd spread his dough around to the various gang leaders to keep people off his ass. Whatever he did, it worked—nobody fucked with him."

"Too bad about that," Jeff offered as he stood and stretched.

"Except, that is, for one incident—at least, from what I heard. After he came outta isolation—and, by the way, he used his time in there to build himself up; he's a lot heavier now and apparently it's all muscle. Anyway, a couple guys jumped him right after they let him outta isolation. He just beat the livin' shit outta both of 'em—broke arms and legs—bit one guy's nose all the way off."

"Jesus, shit!" Jeff said, cringing and sitting down with a thud. Will knew that nothing in Jeff's life had remotely prepared him for the realization that the world contained people like Louis Peel. Now Peel was here, in Carmel, on some psycho crazy fucking mission of retribution. Jeff looked stricken.

Will had no difficulty reading the strain in Jeff's face. He reached across and placed a friendly grip on the man's huge wrist. He was about to offer a few encouraging words when Randolph blurted out, "If this lunatic's been runnin' loose all this time, how come nobody's tried to inform you he might appear on your doorstep?"

Curry, who had moved to the refrigerator in search of a Coke, answered before Will could. "Because, Elliot, the only thing slower'n a whore hittin' orgasm is any and every police bureaucracy. If a note *was* ever sent to Will, it was mailed to the wrong address. But the odds are better that any warning is probably lyin' on some asshole's desk—buried under two feet of reports and requisitions."

"Notice of his escape is in this week's FBI reports, Phil," Will said stonily.

"Yeah, more'n a fuckin' month after he escaped." Phil's snort reiterated his earlier point. He angrily pulled the tab on the soft drink can for further emphasis—as if any were needed.

"How come you didn't catch it then?" Jim asked, looking directly at Will.

"The sheet on Peel was missing from my copy of the FBI weeklies..."

"What!?!" Randolph's face reflected total incredulity. He squinted at Will across the table—the same squint that had earned him great fame and fortune in his chosen career.

"That's right, Gun. One sheet was missing. I think Peel trailed Peach to the post office. When she got the reports, he lifted 'em, tore out his page and returned the rest to the station house."

"Bastard's got three balls!" Ainsley's first words since lunch were a bellow of indignation.

"Huge ones, Tom. But maybe he's a little reckless using them. If he'd just stolen the whole package, it woulda been days, maybe weeks, 'til I missed it. By ripping out his sheet, he told me he's here."

"Maybe he figures it's time for you to know he's here."

"I don't think so, Clint, and I'll tell you why in a minute. But first there's something else his actions have told us." Will's tone was again low and deadly serious. He pulled himself as close to the table as he could.

"Clearly, Peel's been stalking us, individually and as a group, for some time. He knew Peach went to the post office. He knew those FBI reports come out once a week. He knew where Jimmy lived, and I think he was in this house Sunday morning. He sure as hell knew Sari—he trailed her to the beach Saturday. He even knew Emma was the queen of the Garden Club and when the club was gonna meet."

"Bastard's been around here for a good, long time," Phil observed, circling back to his chair.

"No question, partner. Coulda pulled the trigger on any of us, 'cept you, Phil, and been done with Carmel. Fortunately, that's not what he's looking to do. He's out to make me suffer in as many ways as possible. He's got the town in a flat panic. He's killed one of my officers. One or both my kids woulda been next—then he was gonna come after me—prob'ly one on one."

"Jesus, Mary and Joe!" Jim said.

"I'm sure it was Peel at the school yesterday—looking for David and Sari. Maybe to kidnap 'em, maybe to kill 'em—whatever, he was there. By now he prob'ly knows Tom and Clint, too."

Will again sat utterly still for a few beats, then he turned to Phil and said, "You're the only one in this room he doesn't know."

"Well, we're gonna find a way to get the cocksucker to make my acquaintance—that's for damned sure." Phil's tone was sharpened by what Will knew was his friend's eagerness for a session with Peel.

"You're our ace in the hole, Phil. We gotta be careful he doesn't see you—or you'll be just one more target."

"Mama didn't raise her baby boy to be a target or a shield. What's your plan, kid?"

Everyone in the room seemed to realize that the two former partners were the best equipped to find a way to deal with Louis Peel. Phil had eased into a place where he shared Will's dominance over the gathering. The others looked from Will to Curry and back—waiting for more commentary.

"Elliot, when we're done here, two of us'll drive you out to your place. You, Peach and my kids are to stay there, under guard, until we nail Peel."

"Bullshit! I'm not sittin' out there with my thumbs up my ass for a week…" The mayor shook his head and seemed ready to speak again, but Will interrupted.

"It's not gonna take us a week. With any luck, it'll be less than twenty-four hours."

"Still, I don't want…"

Will cut off Randolph's protest. "Listen, Gun. I don't tell you how to mayor—don't tell me how to cop. You'd only get in the way. Christ, you can't even walk a block without ten autograph hunters snapping at your heels. And Peel would just love the publicity he'd get by pickin' off the world-famous Elliot Randolph."

"I got a City Council meeting tonight," Randolph said with some satisfaction.

"Cancel it."

Randolph leaned across the table toward Will, raised his voice and said, "Oh, horseshit! I've never missed…"

Louder still, Will practically shouted, "Cancel the fuckin' meeting, Elliot, goddamnit! We're not in a fuckin' goddamn tea party here."

Will's vehemence and the absence of the deference he normally accorded his boss aborted Randolph's protest. The mayor sat back in his chair. "Okay, Will. This is your shot. I guess I'm just used to being the star."

"Play this one right, and you'll get to play again. Fuck it up, and you'll be the headliner at the biggest funeral Carmel's ever had."

"I gotcha, I gotcha. Jesus, Will, go on. Christ!" Randolph, now just another member of the audience, gazed at his chief of police and waited for any new insight into what laid ahead.

"Okay, then. Sheriff's people are calling every hotel, motel and inn around here on the off-chance that Peel's built himself a nest to stay in the whole time he's been here."

"Would he do that, Chief?" Ainsley asked.

"Maybe. Shrink at Rahway said Peel is extremely organized and methodical. The comforts of home don't matter to him, but having a functional headquarters is very much in line with his profile and his MO." Will folded his hands and tried another shoulder roll to ease the tension in his neck and back.

"Wherever he is, it's prob'ly like a fuckin' armory," Phil interjected.

"Afraid so. The shrink said Peel is just fruity over deadly weapons."

"That's news?" Jim asked. He unwrapped a stick of gum and started to chew.

"Yeah, it really is. Back when he was the 'Slasher,' all he ever used was a ten-inch bowie knife. Over the years, Peel's read everything he could find on weapons—from crossbows to Ninja stars to AK-47s."

"What a great fuckin' assignment this is. Remind me to warmly thank Truitt for sendin' my ass over here," Clint said, lighting yet another cigarette.

"If we live through it," Ainsley threw in.

"He must value you guys highly," Jim said.

"While we wait for Truitt to call, lemme tell you more about Peel. I want you to know what it is we're going after. First, Clint—I don't think Peel's ready for me to know he's here," Will said, placing his still-folded hands under his chin.

"How come?" Clint asked.

"Because Peel's his own best audience. He loves publicity—written, spoken and televised. After we canned him in Jersey, his wife brought me a scrapbook she found. It was entirely devoted to the seventeen murders. She also told me she'd catch him watchin' the late news—something he'd never done before during their marriage. And he'd hustle his kids outta the room whenever the local early newscasts covered the Slasher Murders."

"What's all that got to do with him wantin' us to know it's him or not?" Jim asked.

"I'm thinkin' he's enjoying the huge amount of publicity he's created with his three quick hits. Christ, it's all over TV and the papers." Will paused a beat and continued. "Also, assuming that was him at the school yesterday—he had a helluva close call. I mean I coulda caught him right there with any luck, but he ran. Oh, I think he definitely wants me to know it's him—but only when his timetable, whatever the hell it is, clicks in."

"You think he might back off for a while?" Clint asked. He pushed a heap of butts around in the overflowing ashtray in an attempt to make room for the next one.

"I'm hopin'. The shrink thinks he will. Lemme give you the rest of his profile on Peel." Will rose, stretched and leaned against the door sill separating the kitchen from the dining room.

"Will," Randolph cut in. "Before you do that, back up a little. You said you hope Peel's gonna let up for a while. Other than what the shrink said—what do you base that on?"

"Hope, Gunner. Pure, unadulterated hope." Will's words provided no comfort to any member of his audience, but he continued to hold the undivided attention of every man in the room.

Tuesday Afternoon Wears Down
Chapter Twenty

Before Will could relate what he had learned from the Rahway psychiatrist, the telephone rang. Jim answered, passed the receiver to the mayor. Randolph said, "Hello" once, "Yes" once, "No" once, "Shit" twice, and handed the receiver back. He looked at Will who still stood in the doorway.

"That was Bob at the *Pine Cone*. Tomorrow's *Chronicle* headline's gonna read, 'Hat Trick for Carmel Killer.'"

"Great," Will muttered, shaking his head. "Another trip down the journalistic high road for the *Chron*. Damn that newspaper!"

"Plus, they're gonna feature a nice shot of you keeping me from unloading on Barth."

"Well, that oughta take some heat offa me, anyway."

Randolph's smile was working its way toward his eyes when Jim exclaimed, "Jesus, Gun, don't ever hit Barth in the face. You catch his overbite just right and you could lose a finger or two. Those things aren't teeth—they're tusks."

Something close to genuine laughter moved through the room. Will decided that the change in mood, however temporary, was good. To extend it a few minutes, he suggested a three-minute break for the can and refreshments. Chairs were shoved back and relieved of their burdens. Five men left the room in search of a bathroom. Will and Randolph remained and both moved to the kitchen sink.

Will approached Randolph and placed his hand on the taller man's shoulder. "God, Elliot, I'm sorry for dragging you into this."

"No apology called for. I'd say I owe you thanks for pullin' me off Barth. That woulda made a lovely picture and, knowing that little turd, a dandy little lawsuit." Randolph smirked at the thought.

"Yeah, but if it weren't for me, none of this stuff woulda happened. Peel never woulda come to Carmel."

Randolph looked Will square in the eyes and said, "Listen, kid, we hired you because we wanted a *real* cop here—not some door-rattling old fart ready for pasture. You've done a damned fine job so far. Got that credit card scam last summer and those bastards selling drugs at the high school. You've done good stuff here."

Will shook his head. "This time it's murder, Elliot."

"The people like you, Will, and they're fair. Wrap this up quick, and both our jobs are gonna be secure."

"What about Barth?"

"Fuck him. The more that pus-bag talks, the sooner people're gonna get sick of him."

"Hope you're right." Will glanced at his watch and said so everyone could hear, "Let's get back to business."

Within a minute each man was back in the same chair at the kitchen table. Clint's ashtray was empty. He opened a new pack of smokes.

The emotions that had electrified the air during the previous hour had vanished. Jim's horror, Randolph's anger, Jeff's fear—all were gone, Will thought. Now they could fix on a single goal—stopping Peel. Six sets of eyes turned to Will.

"Okay, guys. According to Dr. Melville Washburn, Peel's the worst homicidal sociopath he's ever seen. Says he's far worse now than when he was doin' Slasher duty. Then he loved to kill—now he lives to kill."

Weight shifted in the chairs. Eyes darted from one man to the next. Clint cleared his throat. Jeff wiped his forehead, damp despite the coolness of the room.

"The man who killed all those women was very cautious," Will told them. "He was a successful stockbroker—wife, kids, sailboat, tennis club, elder in his church, president of the Jaycees—the complete yuppie dream. Whatever drove him to kill was always subordinate to family and career—he *never* took a risk.

"My catching him was a fluke. If I'd missed him that night, he mighta gone on forever. Cops didn't have a single clue to the Slasher's identity. When we put him away, his wife split with the kids. He lost everything. With his straight life gone, so was the motivation to be careful."

Will hunkered down in his chair, paused for a beat and continued. "Now he's driven by hatred for me and for his wife. He won't let anything get in his way. I was easy to find, so he came here first. Washburn believes he'll go after the wife soon's he's finished with me. Washburn said that Peel needs—not wants, *needs*—to kill me to obliterate his own memories of the night I caught him."

"How we gonna find him, Chief?" Jeff asked.

"We're gonna go two ways at the same time..." Will said as he turned toward his young parking officer.

"Now what the hell does that mean?" Randolph bristled. Will could see that the mayor was still struggling with his bit part in the unfolding drama. In an effort to ease Randolph's discomfort, he slipped back into a respectful tone. "Right now we don't know *where* he is. I'm hoping Truitt will call with a lead on that score."

"What's the other path, then?" Randolph asked, somewhat calmed for the moment.

"Just a sec—lemme finish this one, because the two paths are tied together, and once we start, things could move awful damned fast. If Truitt comes up with somethin', Phil, Clint and I will check it out. At the same time, Tom and Jeff will take you out to your place, Elliot. Jim'll stay here and secure the house."

Jim pointed to Tom and Jeff and said, "You boys better haul ass back from Gunner's quick. Bein' here alone does *not* thrill me."

"Plan B is a little dicey," Will was saying. "If it works, it might smoke Peel out. If it doesn't work—well, I can't see that it'll make things much worse than they already are. Unless…." Will looked down at the table briefly.

"Unless what?" Randolph asked with some heat.

"That's the hard part, Elliot. I don't really know." Will looked directly at his boss and gave a small shrug of his shoulders.

"That just isn't good enough, Will," Randolph declared loudly and stood up. "I'm the mayor here, damn it! And you got me tied up like a rodeo calf. You can keep me outta the chase, but I'll be damned if I'll authorize…."

"Enough, Elliot!" Will snapped. The two men locked eyes for a long moment. Will was not enjoying the way he was treating his boss. Then Will spoke again in a slow, controlled tone. "You are not *authorizing* anything, Elliot. Now, sit down and listen!"

Seeing the color rise in Randolph's face, Will added, "Please, Mayor."

Slowly, Elliot's flush subsided. He dropped into his chair and waved Will to proceed.

"I briefed Washburn on everything Peel's done here in the last three days. After some shrink talk he told me Peel is, in his own mind, in a position of control…."

"That's s'posed to be news?" Jim said. "The rate we're goin', he's gonna feel invincible pretty fuckin' soon." Jim's words prompted several nods around the table.

"That's exactly right, Jim. He's got every reason to feel confident. The only crimp we've put in his master plan was my taking the kids outta school—that knocked him off course a little. Washburn thinks he's making a new plan, and that's why nothing's happened since Emma."

"Why doesn't Peel just hunt you down and shoot you?" Clint asked.

"Because, according to Washburn, he wants to take me for a ride— figuratively—like I did to him in Jersey. He wants that total victory. Plus—at the right time—he *wants* me to know it's him, back from the dead, who's destroying me."

"Jesus, what a fuckin' sicko…" Ainsley said. He reached for one of Clint's cigarettes. It would be his first in five years.

"You telling us," Randolph said angrily, "we sit and wait until this asshole starts executing a revised plan?"

"No, Gun. I'm going on TV again, this afternoon. Washburn helped me write a script."

Will flipped through his folder and extracted a single, legal-sized yellow sheet. Holding it at arm's length, he began to read:

"Ladies & gentlemen: I am William E. Kempton, Chief of Police in Carmel. In an effort to halt the recent violence in our city, I have consulted a forensic psychiatrist to build a profile of the perpetrator. The purpose of the profile is to help the police understand, even anticipate, his actions.

As with most serial killers, we seem to be dealing with an individual of relatively low intelligence and low self- esteem—a social misfit who cannot succeed in society.

Serial killers are usually cowards—unable to face a challenge or confrontation directly.

This case is strikingly similar to the vast majority of other random murders we've studied. There is no reason, other than bad luck, for this pathetic person to have selected our area for his depraved actions.

We will continue to work with psychiatric experts. We already have a number of potential clues in front of the medical examiner and should know soon how helpful those clues will be.

I will be reporting to you on our progress on a regular basis.

Thank you."

Will folded the sheet, set it down and looked at each man at the table. Jeff's eyes showed only confusion. Tom, Jim and Randolph struggled to grasp the full implication of what they'd just heard. Clint's brow furrowed.

But Phil seemed to get it right off. He smiled. "Belt him in his ego—smoke him out, or cause him to do somethin' stupid."

"Exactly."

"I like it. If he falls for it, maybe we can find his hole. If he fucks up and blows his cover—we pound the son of a bitch. He ain't gonna like your dandy little profile—that much is for shit sure!" Phil nodded his head vigorously as he spoke.

"Will," Randolph cut in. "Before you read that to us, you said it might be dicey. What's the downside?"

Will leaned back in his chair and stretched his arms in front of him. He shook one of the two remaining cigarettes from Clint's wrinkled pack, lit it and inhaled deeply. It was his first cigarette in thirty-eight months. Through a billow of blue smoke, he said, "Washburn thinks this statement could make Peel respond the way Phil just mentioned. However...." Will crushed out the once-puffed cigarette. "However, he also thinks there's a chance that my comments might set Peel off—push him into a frenzy of murder and—"

"Jesus H. Christ, Will!" Randolph bellowed. "You were keeping that back, for Chrissakes?"

"It's a risk, but—no—I wasn't keeping it back."

Randolph slammed his right fist down onto the tabletop. "No! No, goddamn it! We can't subject this whole peninsula to a blood bath just to support some kinda slick gamesmanship between you and this fucking loony—hopin' it might—possibly—smoke him out."

"Look, Elliot...," Will said quietly.

Randolph pounded the table again. "No, *you* look! Don't give me any more shit, Will. This is too big a risk!" He stood and stomped around the room, obviously preparing to raise the level of his tirade, when Will slammed his fist down with enough force to overturn the heavy ashtray in front of Clint. He looked up at Randolph, whose face was getting redder by the second.

Will's voice was half-growl, half-hiss. "I *know* this man—he's a part of me. We've done nothing up to now, and he's killed at least three innocent people. He's got to be stopped now."

Randolph hadn't moved a muscle since Will had upset the ashtray. The look in Will's eye and the white spittle at the corners of his mouth convinced the mayor to remain quiet. "I'll get him, Elliot," Will said quietly. "Be sure of that. You want to dump me in June—fine. Until then, I'm in charge."

Will could see Randolph struggling. He knew the man genuinely liked him and knew also that he was afraid for his town and hated being treated as an afterthought. Finally, he composed himself and spoke with a voice intended to drain away some of the emotion that choked the room. "Don't want to dump you, Will. But what you're suggesting is just too big a gamble to take. For all we know, it might make him explode—drive down Ocean Avenue at high noon with a machine gun."

"We'd catch him, at least," Will bit off—then wished he could take back the flippant reply.

"Great!" Randolph hollered. "Then where would we be? Carmel'd become a ghost town—nothin' but screwballs, true-crime hacks'd come here, writin' about the Carmel Massacre. Not on my watch, goddamnit! Don't release that statement, Will. There's gotta be another way." Randolph took two big steps and stood over Will.

"It's too late. The local channels have it. If I don't show up to read it on camera, they'll read it anyhow."

Suddenly, Randolph sagged where he stood, looking much more like a fifty-year-old city official than a Hollywood hero.

Will got up and gently guided the mayor a few steps across the room. His voice was low, but audible to all. "Look, Elliot. He's had us goin' nuts for days now. If we don't do somethin'—no matter how risky—he's gonna feel more and more confident, and he's still gonna be killing people. This way we might force him to show himself. Washburn thinks this'll confuse him—maybe anger him—but not to the point of goin' on a suicide spree. He's still too into protecting himself for that."

"Christ, you yourself said Peel's unpredictable…"

"Elliot, he's *crazy*. And, no, I can't predict his every move. But I do know a helluva lot about him and so does Washburn. Peel's got goals. I'm the first big one, and he thinks he's gettin' close. He'll gamble to get me—but not take foolhardy risks, not sacrifice himself—because he wants to get his wife, too."

Randolph slumped wearily against the wall and sighed deeply. Worry filled the deep lines in his tanned face and was underscored by his attempt to press some relief into his temples.

Phil moved between the two men. "He's right, Gun. Nothin's a sure thing, but Will's plan is our best bet in a case like this—and I've seen a lot of 'em. Peel's had it all his own way, so far. If we don't wobble his pins a little bit, he'll keep on making trouble."

Randolph looked from Curry to Will, then tried one more stab at a safer approach. "Why can't we publish the bastard's picture and have a massive, goddamned manhunt?"

Phil grabbed Will's arm to keep him from answering. "Because if we do that, he'd probably disappear."

"That sounds just fine to me, Phil," Elliot answered.

"It'd be great 'til he came back. Peel's got resources. He'd lay low until things blew over, then come back to finish Will off. Meantime, Will's no good to Carmel or you. Couldn't live normal, kids couldn't leave the house. That ain't gonna work, Elliot. We *gotta* draw Peel out in the open. There's no alternative."

The four men seated at the table watched in silence as the drama involving Will, Curry and Randolph played out.

Randolph shut his eyes and remained silent for half a minute. "Okay, okay," he said then, straightening himself away from the wall. "I got no more arguments to make. I just hope to God you know what you're doing. And for Chrissakes, be careful."

Will put his hand on Randolph's shoulder. He understood that things would never be quite the same between them. He hoped that what had been lost would be replaced by something of equal value. But that would have to wait for later. If there was a later. Will's survival was not a sure bet. But there wasn't even time to worry about that now. He had a plan to put into operation.

The phone's ringing cut through the heavy silence in the room. Will spun around and headed across the kitchen to take the call. He answered by giving his name. Two beats. Then: "Yeah, Sheriff, whaddya got?"

Tuesday, Twilight
Chapter Twenty-One

"**A**nd how much longer will you be with us, Mr. Peters?" asked the florid-faced desk clerk at Carmel's Cypress Inn on Lincoln and Seventh. The man across the counter was sharp-featured but otherwise unremarkable in appearance and dress. White Polo shirt, navy slacks, tasseled cordovan loafers. Typical guest.

"Four or five days, I expect," Louis Peel said. "But if I can shake another few days out of my boss, will there be a problem staying longer?" He smiled earnestly at the officious little man.

"Oh, no, sir. No problem at all. Do you need help with your bags?"

"Thanks, but I've only these two and one more in the car. If I can leave the car in the white zone for a couple minutes, I'll get it all upstairs in a jiffy."

"Please feel free. I suspect our police are too busy to be giving out parking tickets." The clerk flicked a piece of lint from the sleeve of his heavy Harris-tweed coat.

"Oh?" Peel wasn't eager for prolonged conversation, but neither did he wish to appear rude or stand out in any way.

"Oh, yes. These last few days with the murders and all….whole city's in an awful snit."

"I've read about that. What a *terrible* business," Peel said, replacing his fake driver's license and fake credit card in his genuine alligator wallet.

"Just awful—terrible, as you said. I've seen nothing like it in forty years here."

"It's probably hurting your business, isn't it?" he said with feigned concern.

The clerk hesitated, but the man seemed more sympathetic than nosy. "Indeed, Mr. Peters, indeed. Four cancellations for next weekend already. It's a pity…."

"Terrible. It certainly is."

"I mean, why are such sick people allowed to roam free?"

Peel's cringe was inward, thus entirely unnoticed by the clerk. "If you ask me, I think it's the courts. Well, if you'll excuse me, I'll start getting my gear upstairs."

Peel took the stairs two at a time. The bags were hardly a burden. He entered his room, dumped the bags on the bed, crossed the floor, opened the curtains and looked out to the street. He surveyed the room he had reserved nearly eight weeks earlier and felt satisfied. There was no reason it couldn't serve his needs for his few remaining days in town.

He bounded downstairs to retrieve his third bag from the car. The large black BMW was the best car he'd ever driven. He especially liked the way the tinted windows made it appear sinister. He looked up at the white-washed façade of the Cypress Inn, then at the boxes full of colorful blossoms running along the length of the building. How peaceful, he thought, as he shifted the bag full of grenades in the trunk.

Goddamn, those things are heavy. Probably don't need them, but one never knows. Back to the lodge for dinner, then move a few more bags over here tonight. Check out of the lodge tomorrow, get into town, find that ugly old bitch and kill her. While Kempton's busy with that mess, find his kids and kill them. Then it should be time to reintroduce myself to Mr. William Kempton. Perfect!

After finishing at the Cypress Inn, Peel walked north on Lincoln to the Carmel Pipe Shop, where he bought three Davidoff cigars for

$34.48. Pausing beneath the steep, artificially-gabled roof of the tiny store, he lit one of the rich cigars.

"Heaven," he said aloud. Though directed at the cigar, his comment also embraced this particular piece of the world. Peel had not failed to appreciate the magnificent scenery in which he'd toiled these past two months.

Nothing like it in the world. A man could be happy here—especially with a tidy sum of money. What a wonderful irony if I returned here to live after finishing my business with Kempton and dear Sandra—that disloyal bitch! 'Til death us do part, Sandy.

That thought produced a loud half-cackle, half-giggle from Peel. The strange sound registered with a few late-afternoon shoppers, who stared in his direction. Quickly, Peel walked the half-block to his car, climbed in and started the powerful engine. He was angry with himself for that public display, however minor. Essential to his plan was staying in the shadows until his work was finished. *Goddamn, Louis, shut the fuck up 'til this is over. Stay sharp. Victory is too close to make a mistake now.*

He swung the car from its resting spot. As he drove across the nearly deserted Ocean Avenue, he kept to the speed limit and watched the large pines fan in the steady wind of twilight. The sky out over the ocean bluffed from pale gray to black. The roiling mass seemed to be moving inland at a rapid pace. The last shoppers on the city's streets quickened their steps. A storm was coming, and it was moving fast.

***

The six men watched as Will wrote with short, rapid strokes. The phone's receiver was balanced precariously on his left shoulder. Will's conversation consisted entirely of monosyllables and grunts until he put the pad down and said, "Thanks, Angus. What the hell? It's a start. No, I don't think we need more troops—least not at this point. No, not yet, but two guys'll be taking him out there soon."

Randolph frowned at Will's words but remained silent. Will signed off with a final word of thanks to Sheriff Angus Truitt and placed the phone in its cradle. He grabbed the note pad from the sink and turned to his men. "Ready to roll, guys. Jim, I want you to join Jeff and Tom takin' Elliot out to his place."

"How come?"

Will looked at him with exasperation. "'Cause it's what I want, damn it. This isn't a democracy—just do it."

Jim's irritation was quickly doused by the torrent of instructions Will issued.

"Okay—you three take Elliot home and—"

"My car's out front, Will."

Will glanced impassively at Randolph. "Leave it—you got a whole fleet at home."

A tense beat. Then the mayor nodded and moved into the back ranks of the group clustered in the kitchen doorway.

"On your way out there," Will said, "call ahead and let 'em know you're comin'. When you get there, check the place out, then get back here. Pull the Jeep and Elliot's car into the garage and cover every foot of the house to make sure Peel's not here."

"Why not have one of us stay here the way you said before—make sure he doesn't get in?"

Ainsley's question was reasonable enough, but no one disagreed when Will said, "Because not one of you guys stands a chance alone with Peel. Don't forget that. Stay together, and don't take any unnecessary risks."

Will stood in front of the six men like the leader of a small chorus. "When you're convinced you're alone, go out the side door and sit there. It's a perfect spot to see all of the front yard and most of the back yard."

"In the fuckin' rain, Will?"

"It's barely misting out there, Jim. But—yes—even if it rains like last week—you guys sit there. Sit quietly and watch for him." Will's eyes played across the members of his team.

"You really think he'd come here?"

"Why not? He's been here. He knows the place and prob'ly knows, or will soon, that this is our camp."

"I still don't see why we gotta sit outside in the rain."

"Because, with Peel, the house'd be a cage for you. Outside, you'll be free—free to see him, escape from him, maybe even catch him. Take a radio with you. There are four of 'em on the living room TV."

"Shit, I'm glad you're sending me home," Randolph said. "At least I'll be inside."

The mayor's jab pushed a smile across Will's face. "Hell, Elliot, I've always thought that house arrest is the best way to treat any politician." The smiles exchanged between mayor and chief were warm, but fleeting. Will returned to his task.

"Phil, Clint and I are gonna hit the road. Sheriff's people came up with eight folks who've been livin' in a hotel or motel more'n a month. No descriptions, but five of 'em are here in Carmel, one's on the strip between here and Monterey. One's in Pacific Grove and one's at the Lodge."

Will saw Jim's eyes widen and watched as his friend turned and picked up the photo of Peel from the edge of the dining room table. He studied the rough copy while Will continued to talk.

"Holy shit!" Jim's voice boomed from the dining room. "This might be the guy I saw in the can the other night at the Lodge."

"What!?!" Will's question was nearly a shout. He took two long strides and stood next to Jim.

"When you were talkin' to the desk guy, I went to take a leak. While I was in the can, there was a guy washin' his hands, and—Jesus—it coulda been the guy in the picture."

"Are you sure, Jim?"

After squinting at the photo for a full three seconds, Jim looked up and exhaled loudly. "God, I can't tell for sure, Will. Picture's so shitty—but it's close enough to scare the shit outtta me."

For a few seconds the only sound in the room was the old clock above the sink. Will felt a new burst of adrenaline with each tick of the clock. Though no one spoke, he sensed the same held true for all in the room. The round of Velcro tearing and the sight of six men checking their side arms proved his theory. The smell of Hoppe's Gun Oil permeated throughout the entry to the kitchen.

"Jim, you guys get Elliot home. Plan's *exactly* the way I laid it out—no deviations. We'll hit the Lodge soon as I pick up the infrared night scopes for the rifles at the station."

"What's the room number at the Lodge, Will?" Jim asked.

Will riffled through the notes from his talk with Truitt, and said, "Room 101. Know where it is?"

"Yeah—sits right out on the eighteenth hole. Part of a six-unit, two-story structure. There's two identical buildings next to each other, but 101 is closest to the ocean. Sliding glass door opens onto a patio fifty yards back from the eighteenth green."

The group in charge of transporting Randolph departed amid wishes of good luck. Phil mentioned bulletproof vests. "Don't have any, partner," Will said, as he closed the front door to his home.

"Got some over in Monterey," Clint said.

Will turned the thought over for five seconds—then shook his head. "Fuck it. I don't want to take the time to go get 'em. I want to move on this guy right now."

Phil and Clint nodded their agreement. Will didn't ask if they were ready. Another minute of doing nothing would blunt the momentum that had built over the long afternoon. A glance at his watch told him his statement would be read, moments from now, on two early local newscasts. He checked his gun a last time and slipped it into its holster. His failure to snap the holster shut was not an oversight.

"Let's go," Will said as he moved briskly from his porch to the car.

The hunt was on.

Tuesday Evening
Chapter Twenty-Two

"Your dinner, Mr. Pearson," said the room service waiter as Louis Peel opened the door of his suite.

"On the table by the TV, please, Lupe." Peel handed a crisp ten-dollar bill to the man. "It's early, but I'm starved."

Peel's tips and easy small talk had made him a favorite of the Lodge staff. The tips were not so high as to set him too far apart from other guests but generous enough to guarantee his wish for privacy—the help had scrupulously heeded his request never to enter Room 101 unless he was present.

As he ushered the stocky Filipino out, Peel told him the dishes would be placed outside the door within the hour.

"Thank you, Mr. Pearson. I will come get, but not to disturb you if they are not there."

"Good, Lupe. Thank you." Peel narrowly missed the man's heels with the closing door.

He worked the corkscrew expertly into place on the bottle of vintage Bordeaux. The intrusion of a news bulletin on television distracted him. The mention of Will Kempton froze him in place.

The relaxed contentment Peel had so carefully cultivated throughout the day was wrecked by the forty-second reading of Kempton's statement.

"You prick!" he said as if his adversary was in the room. The cork bent, then broke off in the bottle.

Peel felt his hands start to shake; his heart pounded loudly in his ears. He recognized the signs and fought to gain control. The bottle slipped from his trembling grasp, bounded against the table and rolled across the carpet, leaving a dark red stain in its wake. He flung the corkscrew into the wall above the bed.

"Coward! Social misfit! You cocksucker! How dare you and your faggot shrink mock me!"

The piercing sound of his own voice jolted Peel back to silence. The tremors worsened and moved into his forearms. His teeth severed the large cigar he'd been enjoying just moments before. He didn't notice as the lit end fell and began to singe the carpet.

Spitting the soggy butt from his mouth, he moved quickly to the closet. Whispering now so no one could possibly hear him, he said, "Okay, Willie—we'll see who's a fucking coward. You're dead, asshole. Louis is coming to get you—now."

Peel grabbed two handguns from the closet shelf and hefted a small but heavy tote bag that lay behind a pile of shoes. He kicked off his tasseled alligator moccasins and pulled on a pair of sturdy, over-the-ankle boots. In two steps he was at the sliding glass door. Panting steadily, he drew back the curtain and peeked out. He saw neither the spectacular, spot-lit view of the ocean, which had so pleased him for nearly two months, nor the struggle of four golfers putting on the eighteenth green under the thin beams of flashlights held by their two caddies. All Peel saw was rain and the lengthening shadows of dusk.

"Darkness. Perfect."

Peel tossed his key on the floor and slipped through the doorway of the room.

***

Will and company commandeered Phil's Cadillac, hoping that Peel had never seen it. As Will drove, he hoped it was the best-armed vehicle this side of Fort Ord. After the brief stop at the station, they headed down Ocean Avenue. The six-block row of quaint buildings and shops looked tourist-perfect—except no tourists were to be seen. It wasn't yet six o'clock. Usually, in all but the stormiest weather, scores of them strolled Ocean Avenue and the side streets, planning their shopping forays for the next day. Tonight the stores were closed. None of the town's several taverns had a customer.

Phil sat in the passenger seat, Clint was in the back, placing the night-scopes on the long guns. No one spoke as the car barreled down Ocean Avenue.

They turned right at Monte Verde and gunned the car past the Pine Inn and the Christian Science Church. Taking a left at the bottom of the hill, he proceeded around a narrow bend, bordered by huge eucalyptus trees, toward the Carmel gate to the Seventeen Mile Drive. The steep, twisting two miles to Del Monte Lodge fronted some of the most magnificent—and expensive— real estate in the world. The guard at the gate recognized Will immediately and waved him along.

Will breached the silence inside the car. "Lodge manager's gonna meet us by the pro shop. Asked him to bring a large busboy's coat, Phil, 'cause you're going in the front door."

"Very considerate, pal— I'd hate to be shot in an ill-fitting frock."

"Don't mention it. After we get the coat, we'll drive down fairly close to Peel's building. Clint and I'll go 'round back and hide near his patio. If he splits, he's gotta go out the patio door, and we'll bring his ass down."

"Shoot for the legs, Will?" Clint asked.

"Take *any* shot you get."

"What if he's not home?"

"Then go in—you'll have a passkey. Manager's gonna telephone the room *exactly* five minutes after we get your coat. You'll be at the front door by then, and you'll hear if Peel answers the phone."

"He might be inside and just not answer it."

"Best I could think of on short notice, partner."

"It'll do—prob'ly."

Will flicked on the wipers—the mist was getting heavier. Rounding the corner near the third tee, he suddenly swerved wide right—just avoiding a large black sedan moving fast in the opposite direction.

"Asshole!" Will shouted as he yanked the car back to the narrow strip of asphalt.

"Another rich fuck thinkin' he owns the road," Phil said. "Where's a cop when you need one?"

Will parked at the rear of the pro shop. All appeared normal at the Lodge. The steady ocean breeze carried the sounds of early drinkers and diners enjoying the comfort of the Tap Room. The laughter and piano music wafting across the green expanse mocked their nervousness. Both Curry and Will thought briefly of their last visit to that trophy- and photo-laden pub. Will reflected on the irony that the Tap Room revelers were in a helluva lot more danger than those who were locked away over in Carmel—if it really was Peel in Room 101.

The session with the Lodge manager was as brief as possible given the man's rabbity fear of involving himself or the hotel in anything that might disrupt the constant flow of pleasure offered by the resort. The sight of two rifles obviously terrified the man—personally as well as professionally. As the manager began a third entreaty for the Lodge's safety, Will grabbed him by the forearm and wrenched him halfway around. "Listen, shithead, if we don't get this guy, your next hundred phone calls're gonna be cancellations. Now you work with me, or I'll run your ass in for aiding and abetting."

Instantly, the manager capitulated and said he'd do everything Will asked. After the four men synchronized their watches, the manager hurried back to his office, and the three cops clambered into the Cadillac.

As the car moved onto the dark path to Room 101, Phil asked, "Is there a mandatory school somewhere that teaches all hotel managers to be snotty candy-asses?"

"At least a test they all gotta pass before they get the job," Will responded. "Manager's gonna let the phone ring a dozen times. If it's answered, Phil bursts in. If it's not answered, Phil goes in after the last ring."

Will parked the car fifty yards from Room 101. As Phil tugged on the too small busboy coat, he said, "I'd look less like a cop if I was wearin' yellow slacks and a pink polo shirt like everyone at the Lodge."

"We're goin' around to the back of the building, Phil. Give us a minute or two, then go to the door of 101," Will said and added, "Good luck, partner."

***

After counting to a hundred, Phil crept away from the soft comfort of his beloved Cadillac. Hope flashed through his mind that he would see the car again. Too old for this shit, he thought, pulling at the starched sleeves of his disguise. As he started down the path to Room 101, his cop instinct told him no one was watching. He very much wanted to trust that.

When he reached the door to Room 101, his heart was thumping— from excitement, not exertion. He'd been here before—there had been a thousand doors like this in Jersey. His hand curled around the butt of his thirty-eight just as the telephone rang inside the room.

***

Will and Clint had reached their positions a minute earlier— covering either side of 101's patio. Will tried to ease his tension by reminding himself that he had been well trained for this type of duty. But that had been nearly twenty years ago. Was he still sharp enough to pull this off? Could he summon up the skills he'd once had?

Hell, I haven't fired a shot outside target practice in five years. All I've done is be a father. Snapshots of David and Sari clicked through his mind. They were all right—they'd be all right. So long as he walked away from this place in one piece.

The first blast of the phone jolted Will back to reality. He signaled to Clint that the phone was ringing. Four—five..

***

At the sixth ring, Curry reached into his pocket with his left hand for the room key. The thirty-eight was cocked in is right hand.

***

Raindrops chilled the warm sweat spilling down Will's back. The phone sounded a tenth time.

***

Before the echo of the twelfth ring had faded, Phil had stepped quietly into the room. It was fully lit. He was almost positive he was alone—but almost wasn't good enough. He threw his wallet hard against the far wall. As it hit the floor, Phil took two paces into the center of the suite. He dropped to one knee in the shooter's pose and swept the gun the full span of the room. Not a sound. The bathroom door was open, showing only darkness beyond. *Shit.* The bed was mounted on a full pedestal, leaving no room to hide there. Phil edged toward the bathroom, keeping the closet's two doors in full view. He'd have to look there after checking out the bathroom. Those were the only places in Room 101 for a person to hide. He reached the bathroom door, noting that the closet was just three feet away. Five of the six pounds required pulled against the trigger of his thirty-eight.

***

At the first ripple of the curtain covering them, Clint and Will trained their rifles on the sliding doors. Light flooded out, revealing the room. As Phil appeared in the middle of the doorway, the rifles were lowered a notch.

***

Phil motioned them up to the patio and whispered, "C'mon in. Nobody's home, but you won't fucking believe what's in here."

"What's the story, Phil?" Will asked.

"Let me put it this way. If this ain't Peel's place, we got two crazy motherfuckers to catch. Place's a fuckin' arsenal."

After Will and Clint were inside, Phil closed the drapes. Still whispering, he herded them toward the bathroom. "Keep your voices down—we'll talk in the can. But take a peek in the closet as you go by—then shut both doors."

With that, Phil walked across the room, picked up his wallet and moved toward the bathroom. Will and Clint looked at one another, shrugged their eyebrows and followed their sturdy compatriot, who was wrestling his way out of the tight, over-starched busboy coat.

Will and Clint stood transfixed by the contents of the closet. Half the inventory Will didn't even recognize, but there was no doubt the entire lot had been brought here with bad intentions. Seven automatic rifles were splayed neatly in the right corner of the closet. Three dozen hand grenades nestled on the floor next to three bricks of plastique, a dozen bound sticks of dynamite, numerous detonators and blasting caps. In the far left corner a large machete was angled against the wall—its cutting edge flecked with a rust-colored scale.

"Jesus! It's lucky we found…"

"Shh! Quiet!" Phil's urgent whisper reminded Will that their work was not even close to being finished.

Will ushered the others toward the bathroom and said, "Guys, we need a new plan, right now!"

"OK, now what?" Phil's question hung in the air while Clint shook a bent cigarette from the pack he'd discovered in an old windbreaker.

As Will tried to focus on the situation, Phil snatched the cigarette from Clint and placed it behind the taller man's ear. "Sorry, Clint," he whispered, "I'm prob'ly being' crazy, but I wouldn't put it past Peel to have a hyper-fine sense of smell. If he comes back here now and opens the door a half-inch, sniffs smoke and manages to escape—or comes in blasting away with an AK-47, I'd be very pissed."

Will nodded his agreement with Phil's warning to Clint and said, "All right, guys, here's our plan.…"

Tuesday Night
Chapter Twenty-Three

Jim, Tom and Jeff, having returned to Carmel from their trip to Randolph's home, were camped at the side of Will's house. Their trip to and from Randolph's home had been quick and uneventful. Tom had groused about sitting in the rain to watch Will's front and back yards, while Jeff exhausted his store of adjectives extolling the beauty of Randolph's compound. Jim explained Will's order that they remain outside.

The first explosion was from above and ripped through the darkness, illuminating the night so brightly that, for an instant, every individual raindrop seemed visible.

"Jesus! What the fuck was that?" Tom shouted.

Before Jim could answer, a second concussion blew the front windows out of Will's house.

"Move to the back, guys, and stay low," Jim commanded. "I think those're fuckin' hand grenades!"

***

Back in Peel's room, Will said, "Clint, train your piece on the front door and we'll look around." He motioned Curry to follow him out of the bathroom.

"Didn't finish his dinner," Will said as he raised the heavy silver warmer from the main course.

"Didn't even start it," Curry said. "Look at the bottle. Shit!—it's a Margaux. I'm sequestering this as evidence…. Oh, the dumb fuck broke the cork." Phil picked the bottle up from the floor and looked at it with genuine sadness.

"Food's still warm…. So's this cigar," Will observed as he moved around the perfectly set table.

They locked eyes. Will asked the question before Phil. "Is it possible he saw us coming?"

"How the fuck could he? We'd'a seen him leaving, wouldn't we? Both doors were locked, for Chrissakes," Phil's whisper was closing in on a wheeze.

"The TV's still warm," Will said quietly, with his palm on the top of the television.

***

Instinct impelled Jim to push his partners face down in the slick ivy. He was joining them when he heard something thud onto the roof above them. There was no time to move, so he flattened out fast, hoping the pitch of the roof would carry what he felt was a grenade away from their hiding place.

The third explosion was deafening. Its accompanying flash of light enabled Jim to see the others' shocked faces.

"Roll under the fence, quick! Fucker's aimin' at the house—he doesn't know we're out here. C'mon, move!"

Two more blasts tore into Will's roof line as the three men scrambled under the split-rail fence into the yard of Will's neighbor. Jim knew he was undeniably in charge of this company, thanks to his tour in Vietnam at the end of the war. One look told him he was the only one of the three who wasn't completely immobilized—though it was close. He recognized the looks on their faces and rasped, "Move it—we're still alive. He's just aimin' at the house. He doesn't know we're out here. Let's just get the fuck away from the house."

Jim shook Tom and slapped Jeff hard, dislodging a tear. Ignoring it, he ordered, "Go 'round back to Eleventh and circle back to the front. There's a car idling up there. I'm goin' straight up the property line here. If you get a clear shot at him or the car, take it—we'll ask fuckin' questions later. Tom, take the radio—call Truitt to get their asses over here. Questions?"

There were none. Jim hoped it was because Tom and Jeff understood his orders, not because they were too stunned to take them in.

"Okay—get going!"

The two ran, hunched over, through the neighbor's back yard. They'll reach the street in about a minute, Jim thought. He belly-crawled in that direction. He figured in about twenty seconds he'd be close enough for a shot.

***

Will locked the sliding door that led from Peel's room, turned back and looked across the table at Phil, who still held the wine bottle. Again, the two shared an identical thought. Years ago, on the job, that phenomenon was a common occurrence and had made them the best team in Narcotics.

"Musta seen 'em read your statement while he was getting' ready to eat...," Phil said, as he carefully set the bottle down on the table.

"...and went nuts," Will completed Phil's sentence and motioned to Clint to join them by the table in front of the television.

"Yep. Shit! This ain't good, gentlemen," Phil said.

Clint joined them and said, "But he left so quick he left all that bad shit'n the closet."

The hope in that sentence was dispatched quickly by Will. "He'll have enough with him to do whatever he's got in mind—car's prob'ly loaded and the fuck's prob'ly got a houseful more, somewhere."

"We gotta get going, Will," Phil urged. "Peel's out there, runnin' loose."

Will heard him. "Clint, call your guys in Monterey and get 'em over here to sit on this room. Have 'em put out an A.P.B. on Louis Peel.

173

Give 'em the best description we got." Then, turning back to Curry, he said, "Phil, gimme your radio. Wanna call Jim and tell 'em to be on the lookout." The instant he punched the "on" button, the radio spit out a tinny, crackling sound, and a disembodied voice filled the luxurious suite with a single, harshly whispered word—repeated over and over.

"Mayday! Mayday! Mayday!"

***

Jim knew it was Louis Peel, fifty feet away, waiting to pick off anyone who might exit Will's house. Jim crawled through the soaked ferns. He could smell the burning house. He wondered if Will's team had missed Peel—or, worse, been ambushed by him at Pebble Beach. He asked God for their safety and crawled faster. Peel wouldn't wait long, and he couldn't let Tom and Jeff hit the street before he was there to provide cover.

Fifteen yards, ten now, to the street. Jim saw the outline of the car, purring like a panther in the darkness. Goddamn it! Where was Peel? Tom and Jeff would be at the intersection in no more than ten seconds.

Jim crawled another ten feet and risked rising to his knees. Willing his eyes to cut through the black mist, he scanned the shadowy shapes of bushes and trees that seemed suddenly dangerous. He saw movement to his right and, fearing for Jeff or Tom, he sacrificed his own position by squeezing off two shots in the air. Then he dove as far left as he could. A staccato burst of fire carved a dozen shells into the side of the neighboring house precisely where he had stood to fire just five seconds earlier.

Jim forced his bulk under the bottom rung of the fence and struggled to replace the two bullets in his thirty-eight, giving him a full load. He heard the automatic fire again and felt the wet leaves and mud kick up just inches from where he lay.

More silence—five, ten seconds. He heard a distant siren—then he saw a blur.

Had to be Peel, Jim thought. He'd heard the siren, too, and was running for the car. Jim leapt to his feet, ran toward the car and put four slugs into the front tires. Peel's rifle roared furiously. At least two bullets hit Jim hard and pounded him into the gravel two feet from the car. The impact stunned him for a moment, but there was no pain.

He rolled to the rear of the car just as a blast of gunfire flashed from the intersection forty feet away. Has to be Tom and Jeff, he thought. Jesus, they're out in the open. He tried to yell a warning, but choked on the dust and exhaust in his throat. He felt dizzy and all movement was tortured. Jim knew he was losing blood. From his place on the ground at the rear of the car, he was able to make out a pair of legs.

Jim recognized the metallic click of the pin being pulled from a hand grenade. He fired three quick shots at what he hoped were Peel's legs. He heard the start of a human shriek above the blare of the fire engine siren—now less than a block away. Then the only sound he heard was an explosion at the intersection of Eleventh and Camino Real.

Jim tried to get up. He had to stop Peel—had to help Jeff... and Tom. He managed to get a claw-hold on the back fender, and pulled his own dead weight, hand over hand, toward the driver's side of the car. Gasping through a face full of exhaust, he found himself looking straight into the furious eyes of Louis Peel, who was on one knee by the driver's door of the car, struggling to regain his grip on the rifle.

Jim sighted his thirty-eight on Peel's forehead. "Don't move, motherfucker," Jim said. He wasn't sure he had the strength to pull the trigger. Before he could find out, the fire truck turned onto Camino Real behind him. Its lights split the night into day with no warning of dawn. Peel was still struggling on one knee. When he raised his head, Jim saw the full face of horror two yards away. Peel's eyes were unforgettable—they were aflame, Jim thought. Peel stared, unmoving, directly at Jim. Those eyes and the mouth, frozen in a rictus of pain and bestial hatred, made the most terrifying mask Jim had ever seen. Sweat mingled with tears and spittle ran down Peel's chin. Inhuman sounds guttered from deep in his throat.

Neither man moved. The pain in Jim's side was agonizing. He finally winced, as though acknowledging the pain would weaken its hold.

The high beams of the fire engine blinded Jim for an instant—and he sensed, without actually seeing, Peel reach for the rifle. Jim pulled the trigger. The siren's blast covered the pistol's report. Jim felt the gun's kick, but he couldn't tell whether he'd hit his target. He tried another shot, but couldn't cock the pistol. Noise and light overwhelmed him. He lost his handhold on the car's bumper and crumpled. All was quiet and dark. He didn't feel the blood pouring from his side. He thought he might have heard a voice call for an ambulance. As blackness pressed down on him, he hoped the ambulance was for Peel.

He didn't hear the shout for two more ambulances after the discovery of two more wounded at the end of the block. He released his gun into a widening puddle of blood.

Tuesday, The Long Night Through
Chapter Twenty-Four

Curry and Forsburg tried to calm Will during the ten-minute wait for the sheriff's cruiser to arrive at room 101. His anxiety over the "Mayday" calls had escalated to dismay when the radio's transmission stopped abruptly. Curry had restrained him from leaving immediately for Carmel. Room 101 and its cache of weapons had to be secured, and Phil was damned if their company of three would be split up by leaving one behind to wait.

When the deputies finally arrived, it took another five minutes to explain the situation and to issue precise instructions. One of the newcomers was Under Sheriff Owen Jackson, a regular in Will's poker group. While Jackson went to his car for evidence bags and a fingerprinting kit, Will, Clint and Phil took a last look around the room. They were interrupted by shouting. Jackson slid the last six feet of the sprint from his car. Will met him at the doorway to Room 101.

"Trouble at your place, Will! Neighbors report explosions and shooting! Three men are down!"

"How bad?" Will asked, as he felt worry scar his face. Curry and Forsburg appeared at Will's side instantly.

"Tom's pretty tore up—Jeff's doin' fair—both in shock. Doc says it looks like shrapnel, for Chrissakes!"

"What about Jimmy?"

"Bad. Gut shot. They say he's lost a lotta blood."

Will stumbled backward into the room. Fighting for control, he heard Curry say to Jackson, "Can your boys cover the hospital, Lieutenant? That crazy fuck's liable to try to finish our guys right there."

"Two there already. They'll stay as long as they're needed."

Will blurted a few words of gratitude, then asked how much the sheriff knew.

"I'll get to Truitt later—he's got all of Monterey to worry about. You handle Carmel, Will—I'll give the old fart a full report in the morning," Jackson said as he leaned against the doorsill of the room.

"Thanks, Owen. I owe you. Truitt'll bite your ass for delayin'." Will took a step toward the doorway.

"Got a *big* ass, Will. Friends are friends—bosses aren't."

Will's smile fell short of the mark. He was overwhelmed at the harm to Tom and Jeff, furious over Peel's flight from a near-perfect trap—and almost physically ill at the news about Jim. Gut shot. Blood loss. His memories of the streets told him that either of those could prove fatal—together, those injuries were damned near insurmountable.

"Go ahead, Will, get over to the hospital," Owen said. He knew, too. He stepped by Will into the room and added, "I'll clean this place up, and when I'm done, I'm gonna personally bring all this shit over to your office."

Will's attempt at a smile came closer to the mark that time. "Jesus, Owen, Truitt'll kill you…"

"Only if he finds out. But this guy Peel's *your* demon. You're gettin' all the shit—y'oughta get all the credit when you nail him."

"*If* I do." Will could feel Clint and Phil behind him, moving forward toward the door.

"You will. Shit, Truitt's never honchoed a case like this—he wouldn't know where or how to start. He's just sittin' on his ass waiting for you to fuck up and hopin' we get lucky and bust Peel so he can take the credit."

Will sensed a return of focus. "How come he gave me Clint and Tom?"

"Because Gunner drove a Cadillac up his ass."

Jackson's vivid image pushed Will's smile all the way to his eyes. But it faded quickly: Owen's description of Peel as *his* demon was absolutely accurate. His and his alone. Half of the company he'd started with that night was out of commission. Jeff was injured—Jim was in trouble—Jennie was dead. Jesus! He was Carmel's remaining functioning cop.

Will's thoughts wandered for a moment. He knew it was time to get Peel. He was pretty sure he could find him. Plan B began to take shape in his mind. And his mind turned quickly back to Jackson.

"We're outta here, Owen."

"Be careful. This guy doesn't sound like a nice man."

Will nodded grimly at the world-class understatement and walked into the drizzling night. This surely had to be the final leg of his pursuit of Louis Peel. But, first, he had to see his men at the hospital. His two men followed closely.

Phil drove and Will settled into the soft leather embrace of the Cadillac's deep back seat. As they bypassed Carmel on their way to the hospital, the malevolence they were leaving behind them was almost palpable. I'm coming, Louis, Will thought.

It was quiet in the car. Will figured each man was reviewing his personal inventory, hoping to find all that would be needed to survive the next few hours. Will knew he had to revert to a level he'd left five years and three thousand miles ago. He was pretty sure Phil's thoughts mirrored his own.

He had thought about that a dozen times today. At first, he was scared. Fear had given way to doubt, then distaste. Now he willed himself to recapture that long-dead piece of himself. The thought was strangely stimulating. He wasn't ready yet—but he was getting closer. He stared straight ahead with unseeing eyes and thought only of Peel—forcing out all thoughts of Carmel and family and hard-earned serenity. He was so engrossed that the fifteen-minute drive to the hospital seemed to take a heartbeat.

By the time Phil parked the Caddy, Will felt excited, downright eager to find Peel. And bring him down—again. For good.

Tuesday, An Hour Later
Chapter Twenty-Five

The six blocks, straight uphill, from Kempton's house to the Cypress Inn took him an hour. Peel felt faint. He knew he needed medical attention, but that wouldn't happen. Not tonight, anyway. A spasm of shivering pain contorted his entire body as he peered through the window into the Inn's tiny lobby.

No action except that same asshole desk clerk. Got to get up to my room without him seeing me. Could go in and kill him—no, he'd be missed— can't have any attention fall on this place. Not till I'm long gone—which'll be soon. No. I've come this far—no hotel clerk is going to fuck things up. Jesus, my leg is on fire!

Standing with weight only on his right leg, Peel looked up to his room, which faced Lincoln Avenue. The window was open, just as he'd left it. He considered climbing up to it but dismissed the thought. His injury made that almost impossible. Besides, even though the street was empty, someone might see him.

That can't happen. I'd lose everything—I will not lose now. Got to fix this fucking leg, kill Kempton, then get out.

He whimpered involuntarily as he shifted his weight to look again into the lobby.

He's gone! Oh, Jesus, let him stay gone. Oh, God, please! Nobody's in the lobby—got to risk it.

Binding his shirt around his left leg to absorb the blood, Peel navigated the short brick stairway into the Cypress, staggered across the lobby and pulled himself up the staircase to the second floor. He entered the room, locked the door behind him and fell onto the bed. The bright jade numerals on the clock read six-thirty, then faded as Peel curled into a fetal ball. He thanked God he'd moved to the Cypress earlier that day. Then he passed out.

***

Will sprinted up the steps to the hospital, with Phil and Clint close behind. The duty nurse, who knew him, pointed left and said, "Room 17."

The first thing the trio saw upon entering the room shared by Tom and Jeff was the latter hobbling back to bed. The gross covering of bandages and gauze on his body made him appear seriously wounded. That was Will's first impression. His second was to wonder if anyone had ever looked more out of place in a flimsy, blue hospital gown. Less than a third of the kid's large, heavily-muscled frame was covered.

Reflexively, Jeff grabbed at the gown's back, trying to pull it closed. All he accomplished was to expose four more inches of thigh.

Will was ecstatic to see his young charge on his feet. He walked toward Jeff and said, "Don't sweat it, youngster, we're not here to look at your ass."

"Chief! Jeez, I'm glad to see you—I was afraid he mighta got you guys, too." Jeff hobbled back toward his bed.

"Not yet. What the hell're you doin' up?" Will grabbed a chair and pulled it near Jeff's eventual landing spot.

"Had to pee—can't go in those little plastic pans they give you," Jeff said, as he gingerly sidled up and onto the hospital bed.

The conversation caused a stir across the room. Tom Ainsley rolled over gingerly and propped himself up on an elbow. "This's a hospital— can't a guy get a little rest?"

Clint crossed the room in three long steps. "How ya doin', buddy?"

"Don't hafta whisper now, Clint. Feel like I fell off a mountain—but I'm ready to be a pallbearer at that pecker's funeral. Did you guys get him?"

Clint shook his head. Tom cursed, then asked for a smoke.

"This is a hospital, partner. Can't smoke in here," Clint said, holding both palms up as though that logic would calm his friend.

"Fuck that. I'll use the kid's bedpan for an ashtray—gimme one."

Clint shook his head as he freed a cigarette from the pack, lit it and passed it to Tom. As Will helped Jeff sit up on his bed, Curry stood by the door, arms folded, and wondered whether the deputies on guard in the hallway were up to the task.

After Jeff expressed a wish for three cheeseburgers, he and Tom recited their versions of the attack on Fort Kempton. With both men competing for speaking time, the story tumbled out in under two minutes. Will felt as if he were at a tennis match, swiveling his head from Jeff to Tom as their recitations played out.

"Your house got pretty fucked up, Chief," Jeff offered.

"House can be fixed, kid. The only thing that matters is that you guys're safe and more or less sound." Will looked squarely at Jeff to impart his meaning with sincerity.

"Swear to God, we'd'a been cooked 'cept for Jim. He got me and Tom outta there quick, then went after the guy. The last grenade knocked Tom and me on our ass, but I think ol' Jim shot him—Jesus! How *is* Jim?" Jeff winced as he bent forward toward Will.

"He's in surgery. Pretty torn up. Don't know…." The iffy prognosis seemed to suck the air out of the room. Will cleared his throat, but his voice came out husky anyway. "He's tough—he's gonna make it." Will looked down and hoped there was truth in his words.

"Damn right, he's tough," Jeff cut in, either from sheer exuberance or because he saw that his boss was on the edge. "I thought I was tough, too—until tonight. You can have all the grenades and automatic rifles you want. Fuck that! I'm about to *seriously* rethink my career plans…."

Will smiled at Jeff and touched him gently on the only part of his shoulder that was untaped. Then he described the arsenal they had found in Peel's room at Del Monte Lodge.

"The son of a bitch had enough firepower to blow up the whole town," Clint added, moving toward Phil, who was still standing in front of the door. "Hope he doesn't have another big stash someplace else. Obviously had a load in his car...."

"Fuckin' BMW was a tank! Christ! Leave it to the Germans," Ainsley said, struggling to sit upright on the bed.

"Firemen found an AK-47 by the side of the car—empty, but there were two full clips in the back seat," Will said. "No more grenades, though."

"Hell, he used 'em all up on us, the asshole!" Ainsley said loudly.

"Any idea how many?" Curry interjected.

Neither veteran of the mini-war with Peel could provide an accurate count, but they agreed there had been at least a half-dozen. Tom allowed as how the "bombs bursting in air" stanza in the National Anthem would forever hold new meaning. Jeff added he'd never enjoy the Fourth of July in quite the same way after the night's display of fireworks.

After saying their goodbyes and warning the sheriff's men to guard the room with vigilance, Will, Clint and Phil walked down the hallway toward the main exit to the parking lot. Thank God, Will thought. Both men would be released in a few days. Will suspected that their wounds would heal long before the memory of tonight's events faded. Now, he thought, a final check on Jim. Then it's after Peel—again.

"Boys're goddamned lucky, Will," Phil said as he quickened his pace to cover the three steps that separated him from Will.

"You got that right, Phil. Hand grenades! Jesus!"

Still Tuesday Night

Chapter Twenty-Six

*H*ot—*unbearably hot—soaking wet. Raining harder outside—no other sound. Pain—sweet Jesus! The pain—throbbing. Shot—the fucker shot me. Got to wake up—get up—get out. So fuckin' hot.*

Peel blinked himself to full consciousness, which made him acutely aware of the shards of pain slicing through his body. He struggled to raise his head from the sodden pillow. An intense shiver raced through his back. It was the first of many.

Carmel. Hotel. Burning house. Leg. Shot. Kempton still alive. Got to get out. How long have I been unconscious?

A huge effort enabled him to turn his head just enough to read the clock. Seven-forty. Another tremor shot through his body.

Jesus! Almost eight! Can't rest—can't stay here. Got to finish—get to Kempton.

Willing himself to move against the searing pain, Peel finally managed to prop himself up on his elbows. For five minutes, he remained like that, searching inside himself for any hidden reserve of energy. Finally, he managed to sit up all the way. He shifted on the bed until he could reach the floor with his right foot. Then, gritting his teeth against the pain, Peel moved his left leg—gently, gently—to the

185

edge of the bed. Taking the wounded limb in both hands, he lowered it to the carpet.

Now he was seated on the side of the bed, but the onslaught of throbbing nearly made him faint. Refusing to give in to a longing for unconsciousness, he forced his breathing to return to a steady rate. Gradually, the intensity of the throbbing ebbed until it was nearly bearable.

Peel stood. The room started to spin around him, and he sat down again without deciding to, grabbed onto the edge of the mattress with both hands.

Whoa! Stop the spinning. Slower this time. That's it. Okay, try to stand.

He waited; the room didn't move. He stood again, crossed the threshold into the bathroom. He didn't look back at the clock, but knew he had wasted precious minutes. Carefully, he peeled the tight, wet Levis from his aching leg. The wound was clean—straight through his calf, with no damage to bone. His face twisted into a silent roar as he emptied the bottle of after-shave onto the leg. He almost blacked out again as he watched tea-colored liquid spill from the hole in his leg onto the tile floor.

No! Stay strong. No time to be weak. Thank God, the bullet didn't break a bone. I'd have to leave—go somewhere to mend. This way, I can stay—finish what needs to be done here. Then I'll rest a bit before I go find Sandra.

Peel pulled himself upright and turned on the water in the shower. He stepped gingerly under the spray and let the steaming water begin to wash away the layers of grime and violated pride accumulated during the evening's activities.

Traces of black hair dye mingled with the blood. He watched the brackish fluid swirling at his feet. Seconds later the water spilling down the drain was clear. So, in that moment, was his mind. *I know what to do next.*

***

Jim's surgeon was firm in his orders that no one be allowed into the recovery room for a half-hour. Though the doctor exhausted his medical vocabulary in both English *and* Latin, Will didn't know any more about Jim's chances than he had an hour earlier.

While waiting to see Jim, Will ignored a second paper cup of pale, semi-warm coffee to call Randolph and brief him on the destruction Peel had wrought. The two men vented for several minutes, then Will spoke for two minutes with David and Sari—one was long enough to boost his spirits.

"Be careful, Daddy," Sari said.

"Was it really hand grenades, Dad?" David asked. Will began to think about finding a new way to make a living. He didn't know what else he could do, but there had to be a better way to protect his family. His doubts were eddying toward self-pity when the doctor reappeared to usher him into the recovery room.

"Just one visitor, Chief Kempton." Will nodded at Phil and Clint, rose and followed the doctor into another hospital room.

Will paused in the doorway to glance across the austere room. A single band of light shone on the mid-point of the unmoving figure on the bed. Approaching, Will saw one tube dripping glucose into Jim's hand, another doing God knows what was in Jim's nose. He assumed the faint beeping he heard was a computer's interpretation of his friend's heartbeat.

Jim looked as if he were sleeping—his unmarked face belied the grave insults to his body. Still, those tubes and the beeping drove home the point that his partner was an extremely fragile commodity right now. This was the man with whom he'd shared a thousand jokes, half a thousand drinks, dozens of rounds of golf, and most of his hopes and fears. Will shook his head and hoped his friend could come all the way back.

Walking to the end of the bed frame, Will deciphered the medical chart: There were more injuries than he'd been told about. Three bullets. The professional in him marveled at the deadly efficiency of those bullets. Will had never seen what an automatic rifle could do to a man. He was too young to have gone to Vietnam, and he had left Jersey's streets before teenage gangs and drug pushers had upgraded their weaponry. He had read and heard enough to know that Jim could have been cut in half by the AK-47. A shiver ran through him, transfiguring the professional cop into a friend once more.

He tiptoed around to the head of the bed. Will wondered why he continued to move so silently. He was here, after all, to disturb Jim—to try to learn *anything* about what had happened. But still he hesitated, staring bleakly at his friend. Gently, he moved a piece of the heavy, curly hair off Jim's forehead.

Jim's eyes snapped open. His voice was strong but distant. "Don't touch me 'less you mean it, city boy."

Will stepped back, then forward again, grinning. Was Jim capable of seriousness—ever? "Guy in your shape can't be real choosy, y'know."

"I'll take my chances." Jim's eyes seemed to fight for focus.

"How you feelin'?" Will said, bending down slightly as if that would help Jim to better hear him.

"Groggy—light as a feather."

Worry played over Will's face. He hoped Jim wouldn't discern that or the tears in his eyes. Jim shifted slightly and felt the pull of the tube imbedded in his hand. "How fucked am I?" he rasped.

"You're here talking, aren't you?"

"C'mon, shithead. I know I been shot. What's broke for good and what's fixable?"

"He got you three times, Jimmy…." Will sat in a plastic chair next to Jim's bed.

"Jesus! Three times…." Jim coughed lightly.

"Guess you're a little slower'n you were in your Purple Heart days."

"Got my Purple Heart from wounds inflicted by a fucking barber in Quang Tri."

"And her name was?"

"Fifi, I think, or Bubbles—so, what's my prognosis?"

"They got you pretty well patched together and gave you three pints'a fresh, wholesome blood…"

"What's the Doc say?"

"He's *real* prouda the work he did…"

"*C'mon*, Will—what's goin' on?"

Will realized that continuing the verbal sparring was worse for Jim than spitting out the truth. Besides, he couldn't lie—Jim would see through that even in his hazy state. "You know these assholes won't predict anything, Jimmy. He's sure you're basically repaired, but the lung's gotta stay full up—the next twenty-four hours are crucial."

"Then get me a nurse in here—young one—to keep me company. I ain't goin' t' sleep for the next twenty-four hours, and a nurse'd help me stay awake." With great effort, Jim turned his head and looked directly at Will.

"Something tells me you're gonna be fine."

"Betcher ass. S'the damnedest thing—lyin' here all shot to shit, and I can't feel a thing. Did you catch him?"

Will shook his head. Jim closed his eyes and groaned. "Goddamn. I'm pretty sure I shot him."

"Can you talk for a minute more?" Will whispered and leaned closer to Jim.

"Yes, and you don't hafta whisper. Noise isn't gonna screw me up any more'n I already am."

Jim's eyes were losing focus, and his words were blanketed with a lazy slur. He made an unsuccessful attempt at a yawn. Will knew the morphine was about to silence his only witness. He called Jim back from sleep. "What exactly the hell happened?"

Jim blinked rapidly like a wino caught at sunrise.

"Got back from Gun's...sittin' outside like you tol' us t'do... ten, fifteen minutes go by'n the fuckin' sky opens up with fireworks."

"Hand grenades?"

Both men were absolutely still. Jim couldn't move, thanks to the drugs and his injuries. Will was frozen in the chair, thanks to Jim's recitation.

"Everywhere—eight or ten. Jesus! How's Jeff and Tom?"

"Fine—cut up, but okay."

"Good. They 'bout shit out there, pally—hadda get 'em outta there quick."

"You saved their lives, Jimbo."

"Yeah." A sleepy grin waned quickly. "How's the house?"

"Goin' over to see it in a minute. Fire guys said the Jeep and Gunner's car are toast."

"Police Chief oughta do better'n a Jeep." Jim chuckled, then coughed lightly. Will saw his friend fading rapidly, taking on more and more the appearance of that drunk at dawn. "*Know* I hit 'im, dropped his ass down to his knees. Shit! I was trained on his head—he'd lost his gun—then the lights came on and all the noise and… hell, I dunno… I musta tapped out."

"Where'd you hit him?"

"Hadda be the leg—s'all I could see from under his car—couldn'ta missed…."

"Let's hope you didn't. We need any kinda break."

"He's the *scariest* lookin' fuck I ever saw—his eyes, man. Jesus!" Jim coughed hard. This time the pain broke through the pharmaceutical haven, Will noticed, forcing a grimace and a slurred curse. Jim shuddered through an attempt to exhale that was broken into parts by an accumulation of fluids in the lung ruptured by Peel's bullet.

Will placed a hand lightly on Jim's good shoulder. "That's enough for now, Jimmy—get some rest. And plan on takin'a coupla days off."

"S'kinda you, boss—I *am* a bit beat."

As Will turned away, Jim said, "By the way—his hair's black now—musta dyed it."

Will took in that piece of information. It didn't seem important now. He began to walk toward the door. Jim called out again. "Got any'a those super cop hunches?"

Will pulled up two steps from the door, turned and said, "I think so, Jimmy. If he's still around here—I think I can meet up with him."

"Be careful, buddy—guy's a fuckin' wild man." Jim raised his untethered hand a foot for emphasis. It fell quickly back to the bed.

"Believe me, I know that." Will turned again toward the door.

"And get that nurse in here—want about a quarta morphine. I'm startin' to hurt in lotsa places."

"I'll tell her," Will said, with a half-turn back to Jim's bed.

"And tell my ex I been shipped to Montana for treatment. Her showin' up here ain't gonna help me recover."

"Jimmy! Get the fuck to sleep, will ya?"

"Nightie night."

Pausing at the door, Will heard Jim's breathing deepen. The heart monitor seemed to beep with more authority than when he'd entered the room. Hoping he was correct, Will stepped into the hallway. He nodded at the deputy posted at Jim's door. The only sound was the faint hum of the fluorescent lighting overhead.

He felt the need for a shot of real coffee, but speaking to the duty nurse came first. Then he'd find the coffee. Then he'd find a way to give the slip to Phil and Clint.

And find Louis Peel.

Tuesday Night Rolls On
Chapter Twenty-Seven

Acting as chauffeur again, Will turned the wipers to the highest setting as he pulled the Cadillac onto Highway One—heading south back to Carmel. Rain pelted the car—much harder than on their trip out to the hospital an hour earlier. This wasn't the teasing sprinkle of an isolated squall—a storm was coming. Magnificent pines and madrones shuddered as if in fear, rather than from the steady ocean-swept winds. This was the only place Will knew where the wind sounded as portrayed by Hollywood. He had a fleeting vision of Laurence Olivier and Merle Oberon crossing the moors in "Wuthering Heights."

They were less than three miles from Carmel. The rain beat down at an angle, as if pulled by an unseen force. There were a few stars still visible directly above them, but the black clouds carrying the storm would soon block them from view. No cars appeared on either side of the highway. And why should they? Will thought. Only a crazy person or a cop would be out on a night like this. Will knew that being a cop did not necessarily exclude him from the other category.

He had related Jim's words to Curry and Forsburg. All three hoped hard for Jim's recovery—and prayed that he had, in fact, wounded Louis Peel.

"Anything to slow that motherfucker down'd sure help," Phil said. He sat in the passenger seat with his arms crossed as if bracing himself against an invisible onslaught.

Clint blew a stream of smoke toward the back window, which he'd cracked a half-inch upon lighting his fifty-seventh cigarette of the day. "Maybe he's laid up someplace and can't move," he said, more from hope than considered judgment. "Rather run into the son of a bitch with him on one leg than at full strength."

"Amen," Curry intoned.

Conversation again ceased as each man prepared for a possible meeting with Louis Peel. At the nurse's station on Jim's floor, they had divided up the list of hotel rooms provided by Sheriff Truitt. The plan was simple—based on the hope that Peel had established a second beachhead upon his arrival in the area. After a brief stop to view the wreckage at Will's house, they would visit the five long-term rentals. Phil and Clint would each cover two, Will would cover one. They would leave the Cadillac, their only surviving vehicle, at a point relatively central to all five rooms—its keys behind the driver's side front tire. In that way the car would be available to the one among them who might need it to transport a prisoner.

It was nearly eight when Will pulled into his driveway. The crunch of the gravel under the tires was muted by the three hours of rain and the drainage from the fire hoses.

The three men exited the car and looked at the wreckage of Will's once tidy home. All the front windows downstairs had been blown out. The porch listed badly to the left.

"Jesus," Will whispered. No other comment was required and no other words were spoken for nearly five minutes. The men stood silently as Will grieved.

They finally moved to what remained of the front porch. It was badly singed and littered with broken glass, splintered window frames and a large chunk of the front door that had been hacked apart by firemen. A jagged piece of the door hung sadly from the middle hinge. As Will pushed into the house, the remnant of the oak door fell with a wet thud onto the entry hall floor, which stood under three inches of water.

Bits of the room leapt to life—pinned in the eerie shafts of their flashlights. All its walls were scarred from shrapnel. Will looked at his favorite chair and realized a grenade must have landed on or under it.

He had a quick vision of himself in that chair. He'd spent many comfortable hours there during the previous week's storm. Had Peel attacked then… but he hadn't. He missed his best chance and now, by God, he would pay.

Will felt his outrage grow as he picked his way through the living room. He spotted his favorite photo of Debbie, leaned down and picked it up from the rubble. It was torn and soaked. He held it in both hands and shook his head. The shards of glass that crunched underfoot and the scarred walls drew a vivid symbol of the ruins Peel had made of Will's existence. His town, his friend, his children—now his home—all damaged. His fury grew.

Will knew that everything in his Carmel life required time and tenderness to repair, and he prayed that he would be there to help the process along. But Peel comes first, he thought. Tenderness is sure as hell not an essential for that job. I have to lose all parts of this Monterey Peninsula life I've so carefully cultivated over the last three years and reach back into a different world.

The three men passed through the nearly unscathed kitchen. As they mounted the slick back stairway, the smells of burned wood and wet carpeting settled in around them. Will's anger took root, marrow-deep. The second floor was a mess. Water seeped through a hundred holes in the ceiling. Rain fell freely onto the landing atop the staircase. Heavy chunks of plaster had sloughed off and lay on the soaking carpet. Sari's room was in decent shape. David's room, directly across the hall, was virtually destroyed. Now, Will thought, he'll have to clean it up.

He peeked into his own room, which was better off than David's, then returned to the far hallway where Clint and Phil were waiting. He felt ready to invoke his Plan B but had to find a way to ditch his men. His first approach was to affect normalcy. "Y'know this guy's really beginnin' to piss me off, gentlemen."

Curry chipped in, "Where's your Christian charity, kid? Give the guy a chance before you form a final opinion on 'im."

"Will, you mind if I have a smoke?" Clint asked. A smile started to loosen Will's jaw—but before he could speak, a loud creak echoed up the back stairway. The three men froze. It dawned on Will that the noise was simply the house settling in against the night's indignity. Old houses—especially this one—played a full score of creaks and groans.

Before he could calm his partners, there was another sound—then another and another. Footfalls on the stairs—the same spongy noise they had made ascending the stairs moments earlier. Something rustled on the stairway below.

The three men crouched as if on cue. Not until he moved to draw his gun did Will realize he still held the photo of Debbie. He took a last, quick look, then set it down gently on the floor behind him. All three drew their guns. The footsteps continued and reached the landing. All of them knew if it were Peel around the corner, he was as good as dead. Each man held his breath, trying mightily to hear anything from their quarry.

Another footstep. Will knew that three more steps would bring the intruder squarely into the opening where the hall turned toward the master bedroom. He couldn't believe Peel would so carelessly set himself up as an easy target. One more step. Suddenly, Will was gripped by the stark realization that if Peel had another grenade or two—he had them perfectly trapped.

At that instant a clump of sodden plaster lost its mooring on the ceiling and splattered on the floor near Clint's foot. Will watched as an involuntary reflex forced Clint to fire his weapon. The bullet buried in the far wall, splintering an ancient wooden stud. Echoes of the gunshot reverberated, nearly deafening the men. Nevertheless, Will heard footsteps rapidly retreating down the hallway toward the back staircase.

Instinct propelled Will forward to follow the intruder. Phil caught him by the shoulder before he could round the corner of the hall where he would become a wide open target.

"Goddamnit, Will! Keep your head…"

Before Phil could finish, a voice echoed from down the hall.

"Will! Will! Is that you?"

Will, still struggling against Phil's iron grip, shouted, "Yeah, it's me—who the hell are you?"

"Christ, Will—it's me. Pete Tuttle."

"Pete, what the hell're you doin' here?" Will tried again to shake off Curry's arm.

Peter Tuttle was the chief of the Carmel Fire Department and had responded upon hearing the fire was at Will's house. Before Will could apologize for the gunplay, Pete's voice boomed up the stairwell.

"Brought 'cha some large, plastic bags for clothes and stuff. Can I come up now without gettin' shot at?"

Pete's question caused Will to realize how ridiculous his bedraggled company appeared at that moment. Clint was still kneeling and holding the literal smoking gun, with Phil behind him with his gun out. Phil released Will. "Hang on, Pete—we're comin' down."

The trio disengaged from the Three Stooges-like pose and headed to the back stairs with what Will hoped was a shred of dignity.

***

They met Tuttle in the kitchen. He was tall and lean. Both Tuttle and the kitchen were illuminated by two CFD battery-powered torch lights. Will made the introductions and apologized for the accidental shot.

"Oh, think nothing of it, Will. 'Course you won't mind if I send you the bill for cleanin' the big wet spot offa my trousers, will you?"

His comment generated a low rumble of laughter, which released a good measure of pent-up tension. "We're all a bit jumpy, Pete," Will said. He walked toward Pete as he spoke.

"I can *see* that. Just glad I hadn't eaten dinner—I'd hafta burn these pants." Pete's humorous inflection changed quickly. "Hand grenades, Will—who'd you piss off?"

"Long story—I'll tell you later." Will introduced Tuttle to his fellow cops, and a brief few moments of small talk ensued. Then Tuttle moved toward the stairway and said, "I'll just go upstairs and bag all the clothes I can and dump 'em by the laundromat on my way home."

"Fuck the clothes. You get home now and stay there. This place's off limits tonight."

Will's ominous tone halted Tuttle's progress. He placed the bags on the kitchen table, walked to the back door, turned to Will and said, "You're the boss, Will. I'm gone."

Will walked across the room, gripped Tuttle's arm and said, "C'mon, we'll walk you to your car. I've seen enough of this place."

They watched Tuttle's taillights fade as his car crested the hill back to the center of town. The driving rain had become an insignificant bother.

"I'm starving—gotta eat," Phil said, and started to move to his car. Will followed him, trailed by Clint, and said, "Sounds good. How 'bout you, Clint?"

"Hungry, but I'm so fucking jumpy I don't know if I can keep anything down."

"Let's go find some food. We can finalize our plan, then go find this cocksucker," Will said. He opened the driver's door and sat down in the welcoming leather seat.

"If he's still here," Phil said as he deposited himself in the passenger seat. Clint folded himself into the back seat.

"He's here, Phil. He's here."

Will turned the key, and the Cadillac roared to life.

Tuesday Night Drags On
Chapter Twenty-Eight

In a town with fifty restaurants, they ended up at a basic coffee shop on a side street several blocks up from Will's house. They ordered and were served quickly. Ravenous as he was, Phil scowled at the feast before them. "Somethin' seriously wrong with eatin' Campbell's soup and dry meatloaf in a place with more four-star restaurants per square foot than anywhere in the world."

Will looked across the table at his friend and said, "Yeah, but I'm buyin', Phil."

Curry grunted, his sour expression effectively discouraging any further repartee from his companions.

With almost no sleep over the last three days, Will knew he should be used up. But he was wholly free of the dead-weight drag of exhaustion. He felt sharp—his senses strong and alert. Had to be adrenaline, he thought. But he'd drawn so deeply from those reserves in the last eighty hours.... How long could he continue to function on nothing but nerves and adrenaline?

"If you've no objection, that is," Clint was saying.

"S'cuse me?" Will yanked himself back to the table.

"I just asked if we could go over it one more time."

"Good idea," Will said. He pushed his dishes to the side of their table and grabbed five bags of sugar from the small white container, then placed them on the red- and white-checked plastic tablecloth. "Basic assumption is Peel's got another place and has had it for a long time."

"That's a coupla pretty big 'ifs,' partner," Curry said.

"If you've got anything better, Phil, I'm all ears," Will said quietly.

Phil's shrug said all he was going to.

Will started in again. "Okay, look," he said now, carefully arranging the sugar bags on the table. "Here's Ocean Avenue. All five Carmel places Truitt's guys came up with are on the south side of Ocean—and they're within five or six blocks of each other."

Clint spoke first. "I got—what—Stonehouse and the Cypress Inn?"

"Yep—and Phil's got the La Playa and the Colonial. I got the Adobe Inn up on Dolores," Will said, placing the pepper shaker among the five sugar bags. "Pepper's the Cadillac. We'll park it right by the intersection of Lincoln and Eighth after we drop Phil off down at the La Playa."

They had agreed that this would be a bust-in operation—no talking to hotel personnel, no knocking on doors. The order of the day was to find Peel and subdue him—whatever it took. Protecting the civil rights of Carmel's few remaining visitors was entirely secondary.

Will's supply of radios had already been reduced to one by Peel's activities. So if anyone found and subdued Peel, he would walk him to the car and get him to the station. If that was impossible, for whatever reason, they had devised a system of warning shots. Phil was to fire one round, Clint two, Will three. Because each knew the general location of the others, the shots would identify who needed help.

The sound of gunshots at this hour in Carmel would be heard easily—anywhere. "I know this is thin, but it's the best I can come up with," Will said.

Phil's sour expression moved from Will's eyes to the bags of sugar and back. "I didn't like this plan when you told us at the hospital, and I don't like it any better now."

Will tensed and was about to respond when Phil continued. "This storm gonna fuck up our great system of field communication?" His sarcasm didn't shake Will's confidence, who shrugged his eyebrows and began to go over the plan a last time.

"Fuck it, kid," Curry said, defiance supplanting sarcasm. "I don't like it. Your plan separates us. I'd rather we all went together to hit these places." Phil sat up in his chair and placed both hands on the table.

"Look, Phil, we covered that at the hospital. Don't tell me I need to remind you there's just three of us left to get this fucking bastard. This way maximizes that remaining force." Will's posture mirrored Curry's.

"Maximizes? What kinda word's that? Sounds like the bullshit I gotta read on campus alla time. Maximize, energize, actualize, conceptualize—two-dollar words for ten-cent thoughts. You'd fit in fine on a campus, kid—alla those pretend doctors talk like that." Phil sat back and crossed his arms over his chest in a particularly non-welcoming gesture.

Silver dollar-size circles of red appeared on Will's cheeks as he glared at Phil. "Your displeasure is noted—but we're gonna do this my way."

Curry locked eyes with Will. His mouth was a thin line drawn tightly over his teeth. Will knew the effort it cost Phil to overcome the urge to continue their argument. But finally he said, "You're the boss, kid."

Clint was obviously uncomfortable as he listened to the verbal sparring. To distract himself, he raised the flimsy curtain next to their table and peered out the window. He used his paper napkin to rub away a rectangle of condensation. "Storm's turnin' into a bitch, guys."

"Maybe it'll help us, Clint—cover any noise we make approaching these rooms." Will's comment was a patently weak effort to calm the human storm he saw brewing in his friend and former partner.

"Hope it don't cover any of our gunshots," Phil said snidely.

"Phil! For Chrissakes!" Will began to rise from his chair.

"Aw right, aw right," Curry said, as he too began to get up.

Will tossed thirty dollars on the table, bid goodnight to the hostess and led his team out to Phil's car. The Cadillac had just begun its descent down Ocean Avenue when a huge clap of thunder echoed up the quarter mile from the beach.

"Great," Phil muttered. "Now we got drums, kid."

Will ignored the needle and navigated the last three blocks to Curry's point of departure. Approaching the La Playa, Will unscrewed the tiny overhead bulb, and, as he coasted to a stop in front of the hotel, he doused the headlights.

"Okay, Phil. Remember, car'll be at Lincoln and Eighth. It's eight-fifteen—we rendezvous at the car in twenty minutes exactly, unless one of us finds Peel. If one of us does, either bring him to the car or fire your gun. Clear?"

Phil grunted his understanding as he heaved himself up and out of the car. Will knew his former partner continued to question the plan that he had so carefully outlined at the restaurant. He also knew Phil would be a good soldier and would follow his lead. Will swung the Caddy left and headed up the hill toward Lincoln and Eighth, where he would park the car and leave Clint to check the long-held room at the Cypress Inn.

One minute later Clint was across the street from the stately old Cypress Inn. The whitewashed adobe glistened under the steady rain. He crossed Lincoln and took the steps up to the lobby by twos—the rain plastering his shirt to his back. Entering the lobby, he let the warmth wash over him—but only for a second before he started up the staircase. His destination was a room that, according to the sheriff, had been reserved nearly two months ago.

Tuesday Night Late
Chapter Twenty-Nine

The tumblers fell easily into place under the credit card, and Peel stepped silently through the doorway. Once inside, he stood rigidly pressed against the doorjamb, and neither breathed nor moved for over a minute. Satisfied that he was alone, he closed and relocked the door.

He waited another minute while his eyes adjusted to the darkness, then moved slowly past the two empty cells. He limped into the main room of the station house—the throb in his leg punctuating each heartbeat. An outdoor lamp sent a thread of light through the front window. The beam broke apart, and he flinched before he realized it was only the wind—splitting the light into angular figures dancing along the walls.

Easy, goddamnit! Not so jumpy. Almost home free. Calm down. Easy now. Okay, move.

He crossed the bullpen to Kempton's office. Closed and locked. Another credit card and he was in. He relocked the door, took two steps toward the desk and heard a faint clicking sound.

Peel froze while a voice filled the room. "Welcome to the Carmel Police Department, Louis—I'll be your tour guide for the remainder of your very short stay."

"Kempton!?!" Peel shrieked, as his heart nearly burst from his body. Peel threw himself to the floor, clawing wildly for the gun holstered in the small of his back. Frenzy destroyed his coordination. When he finally managed to grab the gun, his hand shook so hard he couldn't cock the hammer. Steadying the weapon in his right hand, he pulled the hammer back with the cupped fingers of his left hand. The gun was almost cocked before the combination of sweat and trembling caused it to slip. The hammer's steel point impaled the little finger of his left hand.

The pain was so sudden and intense that Peel's ears rang with a sound only he could hear. The urge to cry out was defeated by his nearly mad attempts to pry the hammer out of his finger. During that frantic effort, his right hand slipped away from the gun. The weapon dangled from his little finger for an instant, then fell to the floor, carrying with it a half-ounce of pulpy flesh from Louis Peel's finger.

***

Phil had no intention of visiting either the La Playa or the Colonial. He paused for a moment to gather his bearings, then began to jog briskly up the hill on Eighth. A crack of thunder knocked him off-stride below Monte Verde. Hastily, he righted himself and returned to an even pace. Five more blocks, he thought.

***

Will sprinted up Seventh—passing Dolores without even a sidelong glance at the Adobe Inn. He knew Peel wouldn't be there, even if it was his second safe haven. He cut right at San Carlos—he was now only two blocks from the station. Unless his instincts had completely deserted him, that was where Peel would be—waiting. A block from the station he heard the thunder and lengthened his stride. A little noise and rain would not faze him now.

***

Peel was terrified. Anxiety and pain blurred his mind—his eyes were unable to focus. Cruel laughter shocked him back to reality. It was an echo from a decade ago. It *was* Kempton! So was the voice that followed.

"You pathetic, little shit. Are you crying, Louis? Run outta women to kill, cocksucker?"

Peel huddled on the floor, trying to suck the pain from his torn finger while his good hand searched for the gun. He fought to focus his eyes on the precise spot from which the voice came. He found the gun—gripped and cocked it. And waited.

"In case you haven't figured it out, Louis, this is a recording. Your good fortune, shithead. But I'll be there with you real soon, so enjoy your last few moments on earth. No point in running away and trying to hide—or going after Sandra. The Feds have her and your kids tucked away so deep, you'll never find 'em. Stick around and let's have a little private get-together, just the two of us."

***

The door marked 212 crashed inward under Clint's weight. He was halfway into the fully-lighted room before the last few splinters from the door sill settled on the pale blue carpet. He swept the entire space with the thirty-eight he held in his two large hands.

It didn't take more than a few seconds to be sure he was alone. The closet door was wide open. So was the bathroom door. Nowhere else for him to hide, Clint thought. He strode to the bathroom. It was still slightly steamy—the mirror over the sink streaked with beads of water. He smelled Ivory soap as he knelt to examine the tangle of towels and clothes dumped between the toilet and shower. One wash rag, one bath towel—both white—and a shirt and a pair of balled-up Levis. All four items were covered with still-sticky blood.

"Holy Jesus," he breathed.

***

Peel heard another whirring sound, then a metallic snap. His breathing, coming in gulps, was now the only sound in the office. Still, he remained frozen, on his knees, for as long as it took to be certain he was alone. When he knew for sure, he struggled to his feet, took two steps—and bumped into Kempton's desk. He reached out and steadied himself against it. Pain punched away at his leg and hand. His heart continued to race at an alarming rate.

How does he know it's me? How could he possibly know? And how could he have known I'd come here? I didn't even know that until twenty minutes ago. Got to get out—if that tape I tripped was rigged into a silent alarm, he'll be on his way. Can't walk—hand's all fucked up. Gotta get outta here…go somewhere…get strong. Come back later and finish him—from a distance.

Peel stood, hunched over the desk, bracing himself with both hands. His head was bent low. He was so deeply confused by this latest brush with Kempton that he failed to notice the tear that rolled down his cheek and onto the desk.

***

In Room 212, Clint wrapped Peel's laundry inside the towel. The amount of blood told him that Peel wouldn't be going too far. He checked his watch, surprised to see that he'd been inside the room less than five minutes. He figured that Will and Curry would return to the car shortly as their respective room assignments could only turn up frightened tourists. The thought, plus his telltale bundle, made him smile.

But Clint's smile vanished when, as he reached the lobby, a huge flash of lightning turned the black night into a bright-as-daylight scene. In that fraction of a second, the small garden of the Church of the Wayfarer, directly across the street, was etched in brilliant detail. Just as quickly, the black curtain of night fell over it again. Clint counted only three beats before he heard the crash of thunder.

Pretty damn close, he thought, as he pushed his way out of the glass door and on down the short, brick stairway to the street. The force of the rain and wind was constant. He walked hunched over, shielding his eyes from the relentless pelting.

He dropped the bloody bundle into the back seat of the Cadillac, wanting nothing more than to climb inside the inviting, dry interior. Instead, he found a shred of shelter under an ancient pine a few feet behind the car. Peel was out there somewhere, and so were Curry and Will. If their paths crossed, Clint didn't want to miss any warning shots.

He struggled to light a comforting smoke and entertained the thought that his wait would be brief.

By the end of his second cigarette, shadows of worry were darkening Clint's thoughts. It was raining harder by the minute. His shelter gave way. Jagged spangles of lightning punctuated by deafening thunder broke into the quiet darkness. Clint edged a couple of steps away from the huge pine.

Where the hell are they?

Tuesday Night Reunion
Chapter Thirty

Peel tried to convince himself that the warm stream oozing from his calf to his sock was merely a distraction. But the pain intensified with each second, and the illusion failed him. The nerve endings in his leg felt as though they'd been skewered and exposed to an open fire.

He lurched across Will's office to the door—each step exacting a terrible price. Collapsing across an old easy chair, he knew he couldn't finish Kempton now. A bolt of pain snapped his head between his knees. Peel sucked air past clenched teeth and rocked forward. *Got to get away.* He made it to his feet again, hopped to the door and grasped the knob. He unlocked the door—and began to wobble. *Steady.* His attempt to ease a little weight onto his damaged left leg created a sucking sound—he realized his shoe was filled with blood.

He moaned—sweat seemed to come from every pore on his body. He turned the knob, and the door began to swing outward into the main part of the station, pulling him after it. The world spun wildly for an instant. Then Louis Peel crashed to the floor.

***

Though he stood in complete darkness, Will knew the door and the lock by heart. His key slipped directly into the deadbolt slot. Before he could turn it, he was violently spun around.

"Catchin' up on your paperwork, asshole?"

"Phil! Jesus—you scared the shit outta me! Don't follow orders too well, do you?"

"Not when I know they're bullshit," Curry's whisper rasped.

Will recovered quickly from the shock of Curry's silent appearance, and actually felt relief to have his help. Now it was two against one—if Peel was inside. "You made me drop the key," he whispered, bending down, feeling around for the gold Russwin. "Go 'round back and cover it, case he tries to get away."

***

The crash of thunder jarred Peel back to full consciousness. He heard the rain beat a steady rhythm on the skylight as he dragged himself across the floor to an open area of the police station. He pulled himself up and balanced on a desk by leaning his hip against a chair. He was trying to figure out how to get from there to the back door when he heard a scratching noise outside—in front. His legs froze in place, and only his hand moved—to the butt of his gun. *Probably just the wind, or maybe a rat looking for a dry place.* Still, he listened—trying mightily to separate the sounds of the storm from any other noise which might be out there.

***

"Oh, horseshit, Will," Curry hissed. "I ain't goin' anywhere. Now get the goddamned key, and let's see if yer right about our friend."

Obviously, Curry was past taking orders—if ever he'd been inclined to. As Phil turned to observe the street, Will squatted to search for the key. When, finally, he grasped it and was starting to get up, he heard the unmistakable report of a pistol. Before his brain could signal any useful reflex, Will felt the considerable bulk of his best friend crushing downward, pinning him to the wet concrete with such force that he couldn't move.

The rain jabbed relentlessly at Will's eyes and face. Thrashing about to free himself, he offered a hasty prayer that he wasn't laboring under a truly dead weight. Before he could push Phil off, the hinges of the station's front door, long ago rusted by the salt sea air, screeched above the sound of the beating rain.

"It's been a long, long time, cocksucker."

Will's body went hollow at the sound. Still pinned to the sidewalk, he looked up at the silhouette in the doorway of the dark station house.

"Get up real slow, you piece of shit," the shadowy Peel commanded. "Both hands in the air. Move wrong and you're dead."

Will's heart pounded as he eased himself out from under Curry as gently as possible. Concern for Phil overcame his fear for himself. He heard no sound—detected no movement from Curry. When he'd made it to his knees, Will placed Phil's head on the wet sidewalk with great care.

"Hands up! Left hand—move the gun outta the holster—thumb and index finger only. Good—now drop it. Quick!"

Will watched his gun clatter into the gutter. The rush of rainwater nudged it forward an inch before the weight of the weapon anchored it against the curb. He felt like a diver whose line had been cut.

"Now, Willy boy, drag the nigger inside."

Will bit his lip. He had not used that word even once since he'd met Phil Curry, but Peel was guilty of worse sins than racism.

"C'mon, move!" Peel ordered. "We don't want anybody tripping over him, do we?"

Will could see only the eyes and teeth of Louis Peel who stood but five feet away. He bent to turn Phil over. Peel hissed, "Grab his ankles and drag him in the way he is. If he's not dead yet, he will be soon. Hurry!"

Will grasped the ankles of Curry's ostrich-skin cowboy boots. It took almost a minute to pull him into the station. The door slammed shut, and Peel threw the deadbolt with the ominous crack of finality. Will reflected on the irony of being a prisoner in his own jail—a place where he'd rarely locked up anyone.

"Step into your office, Chief. We should talk a bit."

Will hesitated, saw Peel's eyes burning through the darkness, and opened his mouth to speak.

Peel's scream interrupted him.

"Just do it, asshole—or I'll cover this whole fuckin' room with parts of you!"

Silently, Will walked toward his office. Though he felt the cold presence following him, he knew Peel was too smart to get close enough for Will to make a move.

"Sit in the chair by the desk."

Will did as he was told. The banker's lamp on his desk was on—the only light in the entire station. It allowed him to observe Peel's uneven gait as he moved behind the desk toward Will's chair. *Good for Jim. By God, he did shoot the son of a bitch.*

Will's chair squealed as Peel fell into it. Looking across the desk at his tormentor, he saw eyes that weren't exclusively human. But he also saw pain and exhaustion mirrored there in roughly equal portions. Will knew it would be wise to hide the contempt he felt for Peel, and he tried.

"Got to give you some credit, Willy boy. Hidin' your kids was smart. Saved their lives—for a little while." Smiling at what he saw in Will's face, Peel added, "Oh, yeah, I'll get them. By the time I'm through here—however long it takes—there won't be anything left...*anywhere*... to remind people that you were ever on this fucking planet."

He switched the gun from his right hand to his left, and pointed it directly at Will's chest.

"Why so quiet, Willy boy? Aren't you happy to see an old friend?" Peel's smile hardened into a twisted grin. Will's eyes never moved from Peel's feral gaze. He knew his life balanced on his ability to somehow engage with the mind of the madman across the desk.

"How'd you like the little ornament I put on your buddy's shower? Bitch didn't look her personal best, did she?"

Despite his determination to show no reaction to anything Peel said, at the mention of Jennie, Will's jaw clenched.

"She was a fine specimen, Willy. I wanted to put her in your shower, but too many trips to your house wouldn't have been prudent—don't you agree?"

Ten seconds of silence followed. Thunder echoed up from the beach.

"Where'd you get the nigger, Willy? He sure wasn't much help. Did you really think all those rent-a-cops could save your ass from me? Got your buddy Jim real good, Will. He had me there for a second, but he crapped out. Is he dead, Willy? No matter. If he isn't—I'll get him. They're all gonna die—every person you care about's gonna die."

Will rubbed the muscle above his aching knee. He knew Peel was revving himself up for action. If he was going to get out of there, he'd better think of a way damned quick.

"You never, ever should've fucked with me, Willy boy. I was doing society a favor back in Jersey, couldn't you see that? All those sluts. I was taking sin off the streets. I was on your side. Nobody worthwhile was hurt. If you hadn't gotten lucky, I'd still be out there, helping. Why did you have to fuck with me?"

Will stared at Peel with a dispassion he did not feel. He had to keep him talking—somehow.

Peel's voice rose in pitch with each sentence, and he punctuated his last question by slamming his right fist on the desk. As if on cue, the picture frame broke loose from the unsteady mortar nail and crashed down onto the lamp. As the lamp tipped over toward the middle of the desk, Peel instinctively reached with his left hand to stop its fall. The gun slipped from his grip. Will felt as though he were watching a movie in slow motion. He flexed his knees and began to rise.

Peel caught the movement from the corner of his eye. He regained his grip on the gun even as the glass shade of the lamp shattered on the desk top. Peel swung his weight to the right and the gun toward Will, who was now on his feet. He was pulling the trigger when his chair lurched wildly to the right. The gun fired.

The lamp and Louis Peel hit the floor at the same time. The last thing Peel saw before the two light bulbs exploded was a wheel of the chair bouncing across the carpet.

Tuesday Night Running Out
Chapter Thirty-One

The impact of the bullet knocked Will back on his heels. Before the room went completely dark, he saw Peel spill onto the floor. *God bless that busted chair.* Will's left shoulder burned where the bullet had lodged. Ignoring it, he got a fingerhold under the top of the desk and surged forward with all of his strength.

The desk tipped up six inches—then a foot. Driving forward with his legs, Will managed to turn the massive desk all the way over on top of the thrashing Louis Peel. He jumped on the desk, hoping the extra weight would squash Peel like an insect.

Rocking on the desk, listening to the screams and curses of the vicious man beneath him, Will felt a strange sense of comfort. He was considering the ways he would finish him off when the flash from Peel's gun went off no more than six inches from his face. Will pushed down with his entire weight, still hoping to disable his enemy. When he heard the gun being cocked again, he decided to continue the battle on other ground.

Will leapt off the upturned desk and across the room. To equalize the fight, he knew he had to get hold of some sort of a weapon. Six rifles were locked in a cabinet in the outer office, but he'd never be able to break it open and load one up before Peel was on top of him.

He pulled the easy chair in front of the doorway and realized that his left arm, though relatively pain-free, was virtually useless. He slammed the office door and ran toward the front door. Over Peel's screams, Will heard Phil's guttural tone.

"Ankle holster, Will…."

Jesus! Phil was alive! "Phil, where are ya!?!"

"Floor behind the counter—can't move—gotta gun in my ankle holster."

As Will vaulted over the counter, he heard Peel thud into the chair blocking the doorway—and let out a stream of world-class curses. He had precious few seconds to find Phil and get the gun before Peel hit the outer office. Down on his hands and knees, Will scrambled frantically—and blessedly ran into Phil's bulk.

"Right leg…" Phil gasped.

Will popped the button on the holster, grabbed the Beretta. As the door to his office was thrown open, Will jumped up and fired two shots. He knew he'd missed when Peel laughed loudly. Two seconds later he heard the shattering of glass from inside the office.

"Out the window—fuck's gone out the window, Will."

"Phil, you okay?" Will struggled to see Phil in the darkness.

"Been better. Go get the shithead—hurry. I'm gonna just lie here and relax."

"Gotta get an ambulance first…"

"*Fuck* that! Gimme a phone down here and get the hell outta here!"

Will grabbed Peach's phone and put it next to Phil's hand. "Can you dial 911? Lemme get some lights on…"

"Fuck the lights. Dark's good as long as that guy's around. Now git. This place's off my vacation list 'til you bury that motherfucker. Gimme the phone."

"Any more bullets for this thing?"

"Trunk of the Caddy."

"Shit!"

"Go!"

Will cracked the front door with great care. As he poked his head outside, a flash of lightning startled him. Before the thunder came, he heard a familiar sound—the Cushman! He headed toward the back of the building where the parking vehicles were kept.

As he rounded the second corner, Will was nearly blinded by the single headlight of the car coming toward him. He dove behind the large garbage Dumpster. A bullet ricocheted off the Dumpster and powdered a brick barely a foot from his head. The Cushman roared around the corner, disappearing from view. Will sprinted to the second three-wheeler, jumped in and prayed that Peel hadn't swiped the keys. Luck was with him! After fumbling with the starter for a moment, Will managed to fire up the overgrown golf cart and, within seconds, cleared the utility area—heading toward Ocean Avenue at full throttle.

***

Clint was halfway through a third cigarette when he heard the shot. Moving quickly to the Cadillac, he listened for another shot—or two. No sound. He fired up the car and spoke aloud, "One shot means Phil——either at La Playa or Colonial Terrace."

He turned the car down Seventh, La Playa first. Hell, he thought, Phil's such a pro he'd probably have Peel cuffed and waiting right out on the street. The Caddy slid to a wet stop in front of the charming old hotel. Clint jumped from the car, looking for any sign of life. Seeing none, he started to run into the hotel. Another shot sounded in the distance, stopping him short. *What the fuck?*

A third shot rang out. Three shots, he thought—that's Will at the Adobe Inn. He raced back to the car. *Shit, that's clear up on Dolores.*

He floored the gas pedal and gunned the car up Eighth. The car fishtailed half a block before finding traction on the slick bed of pine needles and leaves. At the crest of the rise at Monte Verde, he jammed the wheel to the right and slammed on the brakes. Still sliding right, Clint saw someone fly past him behind the wheel of a Cushman. As the Cadillac crunched into a cypress tree, Clint watched a second Cushman, with Will driving, shoot down Eighth. *Holy shit—we got the son of a bitch now!*

Clint floored the car in reverse and felt it slip backward. He pumped the brakes furiously, but the car was out of control. A mailbox and most of a four-foot picket fence were wiped out before the Cadillac came to rest. Clint swore vigorously, righted the car and headed down Eighth, respectful of the slippery track. He pleaded to the right front tire as it rubbed against the crushed fender, "Just get me there—let's catch this asshole and go dry off."

***

Will watched Peel skid left at Scenic. Though he'd ridden faster lawnmowers, this was as close to road racing as Will ever wanted to get. He backed off the gas and started his left turn. He knew hitting the brakes wouldn't he helpful under these road conditions. Despite his precaution, the slick road made his turn more of a skid than a proper turn.

Once on Scenic he could see that the rain was sending thousands of rivulets streaming across the pavement. Peel was out of sight, but Will knew he was up there, around a bend or two on the twisting road. Headlights loomed behind him. *God, I hope that's you, Clint.* After seeing that it was Clint, he pulled left at the driveway of one of the magnificent ocean-view homes and signaled for the Caddy to pass him. *Go get him, Clint—he can't outrun that baby. I'll be right behind you!*

The Cadillac jumped forward with a roar, Will following in its wake. For the first time in this eighty-four-hour nightmare, Will felt he had the upper hand. All things being equal, he and Clint *should* be able to bring Peel down. *Should.* The combination of Peel's savagery and cunning tempered his optimism. *Jesus, the damage that crazy bastard has done in just a few days. Three dead, four wounded, town torn apart by hand grenades, the whole peninsula in a panic—God, what a monster!* It hit Will then that it had been his own bad actions, so long ago, that had brought this scourge to Carmel.

Flooring the Cushman along one of Scenic's few straight-aways, Will told himself to stow all that thinking 'til a later time. Right now his single aim was to disable Louis Peel permanently.

Wednesday Morning Closing In
Chapter Thirty-Two

As he chugged past the tiny twin cottages, Sea Urchin and Periwinkle, on Scenic Drive, Will could see the Cadillac close on Peel's Cushman. They were about three hundred yards ahead of him—obviously his was the one with the bad battery. He was dropping behind at an alarming rate.

"Goddamnit!" he yelled into the storm, punching the pedal to the floor. The cart surged ahead for a hundred yards, then slowed, no longer responsive to the pounding of Will's right foot on the accelerator. It died just short of the driveway of the beautiful home built generations earlier by the Van Löben Sels family. He jumped out and ran along the street as fast as his aching knee would allow. Rounding a bend, he felt sure the Cadillac's taillights would be visible. Up one more hill and....

Nothing but darkness.

He pressed on, just below Tor House, built rock by rock by the bleak poet Robinson Jeffers. Finally, he spotted the Cadillac's lights—a few feet over the edge on the ocean side of Scenic. The driver's door was open—accessory lights played a faint glow over the iceplant.

Then, fifty feet further up Scenic, Will saw the Cushman. It laid on its side on the ledge overhanging the ocean. He approached it cautiously. The pounding of wind-driven waves muted all other sound. As he neared the Cushman and tightened his grip on the Beretta, two shots rang out. He ducked down and pressed himself into the spongy iceplant. The shots had come from well below him and to his right. He tried to tiptoe down the ledge, but slipped. He fell the full ten feet to the rocks below.

Will did a quick once-over of his condition. Surprisingly, the fall hadn't created any new wounds, but it definitely hadn't helped his bad knee. His left arm was numb from shoulder to elbow, but apparently Peel's bullet had missed major veins and arteries. *Thank God. I can't afford any more injuries—I'm running out of working body parts.*

The only lights ahead were those bordering the Gull—one of Carmel's most spectacular architectural legacies. The home, set far out on the rocks overhanging the Pacific, looked precariously balanced— that was part of its magic. On this night, the storm and a very high tide sent huge waves crashing against the retaining walls and the tall casement windows above.

Will tried a few tentative steps—only to discover that gaining a footing on the wet, moss-covered rocks was impossible. Quickly, he removed his shoes and socks and threw them in the direction of the Cadillac. He was creeping along the rocks when another shot thundered from below. Will flinched, muttered, "God, let me kill this son of a bitch, quick!" and kept moving. The fifty yards between him and the Gull were completely black.

Only pure luck allowed him to see the flash as the gun roared again—from down on the ocean side of the Gull. Will picked his way across another series of rocks. That the surface was slick made the going difficult enough—but it was also angled and sharp and tore at his feet. But there was no turning back. He had a long-standing appointment to keep.

Suddenly, Clint's voice floated faintly out to his position. "Will! I'm hit!"

Pocketing the Beretta, he yelled to Clint to keep talking. The wind so warped the sound waves that Will couldn't track the voice of the fallen man. And the driving rain and onrushing tides made progress so slow it was almost like making no headway at all. Then, just as he thought he had a bearing on Clint, Will plunged into a newly formed tide pool—and the freezing, chest-high water shocked all oxygen from his lungs.

When he'd clawed his way up and out of the pool, he had no choice but to rest a few moments on his hands and knees. That was when he saw Clint—he was *under* the Gull, thirty feet short of the back windows.

Will, moving forward again, saw a shadow flutter across one of the spotlights at the far end of the Gull's retaining wall. In the next split-second, Will was certain he saw a figure moving out to the rocks directly below the deck of the house.

There's nothing there but ocean.

"Here, Will—I can see you. Over here!"

In two steps, Will felt the swirling, wet sand between his toes. He clambered up and over a huge rock, cutting both hands as he went. He was nearly on top of Clint before he saw him.

"Where're you hit, Clint?" Will knelt beside yet another of his fallen soldiers.

"Fuckin' thigh. But I got him, too—heard the bastard scream."

Clint's pain was obvious to Will, but his voice was full and he began to sit up.

"Well, he's still out there movin' around— I gotta go after him. Can you make it up the hill?"

"This hurts bad, but I'll try." Clint pulled his damaged leg with both hands until he was standing.

"Just get up to the iceplant—'bout thirty feet. Tide can't get out there in case I don't get back."

Clint grabbed Will's wrist and said, "You *get back*, baby. Prick's got two holes in him. Finish his ass. I'll be okay."

"I'm goin' up and around. I think I saw him down by the rocks under the back windows. I think he's tryin' to get around the house and back up to the street. I'm gonna try to cut him off."

"Shit, Will, there's nothin' but ocean down there. How can he make it?"

Ducking around the slow-moving Clint, Will said, "Nobody normal could. But this fucker ain't normal."

221

Will started straight up the patch of iceplant that bordered the high wall around the Gull. Reaching the street, he ran toward the eight-foot front gate. He cursed because it was locked, found a foothold and climbed to the top. Unable to lower himself down gently because of his left arm, he dropped straight down, landing in a garden bed of white rocks, which felt like a bowl full of broken glass. Ignoring the pain, he got to his feet and ran across the driveway, leaving foot-shaped smears of blood to be washed away by the rain.

He dismissed the idea of breaking into the house. Instead, he climbed up onto the adobe wall surrounding the place. From there, he swung up to the roof. The action reawakened the pain in his left shoulder. He shuddered but kept moving forward. His thought was to get out to the far ledge of the roof, from which he could view the expanse of rocks below the house and, he hoped, see where Peel was. His plan would have been perfect except for the fact that the roof was covered with the same sharp rocks that had torn holes in his feet in the garden.

"Son of a bitch! Jesus, I don't need more goddamned pain!"

The Gull's roof angled sharply upward at its two corners—stretching out above the ocean. On countless treks along Scenic, Will had always loved those wings of the Gull. Now, as every step he took up the left wing punctured his feet, his appreciation of the roof thinned considerably.

What horse's ass designed this goddamned thing?

At last he reached the uppermost part of the roof, furious at his decision to discard his shoes. He looked down from the wing, fifteen feet above the rest of the flat roof. The rocks below the house were fully illuminated by a dozen well-placed spotlights.

Through the rain whipping at his eyes, he spotted Peel dragging himself across the rocks. He had guessed right about Peel's escape plan.

He watched with fascination as Peel ducked under a huge wave. Will felt the spray even on the roof. He had never seen the tide so high. As soon as the ocean began its temporary retreat, Peel, with perfect timing, was off and scrambling up toward the house.

Will watched the remarkable bout between man and nature, again and again marveling at Peel's tenacity. If he had ever doubted Peel's maniacal will to survive, the scene below eliminated all question. He leaned into a gust of wind and peered down at Peel's escape route. There was no way—*nobody* could swim across eighty feet of riptide to the questionable safety of the rocks. A much better option was for Peel to climb up to the Gull's balcony—somehow—and proceed from there to safety.

The next wave washed Peel up under the balcony—out of Will's view. Without hesitating, Will swung himself over the roof and dropped the fifteen feet down to the balcony. Landing, his right knee collapsed under him—pitching Will into an awkward somersault. This time he knew the knee was seriously impaired. He scuttled toward the far corner of the balcony on his ass and pulled himself up to his feet.

Above the sounds of the storm and the sea, Will could hear Peel laboring to pull himself up onto the balcony. Determined to stay put until most of Louis Peel was there with him, Will unpocketed the Beretta, cocked the hammer—and waited.

Wednesday Very Early
Chapter Thirty-Three

Four minutes dragged by. Though Will continued to hear grunts and scuffling from below, he began to worry that Peel might not be able to make it to what Will had staked out as their meeting ground. He was about to peek over the side when, ten feet away, a hand slapped the railing. Then another hand—then a head and two shoulders.

With Peel halfway over the top rail. Will limped forward and aimed the gun at Peel's head. "C'mon up slowly, asshole. Don't for a second think the gun's not loaded."

Peel froze, then turned his head slowly up toward Will. The undiluted hatred in his eyes pierced the dark night and hammering rain. "You won't do it, Kempton—not in cold blood. You didn't then; you won't now."

Will hesitated, as if pondering Peel's words. A thousand images flooded his mind, long-past and recent, all mixed together. In that split second delay Peel summoned a nearly superhuman effort and vaulted up to the balcony and reached for Will's gun.

He was fast, but not fast enough. Will slammed the Beretta into his face. The blow dropped Peel to the floor, but the pistol flew out of Will's hand. His follow-up left hook went wide, but not before it sent a searing pain through Will's body. Then his right knee buckled again.

Now both men were on their knees—two feet apart. Peel, spent from his climb, fought to hold onto consciousness. Will pivoted on his left knee and landed a vicious right hook on Peel's jaw. Peel's head sounded like an overripe cantaloupe as it bounced off the balcony's main balustrade.

Peel appeared limp—completely beaten. Will started to pull himself up to his feet, but nothing worked. His left arm had no strength, and his right knee gave way entirely. He slipped helplessly onto his right side. As he struggled back to a kneeling position, the balcony shuddered under the impact of an immense wave, which shot spray forty feet above the house.

The frigid blast of water resurrected Peel, who started to move. By the time Will got to his knees, Peel was standing—steadying his balance with his right hand on the balcony railing.

The face above Will was as frightening as anything he had ever seen—a grotesque mask of pure loathing. Peel screamed and kicked out at Will with his right leg. The blow bounced off Will's left shoulder, slammed into his jaw and knocked him onto his back and into a slide half the length of the balcony.

Will was conscious but nearly crippled with pain as Peel advanced toward him.

Noticing Peel's pronounced limp, Will silently thanked Jim for his good shot. He rolled onto his right side and shot his good left leg toward Peel's bad left leg. He missed the targeted knee, but his heel pounded into Peel's calf. Another scream, a sound of desperate pain, as Peel spun full circle, slammed against the ten-foot middle window and collapsed in a heap at its base.

Will was struck by the absurdity of being locked in a death dance with his mortal enemy when neither of them could even walk. Hoping that Peel was in worse condition than he, Will rolled to his stomach, pushed up through the burning pain in his left arm and managed to get to his knees again.

Peel stirred, but remained flat on his back. Will wanted to stand. He didn't know why—he wasn't even sure he'd be more effective once he was up—but he needed to stand.

Bracing his right shoulder against the window, he drove upward with his left leg. Salt water burned a hundred cuts in his feet. Halfway up, he reached down for Phil's Beretta. He got the gun but fell hard on both knees. He looked at Peel—sitting now—and cocked the pistol. Peel rolled forward—once again on hands and knees—and looked up at the gun aimed precisely at his forehead.

"Gotta kill me, motherfucker." Peel, still on his knees, made a half-turn and gripped the top of the balcony wall with both hands.

"Not tonight, Louis. Not then, not now. But I'm gonna put your sorry ass back in jail." Will felt almost giddy, but quickly dismissed the intrusion of an emotion so inappropriate to the situation.

"You can't, fucker—I can walk and you can't." Peel struggled to his feet—his tan turned nearly chalk-white with the effort. Now he was the only man standing. Will looked up at him.

"You won't be walkin' if I drop a shot into your right leg, cocksucker. Now, hold it right there." Will had to shout to be heard above the howling wind and crashing waves.

"Better do it quick, asshole, 'cause I'm gone." Peel was holding onto the balcony's top rail with both hands. He bent both legs as if preparing to jump.

Will aimed the gun at the back of Peel's right knee and squeezed the trigger. He was sickened to hear only a click. He fanned the gun through ten more clicks.

Peel smiled at Will. "This weather's a bitch for guns—too bad..." Furious at losing his advantage, Will struggled again to reach his feet. Peel, who had managed to swing his limp left leg over the railing, turned again to Will, who was stuck between squatting and standing.

"Please don't bother seeing me out, Willy boy—I know the way." He laughed. It was a shrill, hollow sound—devoid of mirth or any other normal human emotion. "And I *will* be back, fucker. Believe it. Next time it'll be your kids first. I'm gonna fuck your daughter—and send you pictures. Count on it."

Rage propelled Will to his feet, but he knew one step would crumple him again. He watched helplessly as Peel swung his right leg over the rail. Will wondered how Peel could jump down without killing himself.

Apparently Peel was wondering the same thing. There was no guaranteed safe landing on that side of the balcony. The ocean, wild as it was, would break the roughly fifteen foot fall, but rocks were everywhere. Peel paused. All Will could do was wait.

Will was transfixed as Peel began to swing his legs over the railing back to the balcony. *What the hell?*

A feeling of power seemed to surge through Peel.

Will watched Peel flop his left leg back over the railing. He felt the cold embrace of a chill as he looked into those mad eyes. He couldn't move—without the support of the window, he'd fall on his ass again. *Jesus! What keeps that son of a bitch upright? He's getting stronger.*

Braced for the imminent attack, Will tried to summon any reserve, but there was nothing left. Another chill swept through him—again unrelated to the wind and rain. He watched Peel, seated on the railing, legs swinging slowly, and the precariousness of that position reminded Will of his own mortality.

Peel lowered his right leg, and then Will saw his foe rise three feet. A torrent of frigid salt water hit Will in the face. The storm had sent a tremendous wave up the wings of the Gull—levitating Peel from his perch.

Again, Will watched with fascination as forces beyond his control dictated events. Peel was elevated and turned three hundred sixty degrees in mid-air by the huge wave. Somehow he managed to grab onto the lowest rail of the balcony before he was dashed to the rocks and angry ocean below. Will half-hopped and half-slid across the balcony and pulled himself down to the railing Peel grasped.

Will leaned heavily against the railing—all his weight on his left leg—and peered down at Peel. "Bad way to die, Louis."

"You son of a bitch…" Peel's struggle to hold on was mighty and obvious.

Will could read the terror in the crazy man's eyes. Peel had failed to attain his ultimate goal—Will knew it, and he believed Peel knew it as well.

"Help me, Kempton, goddamnit—I'm slipping."

Will reached around his back and snagged the handcuffs he'd never used since coming to Carmel. The sturdy bracelets fit Peel's wrists perfectly. Will held those wrists as Peel dangled below him.

"Okay, asshole—you're comin' up."

Planting his left leg for leverage, he acted as a hoist. Peel came up a foot, then another. Will's left arm hurt so much he almost cried out. He was sure this insane save of his was destroying every tissue missed by the bullet—but he was determined to save this bastard and send him away forever to a place where straightjackets were standard issue.

With an effort far past his limit, Will brought Peel up another foot. Their eyes met. All Will saw, through his own tears, was pure revulsion in Peel's eyes. He stretched backward—trying to bend Peel up and over the railing. Gasping from the effort and aching everywhere, it occurred to him that once Peel was on the balcony, he might, even handcuffed, somehow overpower Will. Still, he continued to pull with all his strength.

A last heave left Peel teetering on the top rail. Will grabbed his shirt to drag him onto the balcony—and was smashed back into the window by yet another massive wave. Louis Peel slipped backward into the already receding tide. His manacled hands clawed for the railing—missing by inches.

For a millisecond their eyes met again. Will would swear, for the rest of his life, that in that instant a faint smile flickered in those obsidian orbs. Peel disappeared in the swirling foam, then reappeared thirty feet below—captured in the glow of the Gull's floodlights. Just as quickly, the ocean carried him beyond the lighted area. Squinting into the darkness, Will thought he saw a flash of leg far below and to the left. Then, nothing but ocean. He slid slowly down to the balcony floor. For a moment he felt the rain pick at him. He smelled the ripe brine. Then his head fell forward and all the pain disappeared.

Friday Afternoon
Chapter Thirty-Four

Elliot Randolph ushered David, Sari and Peach into the large hospital ward. Though this was their fourth visit in the two days since the last night of Louis Peel, the kids ran straight to their father's hospital bed and hugged him in places that didn't hurt him.

"Are you better today, Daddy?" Sari asked as she clambered gently onto the bed.

"I am, sweetie—careful of the knee...." Will gasped. He hugged his daughter with his good arm and with his hand tousled David's hair in the same motion.

Randolph set down the styrofoam ice chest, looked at the three bed-bound men and said, "This is the sorriest lookin' collection of people I've seen in a long time."

"Since your last City Council meeting, ya mean," Phil Curry said from his bed across from Will's.

"Or the last gathering of your favorite movie critics," Jim chipped in from the other side of the room across from Clint's bed.

Randolph smiled at the spirited responses as he pulled a half gallon of Scotch from the ice chest and set it on the tray angled across Jim's bed. "Anyone?" he asked.

"Four fingers, please, and two ice cubes—and I'll be your friend for life," Phil said.

Three other hands shot into the air, accompanied by a noise reminiscent of the last day of elementary school. Randolph checked his watch—announcing that it was cocktail hour in Texas.

"Good enough for me—same as Phil's," Will said.

Jim and Clint indicated their readiness for a taste from the bottle of Famous Grouse held in the mayor's right hand. Tom Ainsley and Jeff had been discharged earlier that day. Their now-empty beds served as a reminder that things were looking better, and that if being here was a necessary evil to be endured by the remaining injured, their incarceration, too, was only temporary.

Jim had made remarkable progress. As soon as his lung was pronounced fit, he would have surgery on his damaged left knee. Luckily, he had escaped the type of injury that called for an artificial replacement part—such as Will's titanium and Teflon kneecap.

Phil Curry and Clint Forsburg were both well along on the road to recovery. Clint's wound had been less severe than Curry's, and he was scheduled for release within three days. A few weeks on crutches, and he would be nearly as good as new.

A slug had been dug out of Phil's upper back—below his right shoulder. The surgeon said he'd been saved by the overdeveloped musculature in his upper back. Had the bullet been able to move another inch through the tangle of muscle, it would have shattered his spine.

Will's recovery time, set at three weeks, paralleled Curry's. He would have to undergo an additional eight to ten weeks of therapy to rebuild the tissue in his left biceps damaged by Peel's bullet.

Curry raised his glass in a mock toast. "Can't believe I came all this way, and I can't even get out to play golf."

"If you'd'a followed my orders, you'd be out there playing right now," Will said. He tousled Sari's hair with his good hand.

"If I'd'a followed your orders, you dumb shit, you'd'a been dead."

The truth of Phil's comment was known to the small gathering. No further discussion of Tuesday night's activities was required. Each man would carry his own memory of Louis Peel for a long while. All but the mayor would carry physical scars from the night of Louis Peel forever.

***

Wednesday's newspapers had gone to press too early to catch the final hours of Peel's havoc—but radio and television filled in the blanks by Wednesday noon. Once again, Will Kempton was the hero in a short drama with only two central characters. This time his fame was fodder for the minions of the media. By Thursday at lunch time Carmel housed more reporters, cameramen and TV back-up crews than at any time since Randolph's mayoral campaign.

The *San Francisco Chronicle* shamelessly headlined its Thursday issue, "Death Struggle By-the-Sea," and offered thousands of dollars to Will for an exclusive of his battle with Louis Peel. Will had found it easy to decline the opportunity.

Randolph's faith in his chief of police was expressed in dozens of interviews that had sound-bitten their way into hundreds of newspapers and every television newscast for the last two days. Randolph's popularity, political and otherwise, was at an all-time high.

That of Ronald P. Barth was not. The little man, hustled forward by his wife, stood on the periphery of every interview, press conference and photo opportunity he could find. But his unending self-promotional blather was ignored by the star-struck media. Randolph had met and passed his most severe test of leadership—with flying colors. Barth, unable to comprehend the waves of kudos directed at Will and the mayor, circled the edges of a dozen crowds with increasing bitterness. His wife's well-advertised ice cream social for the media was attended by only a stringer from the *Yountville Courier* and the polyester-clad field reporter from channel eight in Des Moines.

***

Back in the hospital ward Will hobbled from his bed to the bathroom. His left arm was in a sling and would stay bound across his chest for at least a month. As he crossed back to his bed, he heard Randolph say "…not yet, anyway—not a single trace."

"No way the son of a bitch ever coulda made it outta the water," Jim said. He spoke with the assurance of one who had spent his life close to the beautiful but treacherous ocean.

Will respected the ocean's power but didn't know it as intimately as Jim. He paused, standing before the window. "Storm seems to be gone," he said.

Through a break in the forest, across the highway from the hospital, he could just glimpse the gray water and pale blue sky far out on the horizon. Though the room was typically hospital-warm, he shivered.

Epilogue
Three Weeks Later

Ten miles south of the Gull lies a strip of perfect white sand. It sits a hundred yards below Highway One, protected by an impassable wall of rocks. It is one of a dozen inaccessible areas between Carmel and Big Sur, no different from the others—except for the birds.

At first there were just a few—then a few dozen. Within an hour hundreds of them had been called together by a medium known only to nature. No one saw them descend. No one observed their midmorning departure. Had anyone happened to notice, he would not have paid much attention because congregations such as this were a not uncommon spectacle along the desolate coast.

The ocean frequently beached trophies of interest only to carrion feeders. The target of this particular feathered frenzy had been wedged between two sharp rocks directly beneath an overhanging ledge. By noon the white bone of the skull cast a brilliant reflection as the sun moved across the tiny beach.

That glint diminished quickly, then disappeared. By two that afternoon the rising tide dislodged the skull. At first, it was rocked rather tenderly against the solid rock cliff. But by late afternoon, winds split the gentle tide into large waves, which pounded the skull repeatedly into the jagged rocks.

At sundown all that remained of the bony object was a piece of lower jaw, containing three teeth.

By midnight, the teeth were dislodged and the jawbone was pulverized, becoming indistinguishable from the bed of sand. The unremitting forces of nature—first the sharks, then the gulls, the sun and, finally, the ocean… always the ocean… had removed every trace of Louis Peel from human observation.